"What If we s feel the same way?"

Bethany's voice was low as she asked the question before boarding the plane.

"That's a risk I'm prepared to take," Robert answered. "With any luck you'll wonder what you saw in this man. It's been two years since you left Italy. Goodbye, Bethany." He kissed her hand.

He continued to hold it as he added, "I should have arranged this before our engagement, but even so, it's not too late to change your mind."

For a long tense moment they stood frozen. Then, with a startling change of tone, Robert said violently, "To hell with this," and pulled her into his arms.

Oblivious to curious onlookers, he crushed her against his tall frame, his lips fiercely demanding. She was still transfixed with amazement as he strode out of sight.

ANNE WEALE

portrait of bethany

Harlequin Books

TORONTO • NEW YORK • LOS ANGELES • LONDON
AMSTERDAM • PARIS • SYDNEY • HAMBURG
STOCKHOLM • ATHENS • TOKYO • MILAN

Lines from the lyrics of *She*, music by Charles Aznavour, words by Herbet Kretzmer, by permission of Standard Music Ltd.

Harlequin Presents first edition October 1982
ISBN 0-373-10541-X

Original hardcover edition published in 1982
by Mills & Boon Limited

CHAPTER ONE

BETHANY was boiling an egg and toasting a slice of brown bread when, through the open kitchen window, she heard sounds which indicated that a bundle of newspapers was about to be pushed through the letterbox in the front door which she and Cressida shared with the tenants of the two other flats.

Wearing a green cotton housecoat over her short summer nightie, and with her thick mane of hair—the rich dark reddish brown of Spanish mahogany—falling loose on her shoulders, she left her breakfast preparations and ran down the carpeted stairs to the well furnished communal hall.

The papers, still folded together, were lying on the large coir mat inside the tall door with its beautiful Georgian fanlight. There were two copies of the *Daily Telegraph* and one of *The Times*. The paper boy had also delivered a monthly magazine for the top floor tenants, and a weekly list of television programmes for the occupants of the garden flat.

She picked them all up and put them neatly on the polished table which was flanked on one side by a hall chair, and on the other by a stand for wet umbrellas.

Having separated her *Telegraph* from the other papers, she then ran back upstairs to the first floor. As she re-entered the kitchen, her toast popped up in the toaster. Quickly she put it on a plate, and turned off the heat under the pan in which the egg was boiling.

Then, with fingers which trembled a little, she spread the paper on a work-top and turned the pages in search of the announcement which should make this, her twentieth birthday, the happiest day of her life.

Yet what she actually felt as she turned past the world news and the leader articles was not the exalted excitement of a girl on a high crest of joy, but rather a nerve-racking fear that she might have made a mistake.

The momentous decision she had taken was made public on Page 14 in the columns headed *Court and Social*. First came the Court Circular issued from Buckingham Palace, describing the Royal Family's activities on the previous day, and also from Thatched House Lodge, the home of Princess Alexandra.

After this came details of memorial services for two important public figures, and a list of the ages achieved by six well-known Englishmen and one notable woman.

Further down was a bold cross-heading *Forthcoming Marriages*, followed by the engagement notices of about a dozen couples. They were not in alphabetical or any other order, and it was a few seconds before her glance was arrested by the paragraph announcing her own engagement. A strange shudder of the kind people attributed to 'someone walking over my grave' ran down her spine as she read it.

Lord Robert Rathbone and Miss B. Castle
The engagement is announced between Robert Edward Andrew, younger son of the Duke and Duchess of Dorset, of Cranmer Castle, and Bethany, eldest daughter of the late Sir John Castle, Bart., and stepdaughter of Lady Castle, of Blackmead Manor, Hampshire.

As she was scanning the words which had cost her many sleepless nights of heart-searching, and about which she still felt uneasy, the telephone rang. It was in the large airy sitting-room between the kitchen and the bedrooms.

Most of the incoming calls were for her flatmate, Cressida Suffolk. But she, having spent half the night dancing at Annabel's, London's most fashionable night-club, was unlikely to wake up for some time yet. Bethany hurried to answer it before the ringing disturbed her.

Very pretty and vivacious, Cressida had a host of young men competing for her attention. Bethany, considered by many to be the most beautiful girl to have appeared on the English social scene for four or five seasons, was of a much quieter temperament. For the past several months she had had only one man in pursuit of her. One by one her other admirers had given up, feeling they could not compete with the son of a duke who was also extremely good-looking, and already in possession of a fortune inherited from his American great-grandmother.

During his courtship of Bethany, more than one gossip columnist had described the man who was now officially her fiancé as among the most eligible men in Britain. Bethany herself had been compared to the former Lady Diana Spencer, now Princess of Wales; and, in many ways, there was a resemblance. Bethany was also an unusually tall girl, five feet ten in her bare feet, with long legs and elegant ankles.

It is rather as if a charming young giraffe had wandered into the Royal Enclosure. Pleasing to look at and to listen to, Lady Diana is also strong-minded, innocent and idealistic—was how *Vogue* had described Prince Charles' bride in its profile of her a short time before the Royal Wedding.

With a life that has been far more private than public, the fact that she adamantly does not smoke and prefers soft drinks to alcohol, she is the antithesis of a go-go bright young debutante.

It was a description which applied equally well to Bethany. Quiet-voiced and gentle in manner, but not without firmness of character, and certainly not lacking in humour, she too exemplified the qualities brought back into fashion, after two decades of neglect, by the popular Princess of Wales.

Bethany's romance had not attracted the remorseless public attention which had been focused on Prince Charles and the then Lady Diana. But even if the English and foreign press had hounded her as ruthlessly as they had harassed the youngest of Earl Spencer's three daughters, they would have had as little success in unearthing anything to her discredit.

Lady Diana, born on the first of July in 1961, had been barely twenty years old on the late July day of her wedding in St Paul's Cathedral.

When Bethany was married to Robert she would be twenty and two months. There was no point in a long engagement. For her, as for the Royal bride, her wedding dress and the antique lace veil being lent to her by her future mother-in-law would be no mere symbols of virginity.

Her bridegroom would be her first lover—if not her first love.

Normally, when answering the telephone, she would give the number and her name. Today, preoccupied with the fact that her engagement was now known to everyone who took the *Telegraph*—although many of the paper's overseas readers would not see today's edition until tomorrow or later—she said only an absentminded, 'Hello?'

The upper class drawl which answered her was the voice of her future husband.

'Happy birthday, dear girl.'

'Oh . . . Robert. Thank you.'

'What are you doing? Having breakfast?'

'Yes . . . almost. I haven't quite started yet. Have you just got back from your jog?'

She knew him to be an enthusiastic disciple of Lt.Col. Kenneth H. Cooper, the United States Air Force doctor who, having popularised aerobic exercise in his own country, was gaining an increasing number of devotees in Europe.

Whenever he was in London, Robert began his day by jogging in Hyde Park or Green Park, both near to his father's town house in Belgravia.

Bethany, too, was an active person, but she preferred walking. Much of their getting-to-know-each-other had taken place on energetic country tramps with three or four dogs at their heels.

Not that she was altogether certain that she did know her fiancé as well as a girl soon to be married ought to know her husband-to-be. In the course of their long winter walks on the Duke's extensive estate, they had talked on all manner of subjects. She knew Robert's views about most things, from serious matters such as religion and politics to trivial ones such as his dislike of dark nail varnish—which she didn't wear anyway—and most root vegetables.

And yet, after all their wide-ranging questions and answers, she felt that in many ways he was and would remain an enigma. As she must be to him.

Most of the people who knew them but were not yet privy to the engagement would be likely, when reading the announcement, to consider them ideally matched; a young couple with everything in common, and every qualification for happiness.

So they were—on the surface.

The fact that, prior to last winter, Robert had had the reputation of being a dedicated womaniser who had never missed any of the opportunities afforded by his position, his wealth and his personal charm, would not be seen by other people as an obstacle to his marriage to a girl as inexperienced as he was experienced.

What not even their closest friends realised was that

Robert's worldly wisdom was limited to sexual relationships. Of affairs of the heart he knew nothing; having never been in love with anyone before her, and making no pretence of being in love with Bethany, except when they were with other people. He liked her. He wanted to go to bed with her. That seemed to be enough to convince his family and other intimates that he was in love with her and she with him.

Not even his mother appeared to suspect that, for different reasons, her son and his chosen bride were incapable of the romantic ardours attributed to them by the columnists who had reported their courtship and forecast their midsummer marriage.

The truth, which would never be known to anyone but themselves, was that Robert was not an emotional person. Bethany was—too emotional. She had been deeply in love; had suffered intolerable anguish, and wanted never to repeat the experience.

'Yes, I got back a couple of minutes ago,' he said, in answer to her question, 'and I thought I'd give you a quick call before having a shower. If you look underneath the sofa, you'll find a little present I hid there last night after the theatre.'

'Robert! How sweet of you. Hold on, I'll go and look for it.'

Carefully, in order not to make a loud noise in his ear, she placed the receiver on the table and crossed the sitting-room.

The sofa, slip-covered with blue and white chintz from Colefax and Fowler, the Mayfair decorators responsible for the interiors of many of England's finest houses, had belonged to Cressida's parents who were no longer alive.

Going down on her hands and knees, Bethany lifted the skirt of the cover and peered underneath. She saw the present immediately, a package about six inches long by two inches wide and less than an inch in depth. It looked like the box for a bracelet. Quickly she unfastened the outer wrapping and cast it aside. On opening the black leather case she found not a bracelet but a watch. The interior of the case was stamped *Watches of Switzerland*, a shop in New Bond Street, and the watch itself was by Vacheron Constantin. It had a round champagne-coloured face with Roman numerals, and was on a gold bracelet. She knew enough about fine watches to realise that Robert must have spent several thousand pounds on it.

Returning to the telephone, she said, 'It's absolutely gorgeous! I shall be terrified of losing it.'

She felt the same way about her engagement ring, which was a magnificent emerald.

'Have you looked at the back of it?' he asked.

'Not yet. It's still in its box. Wait a minute.' She wedged the receiver between her head and shoulder to leave both hands free to remove the watch from its velvet bed.

Engraved on the back was *From R to B on her twentieth birthday*.

It was not the sentimental inscription a man in love might have chosen, but even this factual legend with, beneath it, the date, made the gift a more personal one than if it had been uninscribed.

'You must have been very sure that I'd say "yes" this time,' she remarked.

It was only the night before last that he had finally succeeded in overcoming her resistance to his previous proposals of marriage; and he must know she could not have accepted so extravagant a present had they not become engaged.

'Why d'you say that?' Robert asked.

Bethany explained, adding, 'I can hardly believe you bought this yesterday and had it engraved straightaway.'

'No, you're right. I bought it last week when it caught my eye in the shop window and I thought it seemed rather your style.'

'Did they engrave it last week?'

'Yes, because I *was* certain you'd agree to marry me this time. You know I've been determined for some time, my darling girl.'

It was the first time he had called her anything more affectionate than 'dear girl'. She supposed it must be part of his declared intention to behave as if their engagement was the genuine love match many people would think it.

'Yes, I know, but I still can't think why.'

He had told her why, many times. But for all his praise of her face, her figure and her character, Bethany continued to be baffled by the reason why a man with his assets should have singled her out for his wife. There were literally dozens of attractive, well-bred, amusing girls who would have leapt at the chance to become Lady Robert Rathbone.

As she spoke she could see in her mind's eye her fiancé's tall, loose-limbed figure clad in the dark red track suit which he wore for jogging, and which emphasised his un-English colouring.

Most of his forebears were fair-haired and ruddy-complexioned. Robert's looks were a throwback to the Italian-born American tycoon whose millions had enabled his daughter to marry into the English aristocracy and become the present Duke's grandmother.

Bethany, whose sojourn in Italy had been the happiest time of her life, and who still suffered spasms of homesickness for the apricot house on the hillside above Portofino, had recognised Robert's Italian ancestry at their first encounter.

With his black hair and swarthy skin, and his very dark, smiling eyes she had been quite surprised to find that he spoke with no trace of a foreign accent. He had reminded her of another Italian; but, in spite of their reputation, no Italian had ever looked at her with the predatory light which had glinted in Robert's dark eyes the first time he walked into the flower shop.

'Well, if you still don't know why, I suppose I'll have to tell you again—but not now. Not on the telephone,' was her fiancé's amused response to her last remark. 'I'll pick you up at seven. Okay? In the meantime, take care of yourself. No more jay-walking. Look both ways today. Promise?'

This was a reference to an incident the week before when she had been saved from an accident by Robert's strong hands snatching her out of the path of a taxi which she hadn't noticed speeding towards her.

'Yes, I promise. I won't do that again. And thank you again for the watch, Robert.'

'My pleasure. Till seven. 'Bye.'

He rang off, leaving her to visualise him unzipping the top of his track suit, then shedding it and the trousers preparatory to taking a shower.

She had only once seen him without his shirt on. Thinking about that, it struck her that, on a physical level, their relationship was about thirty years behind the times, if not more.

Except for the one occasion, a long time ago, when he had attempted a pass at her, Robert had never subsequently made more than the most restrained, circumspect love to her.

Now that they were officially engaged, it would be taken for granted, certainly by their contemporaries and probably by most of their elders, that as often as they could they would 'sleep' together. Nor, if they wanted it that way, would it be difficult to contrive opportunities for lovemaking.

Only last night, after their visit to the theatre, they had had the flat to themselves for several hours—or could have done, had Robert chosen to linger.

However, after drinking some coffee—he must have secreted the birthday present under the sofa while Bethany was busy in the kitchen—and discussing the play for half an hour, he had said it was time he went home.

True, he had kissed her goodnight, but it hadn't been a passionate embrace, or a prolonged one. She knew he desired her because he had told her that he did, and sometimes he looked at her desirously, his dark gaze raking her body in a way that made her oddly uneasy.

But his kisses never matched those burning glances. He allowed her to keep her lips closed, and made no attempt to force a more ardent response from her. His restraint was rather bewildering, considering how he had behaved at the outset of their relationship. It still made her flush to remember the things he had done on that occasion.

Soon—as soon as they were married—he would have the right to do whatever he pleased to her. And even though her head told her that it was a futile exercise to deny herself marriage and children because the man of her choice could never be hers, in her heart she still had the feeling that, in yielding her body to Robert on their wedding night, she would be committing a betrayal for which she might never forgive herself.

While these troubled thoughts were in her mind, the bedroom door opened and Cressida came into the sitting-room.

She had not taken off her make-up before collapsing into bed, and her naturally ash-blonde hair was a tousled mess. But the auction house where she worked didn't open till ten, and by nine forty-five she would be on a bus to Piccadilly, her complexion as lovely as the petals of a Madame Alfred Carrière rose, her fair hair a short silky halo, and her blue eyes as clear and sparkling as if she had gone to bed early and slept for eight hours like Bethany.

'Who was that on the telephone? Robert?' she asked, blinking in the brighter light of the east-facing sitting-room.

'Yes. I'm sorry; did my voice wake you? I was going to bring you coffee in bed.'

'It should be me pampering you today. Happy birthday!' From the pocket of her short striped night-shirt, Cressida produced a small package wrapped in the distinctive purple paper embellished with a golden peacock's feather which showed that her birthday present had come from Liberty's.

'They'll change them if you don't like them,' she said, when Bethany had unwrapped a pair of enamelled flower ear-rings.

'Oh, but I do! I love them.'

Her large, long-lashed grey eyes bright with pleasure, Bethany flew to the mirror to try them on.

'They're from China,' Cressida remarked, as she watched her friend fasten the pins with their butterfly catches. 'I really should have my ears pierced. When did you have yours done? In Italy?'

'Yes, in Florence. Francine marked my lobes with a ball-point and took me to one of the jewellers on the Ponte Vecchio. She said it was very important to have them pierced in the right spot.'

'Who was Francine?' asked Cressida.

Bethany hesitated. Usually she avoided talking about the Italian years. It was a time she tried hard to forget because, as the great Italian poet Dante had put it—*There is no greater grief than to recall, in misery, the time when we were happy.*

She said, 'She was a Frenchwoman I knew there who was very kind to me.'

Fortunately Cressida was distracted from asking more questions by catching sight of the Vacheron Constantin watch which her flatmate had left on the telephone table.

'Snakes alive! What a fabulous watch! From Robert, it goes without saying.'

'Yes, he hid it here when he brought me back from the theatre last night. That was why he rang up—to tell me where to find it. It's beautiful, isn't it? Too beautiful for everyday wear. I think I shall keep it for the evening, and go on wearing my ordinary one during the day.'

'I shouldn't. This will be much safer on your wrist than lying about here where someone might break in and steal it.

Anyway, as Robert's wife *les must de Cartier* will be ordinary, everyday things for you. I think you're more to be envied than the Princess of Wales,' said Cressida. 'She, poor girl, has to face a lifetime of incredibly tedious public duties. But even when you're a duchess you'll only have to open an occasional garden fête.'

Bethany's sensitive face reflected her reaction to the older girl's rather thoughtless remark.

For all their wealth and position, the Rathbone family were not strangers to sorrow and misfortune. In his late teens, their elder son James, Viscount Hartigan, had been stricken by a disease of the nervous system which had already confined him to a wheelchair, and made it unlikely that he would marry and produce an heir.

She knew that Robert, who adored James, would have given every penny of his great-grandmother's fortune to restore his brother to health. He had no more desire to succeed to the title than she had.

Probably, had it not been for James' progressive illness, Robert would have remained a philandering bachelor, at least until his late thirties. At present he was twenty-nine, which was young for a man of his inclinations to settle down to matrimony, particularly if he meant to be faithful, which he had assured her was his intention.

In spite of his dubious reputation with the opposite sex, he had never been wholly a playboy. In his early twenties he had trained as an agriculturist, and later spent time in America studying the methods of the organic farming movement.

The conservation of the rich farmlands and unspoilt woodlands which his family had owned since the sixteenth century was a matter of deep concern to him. She had only once seen him look furious, and that was when someone had told him that a wood in Sussex, once the home of the rare butterfly orchid, had had all its undergrowth killed by chemical sprays, an act of vandalism perpetrated by the Forestry Commission.

The sight of him, at a party, listening to a middle-aged woman and looking thunderously angry—his well-cut mouth a hard line, his dark eyes flashing with annoyance—had startled Bethany. Up to that point, she had not known he had a serious side.

Later he had explained the reason for his scowl, and had

talked of his disapproval of modern factory farming, and of the junk foods inflicted on a gullible public by unscrupulous manufacturers and publicists.

It was after she had seen this side of him that she had at last begun to like him . . . and then a little more . . . and more. But liking a man was not loving him.

'*L'amor che move il sole e l'altre stelle.*'

Unaware that she had spoken aloud, she was startled when Cressida said, 'What does that mean?'

'Oh . . . it's just a line from Dante's *Divine Comedy* which popped into my head for some reason,' she said awkwardly.

'What does it mean?' the other girl persisted.

'It means "Love that moves the sun and the other stars".'

'I've been in love plenty of times, but it's never been an all-consuming passion like Dante's for Beatrice,' said Cressida. I don't think I should want to fall in love as intensely as he did. Those great love affairs nearly always seem to go wrong.'

She looked thoughtfully at Bethany. Although the two girls were close friends, having known each other from their schooldays, since meeting again and joining forces, it had usually been Cressida who confided and Bethany who listened. The unrestrained exchange of confidences which they had enjoyed at boarding school had never been fully resumed. Bethany had come back from Italy with a wall of reserve around her, although she had continued to be a sympathetic confidante for Cressida's problems.

Now, venturing for the first time to penetrate her friend's self-containment, Cressida asked, 'Is that how you feel about Robert?—that he moves the sun and the stars?'

'Of course.'

Bethany's reply was an echo of the answer given by Lady Diana when, during a pre-wedding interview, she and Prince Charles had been asked if they were in love. He had said, 'Whatever "in love" means.'

Bethany knew what it meant. For her, being in love had meant a few weeks of bliss, followed by months of misery and loneliness.

Such an innocent bliss it had been; too innocent to foresee the inevitable heartbreak at the end of it.

Remembering how it had ended, and the wretchedness of that first endless winter in England, she said abruptly, 'My toast will be cold. Are you having your usual, Cressida?'

The other girl nodded. 'Yes, but I'll have a shower first.'

She went back to the bedroom, and Bethany returned to the kitchen to eat her egg and wholemeal toast, followed by a sliced orange with yogurt.

It was Robert who had converted her from Cressida's habit of starting the day on black coffee and a crispbread to eating something more nourishing. He himself always ate a huge breakfast, and judging by his inexhaustible energy, and the lean lines of his tall, long-legged frame, his belief in breakfasting like a king, lunching like a prince and dining like a pauper had some force in it.

Like her, he was a non-smoker with unstained fingers and no taint of tobacco on his breath. Nor did he drink a great deal, so that although there were, or had been, hazards for the girls who allowed him to see them home, they did not include drunken driving.

As for drugs, when they had discussed them, his attitude had been that of someone who enjoys life enough not to need any unusual stimulants.

'I prefer the conventional "highs",' he had told her, with a narrowed glance which had made it clear what he meant.

Later, she had wondered if, from a girl's point of view, making love just for physical thrills could ever be totally satisfying.

Usually she set out for the flower shop where she worked half an hour before Cressida left the flat. But today she had the day off and, as her appointment with her mother's solicitors was not until half past eleven, she had time to do some housework before setting out for their chambers.

It had come as a puzzling surprise to her when, a fortnight earlier, she had received a brief letter, signed by one of the firm's senior partners, requesting her to call on him on her birthday.

Evidently Mr Henry Sheringham had seen the announcement in the *Telegraph*. The first thing he said, after she had been shown into his office and he had risen to shake hands with her, was, 'I see you are engaged to be married. Allow me to wish you every happiness.'

'Thank you.' Bethany seated herself in the chair he had indicated, and looked at him expectantly.

He was elderly now, but when her mother was alive he would have been seventeen years younger. She wondered if he remembered Clare Castle.

As if sensing her unspoken question, he said, 'As you were only three when she died, I imagine you have little or no recollection of your mother, Miss Castle?'

As she shook her head, he went on, 'When I met her she was already gravely ill, but still a very beautiful young woman. You are extraordinarily like her, except that you have the good fortune to be in excellent health. One has only to look at you to see that.'

He paused, still eyeing her intently. 'The likeness is quite remarkable . . . really quite remarkable. To describe you as a replica of her would be an exaggeration, but I don't think I have ever encountered a mother and daughter more alike both in colouring and bone structure.'

'Really? I didn't know that. Odd as it may sound, I've never seen a picture of my mother,' Bethany admitted.

If Mr Sheringham found this even more extraordinary, he didn't say so. Probably his career as a family solicitor had inured him to many stranger circumstances.

He said, 'Your mother left in our care a sealed package. She did not divulge its contents. Her instructions were that it should be handed to you on your twentieth birthday. I must ask you to sign this statement that you have received the package intact, and that our responsibility for it is now discharged. After that, no doubt you would like to examine the contents immediately and in privacy. For that purpose I suggest you retire to the office adjoining mine, which is not in use this morning.'

Bethany signed the form, was ushered into the next room, and there left alone with the parcel secured with red sealing wax.

It was strange to have in her hands something left to her by a woman she did not remember, and to whom her father had seldom referred, and then with the utmost reluctance.

From the servants who had looked after her until Sir John's second marriage, she had formed the impression that her mother's fatal illness within a few years of his first marriage had caused him such grief that he could never bear to speak of her.

When she had broken the seals and unfolded the paper, she found the parcel contained two mementoes accompanied by a letter addressed *To my beloved daughter Bethany*.

The memento she examined first was the leather photograph folder. On one side it held a studio portrait, on the other a snapshot of a smiling girl standing up to her knees in tall meadow-grass, cuddling a baby in her arms.

She might have been looking at a photograph of herself. As Mr Sheringham had said, the likeness was almost uncanny.

But when she looked at the portrait, and studied her mother's face in detail, she could see several subtle differences between it and the one which she saw when she looked at herself in a mirror.

The second memento was a shagreen case containing a most unusual pendant. In the centre of it was a deep blue transparent stone. On this had been carved, intaglio, a classical scene of dancing nymphs trailing garlands. The setting of the stone was gold, elaborately enriched with enamel and small rubies. From the setting hung three irregularly-shaped pearls.

Bethany, who had learned a little about antique jewellery from the Duchess, whose interest it was, wondered if the pendant could possibly be a genuine Renaissance jewel, or was merely a clever reproduction.

Either way it was a lovely thing to inherit, although not the kind of ornament she would have imagined her father choosing.

Although, like most old family houses, her childhood home had contained some fine pieces of furniture and paintings acquired by earlier generations of Castles, her father had taken no interest in such things.

In winter he had hunted, being the Master of a well-known pack of foxhounds. The rest of the year he and his second wife were frequently to be seen at race meetings. His presents to the second Lady Castle had taken the form of Hermès scarves with horsey designs, and modern diamond brooches with motifs such as horseshoes and fox masks.

Closing the case and turning her attention to the letter, she broke the seal on the envelope and drew out several sheets of writing paper closely covered on both sides with small, neat, legible writing very much like her own hand.

My darling daughter, the letter began.

Since I knew I could not be cured and would not live to see you grow up, I have spent many days and nights wondering whether to write this to you.

After much thought, I am so deeply convinced that you will either take after me or your real father, and will therefore be a misfit in this household, that I feel I must tell you the truth. No one else in the world knows my secret. Only you, my sweet lovely daughter, whom I can't bear to leave alone in the world. For you will feel alone, just as I have since my darling Benedict was killed.

Your father, whom I loved with all my heart, was Benedict Laurence, the violinist. Perhaps by the time you read this, only other musicians will remember him. But, if he had lived, he would have been one of the great violinists. I hope and pray that you will inherit his genius; although, if you do, you will have a hard struggle to fulfil it, for the man the world thinks is your father is not sympathetic to any of the arts.

It was at this point that the impact of what she had read made Bethany gasp with the shock of realising just what it meant *not* to be John Castle's daughter.

First, and above all, it meant she was not David's niece. The insurmountable barrier of a close blood relationship no longer lay between her and the man she loved.

That she had never stopped loving him, and never would, was demonstrated by the great wave of delight which surged over her as she re-read the opening paragraph's of her mother's letter.

Instead of being dismayed by the discovery of her illegitimacy, or shocked by her mother's deception of the man she had married, she could only feel joy.

How rightly her mother had forecast that she would be a misfit at the Manor. Not only a misfit, but an unwanted interloper.

From the day John Castle had remarried, the child whom everyone thought of as his eldest daughter had been constantly and painfully aware of her stepmother's antagonism. To be sent away to boarding-school at the age of eight had not made her unhappy but glad; glad to be free of the many devious unkindnesses which Margaret had contrived to inflict on her during the holidays.

It took her some time to read the rest of the letter. She

found it difficult to concentrate on anything but the wonderful, almost unbelievable fact that she and David were unrelated.

She was sitting with the letter in her hands, but her thoughts far away from the quiet, book-lined, dark-panelled office, when there was a light tap on the door and Mr Sheringham came in.

'I don't wish to hurry you, Miss Castle, but you've been here some time and I wondered if you might be . . . upset.'

'Oh, no—not in the least upset. I'm . . . overjoyed,' she said radiantly.

He looked somewhat taken aback.

Bethany felt that some explanation was called for, although she could not tell him the real reason for her elation.

'At last I have two photographs of my mother.' She showed them to him. 'And this beautiful pendant which belonged to her.'

The solicitor glanced at the folder, and then at the jewel.

'A very handsome piece of jewellery, and probably of considerable value,' was his comment. 'Strictly speaking, your mother should not have consigned it to our keeping without telling us what it was. I should advise you to lose no time in having it valued and insured, and putting it safely in your bank, Miss Castle. I am no authority on jewellery, but it looks to me as if it might well be worth a considerable sum of money, apart from its sentimental value.'

As she closed the case and slipped it inside her bag, he went on, 'May I ask if the Duke and Duchess are in London at present?'

'Yes, they are.'

'Then if I were you, I should take a taxi to their London house where they will undoubtedly have a strongroom where the pendant will be in safe keeping. Alternatively I can recommend Harvey & Gore in Burlington Gardens as a highly reputable firm with whom we have had many dealings. They are experts in the appraisal of antique jewellery, and would undoubtedly be able to date and value the pendant for you. Will you allow me to have a taxi-cab called for you?'

'Yes, thank you, if you would,' she answered.

His reference to her prospective parents-in-law had brought her abruptly down to earth.

Before he entered the room, disturbing her reverie, she had

been thinking in terms of flying immediately to Italy. For a short time all thought of Robert and her engagement to him had been driven from her mind by the revelation in the letter. But now, remembering her fiancé, she realised she had been freed from one trap only to find herself caught in a different kind of snare.

It seemed much longer than a few minutes before the cab arrived and she was able to take leave of Mr Sheringham. Fortunately the taxi-driver was not disposed to chat to her over his shoulder as many of them did. Perhaps he, too, had things on his mind. Grateful for his silence, and for the heavy traffic which prolonged the journey and gave her more time to pull herself together, she sat in a corner of the back seat, gazing unseeingly at the bustle of central London shortly before lunchtime.

Suddenly, about half way to her destination, she saw a way out of her dilemma. Because one-parent families were a commonplace of contemporary life, and illegitimacy no longer the stigma it had once been, the fact that she had no right to the surname Castle had not come as a shocking blow to her.

But looking at her parentage from the viewpoint of the Duke and Duchess, she saw that it would be a matter of much greater moment to them.

Probably, if the truth were known, they would have preferred Robert to choose his bride from a family which ranked their own. Baronets, although their titles descended from father to son, were neither noblemen nor peers. Even so Robert's marriage to a baronet's daughter could hardly be considered a mésalliance, even though Sir John had married beneath him, his first wife being the daughter of a nouveau-riche businessman who had bought a large house near Blackmead Manor.

Bethany had been made aware of her mother's lack of breeding by her stepmother; and perhaps, if her maternal grandparents had still been alive, Robert's mother and father might have jibbed at the connection. Only when very large fortunes were involved did the English aristocracy set aside their distaste for parvenus; and while Clare Castle's father had been a well-to-do man, he had not been sufficiently rich to make him acceptable at any level.

Full of hope that, even with the engagement now public

knowledge, the Duke and his wife might prefer the temporary scandal of a broken engagement to an unsuitable daughter-in-law, Bethany braced herself for the difficult interview ahead of her.

As far as Robert was concerned, he had never professed to be in love with her, so he could only be inconvenienced, not hurt. If there had been any question of hurting him ... she was not sure what she would have done.

She had been through too much herself to inflict the same pain on another if it could be avoided.

If only Mother had arranged for the letter to be given to me on my eighteenth birthday, when I came of age, all this need never have happened, she thought, with a sigh. But I suppose in her day people weren't officially grown up until they were twenty-one, and she thought eighteen was too young.

The taxi turned into the crescent which was one of London's most prestigious addresses. The houses at either end, and the one in the centre, were considerably taller and wider than the rest of the long curving terrace of well-kept, white-painted houses.

The Dorsets owned the large centre house. It had bay trees in tubs on the black-railed balcony outside the first floor drawing-room where, tonight, a party, which might not now take place, was to have been held.

The full length of the pavement outside the houses was solidly packed with parked cars, not necessarily belonging to the people who lived in the houses but to anyone who had the luck to find a vacant space.

Even a street inhabited by some of the most privileged people in the world could not escape parking meters and prowling traffic wardens. But although they robbed the crescent of some of its former elegance, the cars did not irritate the Dorsets as much as some of the other householders who no longer had their stable buildings to use as garages.

Having paid the fare and added a tip, she crossed the pavement to the portico with the number of the house painted on its columns.

A few moments after she had pressed the shiny brass bell push, the door was opened by a young man whom she recognised as one of the footmen from the Castle. He was dressed in the discreet dark green livery worn by all the Duke's household staff except his butler, who wore a black coat and striped trousers.

'Good morning. Is the Duchess at home?' she asked.

She knew that Robert was not. He had told her he was having lunch at his club with a man who had been at Eton with him and now farmed in the north, coming to London only rarely.

'I believe so, Miss Castle.'

He waited for her to step into the hall which was paved with squares of black and white marble, like a chessboard. From the centre of the floor a staircase swept up to a low landing and then branched into two curving flights to another, larger landing, and to the two double doors which led into the sixty-foot drawing-room.

On either side of the hall were doors leading, on the left, to the Duke's study, and on the right to a morning-room. It was from this room that the Duchess emerged, saying, 'I saw a taxi drawing away and thought it was Jack'—meaning her husband. 'I didn't expect to see you until this evening, Bethany.'

A woman of average height, and consequently some inches shorter than her son's long-legged fiancée, she offered her cheek for a kiss.

Even at their first meeting, Bethany had not been in awe of the Duchess, and since then they had established the easy relationship of two women who, in spite of a thirty-year age gap, are otherwise on the same wavelength.

The Duchess had short crisp grey hair, wore a minimum of make-up and, when in the country, was usually dressed in jeans or a blue denim skirt with a cotton shirt or a sweater, according to the season. Today, having spent the morning shopping in Knightsbridge, she was wearing a red linen suit with a red-spotted navy silk blouse with streamers which tied in a floppy bow. Shod by Magli in navy blue calf with heels not so low as to be dowdy, but not so high as to prevent her from walking at her normal brisk pace, she wore on the collar of her jacket an early Victorian gold brooch in the form of a coiled serpent.

'I'm just on the point of having a very light lunch. Will you join me? If you wanted to see Robert, I'm afraid he's not here. He and Jack are both out to lunch today. That's why I was surprised to see the taxi.'

'Yes, I know Robert is out. It was you I w-wanted to see,' said Bethany, stammering slightly because her mouth was suddenly dry with nervousness.

The Duchess turned to her footman, who was still hovering in the background, and asked him to ask the cook to send up enough lunch for two. Then she led the way into the morning-room, saying, as Bethany closed the door, 'You look a little weary this morning. Did Robert keep you out late last night?'

'No . . . no, he left me quite early. I—I think it must be that I've just had rather a shock. I'm afraid I have something . . . unpleasant to tell you.'

'In that case you'd better sit down and have some sherry to fortify you,' said the Duchess. 'And I'll fortify myself,' she added, in the cheerful tone of someone who is not expecting to be told anything too serious.

The Duke's favourite sherry was a completely dry fino, and the first time he had given her a glass of it Bethany had had the feeling that, if she didn't like it, she might be failing an important test. Later she had discovered that the Duchess preferred a golden amoroso, which was much more to her own taste. But at the moment she was in no mood to care what she was given. As she raised the glass to her lips, her hand began shaking so violently that she spilled some drops on her skirt.

'My poor child, you are in a state,' the older woman said kindly, as she sat down next to her on the sofa. 'Tell me at once what the trouble is.'

Bethany's soft full lips were quivering now, and she felt like bursting into tears. But she managed to keep some control, and to say, coming straight to the point, 'I've discovered that my father wasn't my father. My mother was pregnant when she married him. My real father had been killed in a plane crash, and she panicked and married the man I thought was my father.'

The Duchess was silent for some seconds. Then she said, 'Are you sure of this? *How* did you discover it?'

Bethany explained about her visit to Mr Sheringham. She had mentioned the appointment to Robert, but apparently he had said nothing of it to his parents.

'I must say I can't think what purpose your mother felt it

would serve to break it to you at this juncture,' the Duchess said, frowning slightly. 'Most unwise of her, in my opinion. Let sleeping dogs lie, especially those of this nature.'

'Oh, no!—I would rather know the truth,' Bethany protested. 'It explains why I never felt fond of my official father ... why I often felt like a ... a changeling. I only wish I'd found out a few days sooner, before the engagement was announced. Because of course I do realise that I can't marry Robert after this,' she added, in a low voice.

'Can't marry Robert?. Why not?' The Duchess sounded genuinely astonished.

Bethany gazed at her for an instant. 'Well ... because I'm a bastard!' she exclaimed.

'I prefer to use the term love-child, and if you seriously believe that the circumstances surrounding your birth will make one iota of difference to Robert's attitude towards you, you underrate him, Bethany,' the Duchess said rather sternly. 'I don't usually sing his praises, but my son has a much finer character than he is sometimes given credit for. He has always been intensely loyal to the people he loves. The fact that, in the past, he has been a flirt doesn't mean that he will be in future. Now that he has found the right girl, I shall be very surprised if he ever looks at anyone else. As for breaking off your engagement, that is quite nonsensical, my dear. I hope you won't suggest it to Robert. He expects you to trust him in all things.'

'I do trust him. I'm sure he will say all that you've said, because it's the decent reaction, and because he's pledged himself to marry me. But the decent thing for *me* to do is to take off this ring and give it back to him.'

As she spoke, Bethany pulled off the emerald and held it in her right hand.

She said, 'You haven't had as much time to think about it as I have. I know my father was felt to have married beneath him the first time, and if he wasn't my real father it means——'

The Duchess interrupted her. 'Does your mother say in her letter who was your natural father?'

'Only that he was a musician named Benedict Laurence.'

She waited to see if the Duchess, who often went to the opera, and to concerts at the Festival Hall, would remember the name. Probably her mother had overestimated her lover's talent.

'Well, since both your real parents and the man who gave you his name have all been dead for many years, I think you should put the whole thing out of your mind and go on as if nothing had happened,' said the Duchess. 'You can mention the matter to Robert, as I shall mention it to Jack; but I can assure you that neither of them will attach the slightest importance to it. As far as my husband and I are concerned, all that matters to us is that Robert has chosen a girl with all the qualities we hoped to find in our daughter-in-law.'

Leaning forward, she took the engagement ring from between Bethany's fingers and replaced it on the third finger of her left hand.

'I have every confidence that you'll make him an excellent wife, my dear,' she said affectionately, as the door behind her opened and the footman wheeled in a trolley.

Had she been in love with Robert, Bethany would have been relieved by the Duchess's attitude. It was only because she had been ready to clutch at any straw that she had allowed herself to hope the Dorsets would take a different view. Coming here in a clearer frame of mind, she would have known that Robert's parents were not the kind of people to be influenced by any factors other than her own personality and behaviour.

While the footman placed a small table near them, and spread it with a cloth and set out their luncheon, the two women sipped their sherry and the Duchess chatted about her shopping.

'Which reminds me, I haven't wished you a happy birthday or given you your present,' she exclaimed suddenly. 'I was going to give it to you tonight, but as you're here you shall have it now. Roger would you go upstairs and ask Mrs Crane to give you the parcel I left on the writing table in my bedroom, please?'

'Yes, Your Grace.'

The footman withdrew and the two women helped themselves to a pale green cucumber mousse speckled with chopped chives, parsley and grains of black pepper. It was accompanied by hot wholemeal rolls and butter from the Duke's home farm, and to drink there was chilled white wine or home-made iced lemonade.

But although it was deliciously creamy, Bethany found it difficult to eat even a small helping of mousse.

'Is that the watch Robert gave you? I like it,' the Duchess remarked. 'I've never cared for those very small women's watches, and they're useless as one gets older and starts wearing spectacles.'

'Yes, I like it too. It's gorgeous,' said Bethany hastily.

She realised it had been remiss of her not to mention Robert's present much sooner, but her mind was obsessed by her dilemma.

Until today it had seemed that no power on earth could alter the cruel misfortune of falling in love with a man who, although she had never thought of him as such, had been, genetically, her uncle.

It seemed to her bitterly ironic that, after holding out against Robert's relentless besiegement from last autumn until now, early summer, she should have surrendered only forty-eight hours before learning that David was really no relation at all.

The footman returned with a small parcel which proved to contain an object which Bethany had seen before when the Duchess had been showing her a collection of miniatures at the Castle. Many of them had been family portraits, but some had been bought by the Duchess, including the one she was giving now to her son's fiancée.

Instead of being a complete portrait, it was what was known as an eye miniature, the artist having painted only one of the sitter's eyes and a ringlet of hair. Painted on ivory, and mounted in a circular gold bezel, it could be worn as a brooch.

In shape and colour, and in the sweeping curve of the dark brown eyebrow, the eye was very much like one of Bethany's and the curling lock of hair above it was the same rich colour as her own.

'Oh, but this is part of your collection,' she protested, when she saw what it was.

'Which you can replace by having one of your pretty eyes painted for my next birthday,' said the Duchess, with a smile. 'Although I would rather have a whole face miniature of you. Happy birthday, my dear.' She kissed her. 'By the way, don't wear any jewellery tonight, because Jack is going to give you a very charming set made for Charlotte, the fifth Duchess.'

Bethany felt sick with embarrassment. 'You're all much too kind to me,' she murmured uncomfortably.

'Not at all, but in any case I think you deserve a little spoiling. I suspect it was decidedly lacking when you were a small child. Being sent away to school at eight is far, far too young, in my view.'

The Duchess must have heard about this from Robert, as Bethany had never mentioned it to her, and had only told him in answer to a direct question.

Reminded of her mother's pendant, she showed it to the Duchess who, after looking at it carefully through the magnifying glass which she kept in her bag, said, 'I should say this was probably made either by Carlo Giuliano or by one of the Castellani family.'

'You think it's a genuine Renaissance piece?'

The Duchess shook her head. 'The Castellanis and Giuliano were Italians, but not of the fourteenth century. The Castellani workshop opened in Rome in 1814, and Giuliano came to London from Naples in Queen Victoria's reign. They specialised in very accurate reproductions of the jewels of much earlier periods, but now one can generally distinguish between their work and the originals because they were so accomplished technically that their pieces have a perfection which even the finest early jewellers couldn't match.'

She laid down the glass and looked up. 'You must take this to the Victoria and Albert Museum, Bethany. They are the people to tell you about it. I will take it in for you, if you like, as you haven't much time while you're working. Have you told Mrs Hastings that she'll have to replace you before long?'

'Yes, I told her yesterday. She said she was sorry to lose me. But I'm sure she'll have lots of people applying for my job. She's such a sweet person to work for, and most of the customers are nice, too.'

For the past eighteen months Bethany had worked in a shop in Chelsea which sold beautiful arrangements of hand-made silk flowers and dried flowers. It was a job which David had organised for her; his last act as her friend and protector before, during his final telephone call from Italy, he had told her it would be best if they had no further contact beyond an occasional postcard and a card at Christmas.

For a year after that he had travelled in India and the Far East. After his return to Italy, the postcards had dwindled. Since receiving a Christmas card from him, Bethany had heard nothing more.

In a way, she had been glad of his silence. She had felt that her wounds were healing; that the day might come when she would be able to think of him without even a twinge of pain, remembering only the happy times they had shared.

Today that belief had been proven false. In a few hours all the old love and longing had gushed up like a spring which had never truly run dry.

It was half past two before she could make her escape, and walk slowly back to the flat, her mind in a ferment of uncertainty. Clearly, there was only one thing to be done, and that was to tell Robert the truth. He already knew there had been a man she had loved and lost, but he didn't know the man's identity.

However, although her common sense told her she must be frank with him, and without delay, something in her shrank from the task. Perhaps it was merely moral cowardice because he was certain to be furious, and the glimpse she had had of his anger had suggested that, when he was really roused, he would be even more daunting.

Yet it wasn't only his wrath she was afraid of, but that he might not accept that her long-standing love for another man had priority over her present relationship with him.

He couldn't hold her to their engagement by force, but he could refuse to give her up and exert great mental coercion. In a sense, he had won her by force—the force of his own powerful will to which, finally, she had bent.

But what, deep down, she feared most was that, if it came to a battle between them, he might unleash his self-control and behave as he had once before, on the night he had made a pass at her.

On that occasion, as soon as he had realised her resistance was genuine, he had stopped, had even apologised. This time, motivated by temper as well as passion, he might be less tractable. And if that happened, and he used his strength and his sensual expertise to make love to her, in a last-ditch attempt to bind her to him, afterwards she would hate him, and he would hate himself.

The Duchess had advised Bethany to spend the afternoon resting.

'My mother always insisted that we go to bed for at least two hours on the afternoon of a dance or a ball,' she had said. 'Of course that's impossible now when nearly every girl works. But as you have a free day today, there's nothing to stop you from resting. When you get home, do lie down and try to sleep, my dear. It's been an upsetting morning for you, and sleep is the best possible restorative after a shock of any kind.'

When she got back to the flat, Bethany made herself a pot of tea. Had matters stood as the Duchess imagined they did— her fears allayed, her future secure—she would have gone to the bedroom, and drawn the curtains, and set the alarm clock for five.

As things stood, sleep was impossible. Robert was coming to collect her at seven o'clock. At eight other members of his family and many of his and her parents' closest friends would assemble for a celebration supper party in the spacious blue and gold drawing-room which was said to be one of the most beautiful rooms in London.

She had taken the tea tray into the sitting-room, and was slumped in a chair, distracted with worry, when her eye fell upon the telephone.

Suddenly she felt an overwhelming longing to hear David's voice, to tell him the shattering news that she was not his niece as he had thought.

She had not forgotten the number. It was almost the same as the number of the luxurious Hotel Splendido on the wooded heights behind the harbour. Sometimes they had received calls intended for the hotel.

First she had to dial the overseas call code, followed by the number for Italy, and then the trunk dialling code. Finally, the number of the house.

'Sette . . . nove . . . uno . . . nove . . . quattro.' As she swirled the dial with a pencil, she murmured the numbers aloud in the musical language which, in less than a year, she had learned to speak as fluently as David did.

As she waited to be connected, hoping not to hear a recorded voice explaining that the lines were busy and asking her to try again later, her heart began to pound with excitement. In a moment she would hear his voice for the first time in two interminable years.

But when the connection was made, and she could hear the telephone ringing in the room which, when the shutters were closed, was like a cool, dim, deep-sea cavern, it was not his quiet voice which answered the call, but that of an elderly woman speaking with the local accent.

'May I speak to Signore Castle, please?'

'He is not here. This is his housekeeper, Anna.'

'When do you expect him to return?'

'Tomorrow night, if he isn't delayed.'

'He's away from Portofino?'

'Yes, in France. I can't give you his number. He's touring in his new *automobile*. Is there a message I can give him when he comes back?'

Bethany hesitated. Should she leave her name and number? Almost David's last words to her, when they had said goodbye at Genoa airport, had been that, in a dire emergency, she could telephone him. But there hadn't been a dire emergency—until now.

'No . . . no, thank you. I'll call again. *Grazie. Arrivederci.*'

'*Prego. Arrivederci.*'

Slowly, she replaced the receiver on its rest. So David was motoring in France, as he once had with her on that unforgettable journey from the Italian frontier to the Pyrenees.

Was there someone else with him this time? Or was he alone, with only his sketch block and paintbox on the seat beside him?

Suddenly, and for the first time, it struck her that it wasn't impossible that he, weary of transitory liaisons, might have decided to take a wife. If she could contemplate marriage, why should he not?

Tortured by the thought that he might have preceded her into a second-best marriage, she began to pace up and down.

Should she ring back and ask Anna if he was married? If so, what was the point of making Robert look foolish, embarrassing his parents, and throwing away her chance to have children and lead a congenial country life in a wing of the castle?

No, no . . . even if David *were* married, she still had to tell Robert about him.

She had given him to believe—because she had believed it

herself—that her unhappy love affair was now a thing of the past. But that wasn't true any more. Today had shown how easily her love could be reanimated; like an ember needing only a breath of breeze to make it glow red-hot again.

For the second time she dialled the number of the house at Portofino. But this time, to her dismay, she heard the recorded voice saying the lines were busy.

For how long?

In a little more than three hours, Robert would ring the bell, expecting her to be ready and waiting in the black silk taffeta skirt and snowy white lawn and lace blouse which he liked best of all her evening clothes.

'Oh, God! What *am* I to do?' she exclaimed aloud, close to tears.

This time she could not fight them back. Her eyes brimmed and overflowed, the tears pouring down her cheeks as she rushed to the bedroom and flung herself on the bed.

For three or four minutes she abandoned herself to her emotions. Afterwards she felt calmer, less frantic and panic-stricken.

There was a box of tissues on the night table. She dried her eyes and blotted her cheeks, and then she lay back with her head on the mound made by the pillow, and gazed at the ceiling.

There were several fine hairline cracks in the plaster. As she looked at them, she remembered similar cracks in the ceiling of her room at the Manor. In the early years of her teens she had spent a great deal of time lying on her bed, reading or daydreaming.

She had been in her room the afternoon John Castle had been killed by black ice on a road near his home.

A few days later David had come into her life.

CHAPTER TWO

BETHANY was writing to her best friend, Cressida. They exchanged long letters every week throughout the school holidays. Cressida recorded the progress of her current grand passion—currently the young and good-looking locum who was holding the fort for the Suffolks' family doctor while he recovered from a heart attack—and Bethany wrote about her long-standing love for the son of the local veterinary surgeon, and her difficulties with her stepmother.

These promised to become even worse now that her father was dead. It was six days after the accident which had abruptly ended his life, and yesterday he had been buried in the village churchyard. His widow and her two daughters were still red-eyed from weeping for him.

Only his eldest daughter had been unable to cry for a man who had never once kissed her. However, although he had never demonstrated the slightest affection for her, she had felt that he would not allow her stepmother to be too nasty to her. But now that he was dead . . .

Nanny Evans came into the room.

Although Bethany was sixteen, no one treated her as a young woman with a right to privacy. When Susan, aged ten, the elder of her two stepsisters, had reported to her mother that Bethany had locked the door of her room, Lady Castle had swept upstairs, demanded that the door be unlocked immediately, and pocketed the key.

'You're not smoking pot, I hope?'—sniffing the air suspiciously.

'Of course not! I just don't like Susan and Julia bursting in without knocking.'

'There will be no locked doors in this house. You spend far too much of your time up here. No wonder you're so pale and peaky! You should be out in the fresh air, getting some healthy exercise.'

Taking her cue from her employer, Nanny Evans, who had been at Blackmead Manor since Susan was a month old, usually treated Bethany as if she were still a child to be ordered about, reprimanded, and given no say in how she occupied her time.

'I thought I should find you up here,' she said crossly, as if, on a wet afternoon, the girl had no right to be writing a letter in her bedroom, but ought to be doing something else. 'There's someone downstairs who claims to be Sir John's brother. I didn't know he had a brother. As your mother's not in, you'd better come down and see him.'

She always referred to Lady Castle as 'your mother' which, considering that Bethany had no memory of her own mother, and that her father had remarried within a short time of his first wife's death, should have been the way Bethany regarded her.

It was Margaret Castle who had chosen the role of the traditionally unpleasant stepmother. From as far back as Bethany could remember, Margaret had shown her nothing but veiled antagonism, sometimes erupting into overt hostility.

For a moment or two Bethany was as surprised and puzzled as her stepsisters' nurse. Then she remembered that, a long time ago, Cressida had regaled her with some gossip which she had overheard at home.

It appeared that Bethany's grandparents had had two sons. After the elder had succeeded to the baronetcy, he and his brother had quarrelled, and the younger one had left England and never come back.

Although Cressida had urged her to do so, Bethany had never questioned her father or stepmother about the truth of this story. She had already learnt that even to mention her own mother was something better avoided. Very soon she had forgotten the tale.

Now her interest revived. Exceedingly curious to see what her father's brother might be like, she pushed back her chair and stood up.

'All right, Nanny, I'll come down at once.'

'I showed him into the library where there isn't much for him to steal if it's some kind of confidence trick,' said Miss Evans, still breathing heavily from the exertion of climbing up to Bethany's eyrie on the attic floor of the rambling old house. 'He looks and sounds like a gentleman, but there's no resemblance to your father that I can see. He may have read about Sir John's accident in the papers, and seen an opportunity to get in here and lay his hands on some valuables. He's got one of those big grips with him—it looks full, but it may be stuffed with newspapers. You can go faster than I can. You'd better run down quickly and see what he's doing. If he's up to anything suspicious, you must scream and I'll call the police.'

A conscientious woman, well qualified for her job but not otherwise too intelligent, Miss Evans spent much of her leisure engrossed in the sensational newspapers, and consequently was inclined to see life through crime-coloured glasses.

Bethany sped down the stairs, not because she expected to find a sneak-thief at work, but because she didn't think Cressida would be much interested in an account of the accident or the funeral, and this would make something more exciting to write to her about.

When she entered the library, which no one but herself made much use of, at first there seemed to be no one there. Then a pleasant male voice said, 'Hello,' and she looked up to see him perched on the top of the rubber-wheeled library ladder which gave access to the highest shelves.

'Good afternoon,' she said formally.

He was *not* like her father; not at all.

Instead of being florid, with little purple veins on the nose and cheeks, his face was a deep golden brown, and his fair hair had sun-bleached blond streaks. Sir John had had very pale blue eyes. This man's eyes were the colour of cornflowers.

He closed the book he was holding and thrust it back into its space. Then he came lightly down the ladder, not turning round to face it as she did, but descending it with his back to it, in the manner of a man long accustomed to the narrow steps of companionways—although, at the time, she didn't recognise the ability for what it was.

It wasn't until he reached the floor and began walking towards her that she realised how extremely tall he was.

A beanpole herself—'I hope you're not going to grow any taller. It's a great disadvantage for a girl to be even your present height,' Lady Castle had remarked more than once—she was not used to feeling quite small, as she did by comparison with his inches.

'How d'you do? I'm David Castle, and you must be Miss Castle,' he said, as he offered his hand.

He was the first person who had ever addressed her by the title which was her right as her father's eldest daughter.

'Yes. How do you do?'

She put out her hand and had it enclosed in a warm, dry, sinewy grip.

'As you've probably never heard of me,' he said, 'perhaps I'd better identify myself.'

He released her hand to feel in an inside pocket of the her-ringbone tweed coat he was wearing over a thick navy sweater.

The weather was still very cold, even though it was now early April, and obviously he must live in a much warmer climate to keep that deep tan through the winter.

The identification which he handed to her had *Mr D. W. Castle* written in the space above the gold-printed words *British Passport* and the crown, lion and unicorn of the Queen's coat of arms.

After glancing at the name on it, Bethany would have handed it back to him, but he said, 'Hadn't you better check that the photograph inside is of me.'

She turned to the page bearing a small coloured photograph of the same lean and sunburned features as those of the man smiling down at her.

Her eyes flicked to the opposite page where, under *Description—Signalement* there were brief details about him.

Occupation	*Artist*
Place of birth	*Blackmead, U.K.*
Date of birth	*9 September 1943*
Residence	*Italy*
Height	*1.87 m.*

The space against *Distinguishing Marks* had been left blank. The spaces for *Spouse* and *Children* had diagonal lines dashed across them. At the bottom of the page he had signed his name in black ink and a bold, stylish hand.

Bethany closed the passport and returned it to him.

'Welcome home,' she said, a little shyly.

She had left the door open behind her, and now they were joined by Miss Evans, her expression worried and wary.

Suddenly Bethany felt very grown-up and self-possessed; very much 'Miss Castle'.

'Mr Castle has just identified himself. Your suspicions were quite unfounded, Nanny. He must be cold and tired after his journey. Would you ask Mrs Herring to make us some tea and toast, please.'

'Oh . . . very well.' Looking put out, the nurse withdrew.

Bethany turned back to him. 'Or perhaps you would rather have a whisky and soda?' she suggested. 'The drinks are in the drawing-room, and it's warmer there. It's freezing in here, I'm afraid.'

'It was freezing all over the house when I was growing up here. But I noticed the hall felt warm just now, and I saw a couple of radiators indicating that things had improved since my time.'

'Yes, except in this room which is hardly ever used—except by me.'

'Do I gather that Nanny took me for a suspicious character, and put me in here as a precautionary measure?'

Bethany nodded.

'Little does she realise that some of the most valuable and easily saleable things in the house are here,' he said dryly. 'So you're a bookworm too, are you?'

'Yes.'

She led the way to the drawing-room, an apartment now less attractive than it had been a few years before when a faded dark rose-red paper which had hung there for eighty years had been stripped and replaced by a reproduction of a William Morris paper in shades of ice green.

'Good lord! *Not* an improvement!' was her companion's comment, when he saw it. 'Who chose this, for God's sake?'

'My stepmother chose it,' she answered, her face expressionless.

'I'm sorry—that was very rude of me. You must forgive my bad manners. Only I used rather to like the old red paper, and it was a shock to find it replaced by this . . . pattern.'

She suspected him of biting back a less noncommittal term.

'I liked the old paper, too,' she admitted. 'Please . . . help yourself to a drink, and I'll light the fire. Even with central heating this room is never really cosy unless the fire's alight.'

With a gesture towards the drinks tray, which perhaps had

not been where it was now before his estrangement from her father, she went to put a match to the rolls of newspaper and kindling twigs under the logs on the hearth.

'What'll you have? Sherry?' he asked her.

'Er . . . yes, please.'

Her hesitation was caused by the fact that, except when staying with Cressida, she was never offered any alcohol. At the Suffolks' house she had had wine and, once, on Mrs Suffolk's birthday, a glass of champagne. But here, even on the rare occasions when she was introduced to her father's guests, she was always expected to have a soft drink like her much younger stepsisters.

He came to join her at the fireside, a tumbler of whisky in one hand, her glass of sherry in the other. She noticed his well scrubbed, short nails.

'How is your stepmother taking it? Were she and your father very close?'

'Yes, very. The only reason she's out today is that the girls had dental appointments, and Nanny doesn't drive so she couldn't take them. They should be back about five.' A thought occurred to her. 'I shouldn't have called you Mr Castle. You're Sir David now.'

He shrugged. 'I shan't use the title. It will die with my brother—unless I have a son, which isn't likely. That's the chief reason I've come over; to make it clear to your stepmother that I've no intention of usurping her place here.'

'You can't usurp what is yours. This is your house now,' said Bethany.

'Which I don't want; having a much nicer house in a much nicer place,' was his answer. *'Alla salute!'*

'Alla salute,' she echoed, not knowing what it meant but guessing it was an Italian toast. 'My name is Bethany,' she added, because although it had pleased her to be called Miss Castle, very soon he was going to find out that she wasn't as old as he seemed to think her. 'Where do you live in Italy?'

'In a little place called Portofino, a fishing village on what's known as the Ligurian Riviera.'

'Is that on the east or the west coast?'

'On the west coast, right up at the top, stretching from the border with France round to Viareggio, which is where

Shelley's body was washed up after his boat overturned in the gulf of Spezia.'

Shelley was one of Bethany's favourite poets. She knew that soon after being sent down from Oxford University for publishing a pamphlet on atheism, he had, at the age of nineteen, eloped to Edinburgh with a girl called Harriet Westbrook. It had been an ill-advised marriage, and he had again eloped, this time to the Continent, with the much more compatible Mary Wollstonecraft Godwin. Later Harriet had drowned herself, enabling Shelley and Mary to marry. They had lived in Italy until, when only thirty, he had drowned on a July day in 1822.

Although Sir John and his widow must have heard of Shelley, and perhaps known the first two lines of his famous ode To a Skylark, she knew she could never have discussed the poet's short, stormy life with them.

But David looked as if he knew all about Shelley, and perhaps had something in common with him. She wondered what he and her father had quarrelled about, and why he wasn't married, as most people were at thirty-five.

Not that he looked as old as that. Seen from behind, with his thick hair, wide shoulders and lean hips, he didn't look older than Peter, the vet's son, who was twenty.

It was only the lines round David's eyes, and something in his expression, which made him look older than Peter from the front. Bethany thought it might be that Peter took himself very seriously, but David looked as if he didn't take *anything* too seriously. Even in repose, his mouth had a humorous quirk, as if it wouldn't take much to make him laugh. Laughter was something which, having joined in gales of it at the Suffolks' house, she missed and longed for in her home life.

'Have you lived in Portofino a long time?' she asked.

'Five years. Before that I was a gypsy, moving from place to place as the fancy took me. I still travel a good deal, but Portofino is my base. Unfortunately it's such an attractive place that at certain times of year it's infested with tourists, and the shopkeepers go mad with greed and charge eight hundred *lire* for a bottle of water which would normally be about two hundred. But I get my supplies from Rapallo, which is just along the coast, and my house is out of the way of the trippers, most of whom only come for a few hours. I sometimes wish I had known Portofino twenty or thirty years ago, but

I'm still very happy to live there as it is now. I've never found anywhere I like better.'

At this point they were interrupted by the entrance of Nanny and another woman carrying a tray.

'This is Mrs Herring,' said Bethany.

'Good afternoon, sir.' The Castles' cook-housekeeper gave him the smirk which was as close as she came to a smile. Her eyes were beady with curiosity.

'Good afternoon. Those look splendid cakes. Are they home-made?' He was looking at the cakes, two cut and one uncut, which Nanny was carrying on a tiered stand.

'Yes, sir, everything's home-made.'

'I haven't had an English tea for over ten years. With breakfast, it used to be my favourite meal.'

To Bethany, when they were alone again, he added, 'But I seem to remember that lunch and dinner were nothing to write home about. Greasy mutton, boiled vegetables and lumpy custard are the things which stand out in my mind. But probably Mrs Herring is a much better cook than the old girl we had in my time.'

'She isn't very good at vegetables or salads. I like Mrs Suffolk's cooking—she's the mother of a friend of mine—but she uses garlic and herbs, and Father and Margaret don't like French cooking. Is Italian food good?'

'It was from Catherine de Medici's Italian chefs that the French first learnt their expertise. Italian food can be superb, but when I was a student in Florence, I used to live mostly on pizza. There was a place near the Duomo where you could watch the cooks kneading the dough and sliding your order into a huge wood-fired oven.'

'I've had pizza. It was delicious. Mr and Mrs Suffolk took Cressida and me to a restaurant in London called The Chicago Pizza Pie Factory. It was a treat for Cressida's last birthday. I sometimes stay with them in the holidays. They live in a lovely flat on Chelsea Embankment.'

'Have they taken you to the Tate Gallery?'

Her thin face alight with remembered enjoyment, she said eagerly, 'Oh, yes—and to the National Gallery and the Courtauld Institute. Last year Mrs Suffolk took us to see the Summer Exhibition at the Royal Academy. Have you exhibited there?'

'Yes, but not for some time. Nowadays I sell most of my stuff through a gallery called Colnaghi's.'

Bethany remembered hearing Mr Suffolk talking about a painting at Colnaghi's which he would have liked to buy but couldn't afford.

'That's a very grand gallery, isn't it? Are you a famous artist?'

'Not famous. I sell fairly well. My nom-de-brosse is David Warren—Warren being my middle name.'

'What kind of artist are you? I mean, do you paint landscape or portraits?'

'Do you know what a genre painting is?'

Bethany shook her head.

He said, 'It's a painting which shows everyday life; not idealised life, but real life. You can see small touches of genre in Italian Renaissance pictures, and in some early Flemish painting. But it first got a really strong hold in Holland in the seventeenth century when artists like Vermeer and de Hooch painted tavern scenes and musical parties. Chardin was one of the best known French genre painters and, in England, there was Hogarth. Degas's pictures of ballet dancers practising at the *barre* and fastening the tapes of their shoes are examples of genre painting. I mostly paint beach and harbour scenes.'

'In watercolours or oils?'

'Watercolours mainly. Sometimes I use pastels. But enough about me. Tell me something about yourself. What, apart from reading, are your interests? Have you discovered your métier yet?'

She shook her head. 'I'm doing quite well at school, but I don't seem to have a bent in any special direction. I'd better pour out the tea or it will get cold.'

It was the first time she had handled the large and heavy silver teapot. But her wrists, bared by the cuffs of an outgrown guernsey, were not as fragile as they looked. She managed to fill the cups without spilling any tea in the saucers or on the old-fashioned white traycloth.

She was conscious of David watching her, but his scrutiny did not make her nervous. She felt comfortable with him, as she did with the Suffolks.

'What are your best subjects?' he asked her, helping himself to toast and a buttered scone from the two covered silver dishes which had hot water compartments beneath them to keep their contents warm.

'French and German.'

'Perhaps you're a linguist in the making. That's a bent with a great deal of scope. For a girl with two or three languages the world is her oyster.'

'Is it?' she said, somewhat surprised.

Although she had received more encouragement from her schoolmistress than from her parents, the emphasis at school was on the intense competition the girls would face when they left it. No one had ever suggested that the world might be her oyster.

They talked without pause all through tea. Encouraged by David, who himself ate large slices of all three cakes, Bethany indulged her hearty appetite. Margaret, who ate little, disapproved of her stepdaughter's tendency to 'wolf everything in sight', as she put it.

But Bethany couldn't help feeling ravenous much of the time. She supposed it was because she was still growing, and worry about her eventual height would be added to the pangs of unsatisfied hunger.

Today, however, with David's much longer legs stretched out towards the now blazing logs, even her lankiness didn't bother her. Feeling comfortably full for a change, she curled up on the sofa opposite his chair, and chatted with a vivacity which, although she was unaware of it, infused her adolescent looks with hints of a beauty as yet undeveloped.

Her animation was swiftly extinguished when the door opened and Lady Castle walked in, still wearing her outdoor clothes, suggesting that Nanny had been waiting to tell her about their visitor as soon as she set foot in the house.

David, who by now had shed his tweed coat with its leather elbow patches, rose at once to his feet, but not as quickly as Bethany uncurled herself.

After nervously clearing her throat, she said, 'Margaret, this is Father's brother David.'

'How do you do, Lady Castle.' He walked towards her, hand outstretched, smiling.

Margaret looked at him with the same cold and critical expression she often fixed on her stepdaughter.

'Good afternoon,' she said frigidly. 'I've been expecting

you—but not quite as soon as this.'

The inference that he had come to claim his inheritance with indecent haste was clear in her rather harsh voice.

Bethany was astonished at her showing such animus towards him, until she remembered that Margaret probably knew the cause of the permanent breach between her husband and this man, and naturally she would share her husband's attitude towards him. Even so it seemed undiplomatic to be hostile towards someone whose good-will could smooth her widowhood.

'I came as soon as I heard of my brother's death, thinking it would relieve your mind to know that I have no intention of interfering with your life here, Lady Castle,' he said pleasantly.

'I have established a life style which I don't wish to change. Although the estate is entailed, I am not obliged to live in this house and give up the work I prefer in order to manage things here. If you can take over the reins, well and good. If not, you will have to engage someone who can handle them for you. I shall never come back to England. Although, having said that, it isn't entirely impossible that I might have a son, and that he might want to follow in the footsteps of his forebears. But that's an eventuality many years ahead.'

Margaret Castle looked taken aback. Clearly, she had not only anticipated his arrival but felt herself threatened by it.

It was typical of her that, when she recovered herself, she made no attempt to redress her initial coldness with a more gracious attitude.

Her tone more peremptory than conciliating, she said, 'Are you prepared to support that assurance with a legal agreement?'

Bethany saw his mouth and jaw harden, but there was no change in his voice as he said courteously, 'I don't think that will be necessary. You have my word that the only person who might ask you to look for somewhere else to live would be my son. At present I'm a bachelor, and likely to remain one.'

When she didn't respond, he added gently, 'Isn't my word enough for you, Lady Castle?'

A flash of anger showed in her brown eyes. She glanced at her stepdaughter.

'Will you leave us, please?'

In the hall, Bethany found Nanny lurking.

'Is he staying the night?' she asked, in a conspiratorial undertone.

'I don't know.'

Privately, she wished he were staying permanently. Life would be very different with David as head of the household.

On the first floor landing she was intercepted by her stepsisters.

'What is the mystery? Why did Nanny whisper something to Mummy, and then shoo us upstairs and tell us to stay in our room?'

'You came out of the drawing-room. Who was in there with you?'

'A visitor for your mother.'

'Who?'

'If she wants you to know, she'll tell you.'

Bethany made a dash for the only room where she could still lock herself in. She perched on the old-fashioned polished mahogany lid, knowing that Susan and Julia would soon tire of accusing her of being a meanie from the other side of the door.

When she judged the coast to be clear, she slipped up to her room on the top floor. She was continuing her letter to Cressida when footsteps on the stairs warned her that Margaret was coming up.

'May I ask you why you took it upon yourself to order tea and light the fire in the drawing-room?' she demanded, as she entered the bedroom.

Instinctively Bethany stood up, just as she would have done had Margaret been one of the mistresses at school.

'I—I thought you would want me to make him welcome. He is Father's brother.'

'Whom you have never set eyes on, or heard us mention. A person with any intelligence would have realised there must be some reason why he was persona non grata in this house.'

'He seems a very nice man,' Bethany ventured.

'So do many undesirable people. As a young man he behaved disgracefully.'

'What did he do?'

Her stepmother hesitated. 'He betrayed your father's trust

in him in a way which was quite unforgivable.'

'Perhaps he has changed since then. He seems to be a very successful artist now.'

'You have only his word for that.'

'But if he were not successful, surely he would jump at the chance to come back here and take Father's place.'

'He could never take your father's place. He isn't a man of the same calibre,' Margaret said impatiently. 'I've no doubt he much prefers a free and easy life abroad where he doesn't have to set an example and uphold certain standards as we do. He has a most dissolute face.'

Bethany said nothing. His face hadn't struck her as dissolute. He looked as if his consumption of whisky was considerably less than her father's; and in spite of the large tea he had eaten, his middle was as flat as her own, and his jawline was clearly defined by his taut teak skin.

'However, as I seem to have no option but to put him up for one night, I must make the best of it, I suppose,' Margaret went on. 'You can have your supper with Nanny and the girls. There's no need for you to come down again. And I don't want to hear a second time of your speaking sarcastically to Nanny, as I'm told you did this afternoon.'

She walked out, leaving Bethany to sink back into her chair, very disappointed that she was not going to see David again, perhaps not even to say goodbye to him the following day.

Late that night, she was sitting up in bed with her sweater over her pyjamas—the central heating did not extend to the attic floor—reading *Under The Red Robe*, when a tap at the door made her start up in momentary fright.

The door opened and David came in.

'I thought you might still be awake. I used to read half the night. Are you hungry?'

'Have you brought some food?' she asked, brightening.

'Dinner wasn't too filling, so after your stepmother had gone to bed I raided the pantry for a bedtime snack. I thought you might feel peckish too.'

He was carrying a plastic bag from which, sitting down on the bed, he unloaded some apples and biscuits, a large hunk of Cheddar, and the remains of the ginger cake.

'This room's like an ice-house,' he remarked. 'Why do you

have to sleep up here? There are plenty of bedrooms on the next floor.'

'Father and Margaret used to have quite a lot of visitors, and Nanny and Mrs Herring can't sleep on this floor because they don't like climbing stairs. I like this room . . . although it would be nicer if I could paper it with one of those spriggy papers,' she said wistfully.

Margaret had vetoed this suggestion.

'It's not cold with bed-socks and a hot-water bottle,' she assured him.

'Good God! Couldn't they run to an electric blanket for you?' he expostulated.

Bethany bit off a piece of biscuit. A midnight feast with this nice man was an unlooked-for treat.

He said, 'Frankly, I don't like your stepmother, and I get the impression you and she don't see eye to eye either.'

'Well . . . no, we don't get on very well. I have tried to, I really have. But somehow it seems to be impossible.'

He cocked a quizzical eyebrow. 'Do you think you could get on with me?'

'Oh, yes, that would be easy. Have you changed your mind? Are you staying?'

'No, I have a better idea. How would you like to come back to Portofino with me?'

About to bite off more biscuit, Bethany checked, her eyes huge with astonishment.

'You mean . . . live in Italy . . . for good?'

'If not for good, for as long as it takes to add Italian to your repertoire of languages.'

'Oh, David . . . I'd love it. *I'd love it!* You aren't joking, are you?'—in alarm.

He shook his head. 'Couldn't be more serious.'

'Have you talked to Margaret about it? Will she let me go with you? She said——'

'She said what?' he prompted, after she had stopped short.

Bethany looked embarrassed. 'She doesn't approve of you. She . . . she said you had once done something "quite unforgivable".'

'That's true. I did,' he said gravely. 'But it was a very long time ago, and there were extenuating circumstances which perhaps she wouldn't understand.'

'Do you think Father would have forgiven you, if you'd come back before he was killed? Did he know where you were? Could he have written to you?'

'No, he didn't know where I was. If he had, he wouldn't have written. What I did was unforgivable from his point of view. I can only say that it wasn't something which need make you feel dubious about coming to Italy with me. I'm not an unsuitable person to have charge of a minor.'

He paused, reconsidering this statement. 'Perhaps some people might think so; but it seems to me that your present circumstances are far from ideal.'

'No, they aren't,' she agreed. 'I would much, much rather come with you. But are you sure I shan't be a nuisance? I'm bound to be an expense.'

'You can earn your keep by cleaning my brushes and keeping the studio tidy. You can be my general factotum. You realise it will mean leaving school? I'm not proposing to take over the payment of your school fees, plus the cost of flying you backwards and forwards half a dozen times a year.'

'Oh, no—I wouldn't expect it. I shan't mind leaving school—except for missing Cressida. But she's leaving at the end of next term, unless she flunks her O-levels and has to re-take them at Christmas.'

'I'd forgotten about those,' David said, frowning. 'I don't think you ought to leave before you've had a crack at O-levels. When does this holiday end? When should you go back to school?'

'On Saturday week. But——'

She had been about to say, not quite truthfully, that she didn't care about missing the examinations, but he interrupted her.

'Right: then there's plenty of time for you to come to Portofino and see how you like living there. Presumably your school fees have been paid to the end of the academic year, so there's no point in wasting a whole term's board and tuition. You can take your exams in June, or whenever they're held, and leave at the same time as Cressida. How does that plan strike you?'

'It strikes me as absolutely perfect. Oh, David, I . . . I . . .'

Unable to put her feelings into words, Bethany seized the long brown hand nearest to her and pressed it to her thin cheek, her grey eyes shining with inexpressible gratitude for this whirlwind change he had wrought in her lonely home life.

Suddenly, to her dismay, her eyes filled with tears. Before she could blink them away, some had rolled down her cheeks and dripped on her hands and his.

It was the first time in all her life—except perhaps when she was tiny—that she had cried in the presence of another person. She had shed many tears in private, but never in public. She expected David to pull his hand free, and to look as embarrassed as she was by this uncontrolled show of emotion.

The next thing she knew was that he had shifted his position to enfold her in a comforting hug.

'Poor little Bethany . . . poor little wretch,' he said gently, patting her back.

The effect of this was to make her break down completely, the pent-up misery of years at last finding release in a storm of uncontrollable weeping.

She seemed to cry for a long time, but David showed no impatience. He did not say there was nothing to cry about, or abjure her to pull herself together as, afterwards, she felt sure any other man would have done. He merely held her against his shoulder, and stroked her short thick brown hair, as if she were six years old and entitled to an uninhibited howl when something upset her.

When at last she could speak coherently, she muttered, her face still hidden, 'I'm s-sorry . . . I f-feel such a f-fool.'

David said calmly, 'It does women good to cry. It's because men don't—or not often—that they get ulcers and coronaries. Want a handkerchief?'

A large clean white cotton handkerchief was put into her hand. With his right arm still lightly round her, she mopped her eyes and her wet cheeks.

Presently, he said, 'I think what you need after that is a hot drink laced with a little whisky to help you to sleep. I'll nip down and find some cocoa or chocolate or something. I shan't be long.'

When he had left her, going down the stairs as silently as a cat burglar, Bethany blew her nose and waited for her shaky breathing to revert to normal.

He was the nicest, kindest person she had ever met, she thought. She couldn't believe that he and her brusque, unaffectionate father had been brothers. They were as unlike in nature as in looks. She felt sure that, had the estrangement between them been caused by an offence on her father's part, by now David would have forgiven him and made some attempt to repair the breach.

By the time he returned she had slipped out of bed to the hand basin, and washed her tear-sticky face.

Brushing her hair, she had realised that, once free of Margaret's governance, she could follow Mrs Suffolk's suggestion that longer hair would be more becoming to her.

'You have an enviably long neck, Bethany,' her friend's mother had said to her. 'A long neck and long, slender legs are the essence of grace in a woman. But just at the moment, while you're growing and are still a bit coltish, that very short cut is too short. Hair down to your shoulders, and possibly longer, is what I think would suit you. You could wear it in a pigtail in term-time.'

But Lady Castle had not agreed. 'Short hair is neat and practical. You're untidy enough as it is. With long hair you'd look like a hippie,' had been her arbitrary response to Bethany's request.

Her accusation of untidiness was not unjustified. Bethany had to admit that sometimes she didn't keep her bedroom as neat as it should be. Cressida's lapses were even worse. But although her mother would remonstrate with her, in general she took a much more tolerant view of teenagers' shortcomings than Margaret Castle. But then Mrs Suffolk loved Cressida, whereas Margaret was not a loving person, even with her own daughters.

I wonder if she'll forbid me to go with David, Bethany pondered worriedly, after she had climbed into bed and was absently munching an apple.

When David returned, he brought a mug of hot chocolate for her, and a glass of whisky for himself, a little of which he tipped into the chocolate.

When she expressed her anxiety to him, he said, 'I shouldn't worry your head about that. Your stepmother is far too preoccupied with her own welfare to want to cross swords with me on your account. How long will it take you to pack? We shall have to leave early tomorrow to catch the noon flight to Genoa.'

'It will only take a few minutes. I can pack tonight, if you like.'

'No, no, leave it till the morning. You'd do better to go to sleep now, and get up early. Have you got an alarm clock?'

She shook her head.

'Then you'd better have my watch.' He unstrapped it. 'I'll set it for a quarter to seven. Okay?'

'Okay. But how will you wake up without it?'

'There's a calculator in my baggage which has an alarm. I'll have to show you how to use it. If you're going to be my factotum and do the shopping, a calculator will help you to convert lire into pounds, and to check that you aren't being diddled.'

'Are the Italians a nation of diddlers?' asked Bethany.

He grinned. 'In my experience they're among the most warmhearted, friendly people on the Continent. A tiny minority of kidnappers and bag-snatchers have given the country a bad name, but violence and vandalism are the exception rather than the rule, and only a few unlucky tourists have their bags snatched—a thing which happens in most countries. I'm sure you'll like the Italians—their language, their food, their marvellous eye for good design.'

'I can't wait to arrive,' she said happily, confident now that he was more than a match for her stepmother.

David laughed, and tossed back his whisky. 'I'll say goodnight now. Sleep tight.'

He leaned towards her, put his hand under her chin, and kissed her on the tip of her nose.

A little more than twelve hours later, Bethany went ahead of him up the steps of the aircraft which would fly them to Genoa.

Sir John and his wife had not cared for holidays abroad, so it was her first experience of roaring down a runway and soaring into the sky. Soon they were above the clouds which made it a grey, cool day at ground-level, up in the ethereal world of perpetual sunshine or starshine.

In spite of the hot chocolate nightcap, she had passed a rather restless night. After the meal had been served, she began to feel very drowsy.

The next thing she knew was that David was shaking her arm.

'Wake up, Bethany! We're nearly there.'

He had left his car, a streamlined bronze-coloured two-seater, in the car park at Genoa airport. The sprawling seaport, birthplace of Christopher Columbus, was not called Genoa in Italy, but Genova.

Soon they were on the *autostrada*, speeding south through a series of tunnels which pierced the green wooded hills, their outlines punctuated by the tall dark exclamation marks of columnar cypress trees.

'How far is Portofino?' she asked.

'Only thirty-six kilometres from Genova, which is about twenty-two miles. Ten minutes on the *autostrada*, and about the same after we leave it at Rapallo. Half an hour from now we can be up to our necks in the pool.'

'You have your own swimming pool?'

'Yes, it's a necessity in the hottest weather. Today is cool compared with July and August.'

But the day was hot compared with England; the sky as blue as his eyes, not a cloud to be seen.

The motorway exit for Rapallo led into the back of the small town, but soon they were passing the northern end of the sea-front where a crescent bay had once been dominated by a sixteenth-century castle built a short way off-shore.

Now it looked small and unimpressive in relation to the buildings behind the palm-lined promenade. Although nowhere could Bethany see any of the high-rise apartments and hotels which Mr and Mrs Suffolk said had ruined many Mediterranean resorts.

'The castle was built after Rapallo was sacked by an Algerian pirate called Dragut in 1549. He took about a hundred captives, and the castle was put up to stop a repetition of his visit,' David explained, when she asked him about it.

His own attention was fixed on the road which now wound along the narrow space between the sea on her side and the steep escarpments on his.

A few minutes later they passed through another resort which he told her was Santa Margherita Ligure, the Ligure being to distinguish it from another town of the same name elsewhere in Italy.

After this came a tiny place called Paraggi, soon after which he turned the car off the coast road and they snaked up a steep narrow lane which led past the gateway of several large villas and eventually to his own gate.

The house was called Villa Delphini after the Roman name for Portofino, Portus Delphini. For Bethany it was love at first sight. The exterior walls were painted the colour of ripe apricots. To her surprise and amusement the glowing colour was embellished by the most clever trompe l'oeil stonework. Although the façade of the building was really very simple, it appeared to be much grander than it was with carved stone surrounds to the windows and a handsome pediment over the entrance, all of which looked convincingly three-dimensional but were actually no more than skilful applications of paint.

Later she was to see many of these trompe l'oeil façades; some of recent origin, and some almost weathered away by years of hot summer sun and the rains which made the whole region so verdant.

As she climbed out of the car, David came round from his side, dangling a large old key with which to unlock the tall double doors. These, like many doors and shutters on older houses, were painted a dark blueish-green.

When the door was unlocked, he held out a hand to her, saying, 'Close your eyes and let me lead you for a minute or two. There's something I want you to see in one burst, as it were.'

Obediently, Bethany put her hand into his and shut her eyes tightly while he led her over the threshold and across a tiled floor. She heard another door being unlocked, and was guided from the coolness of the interior into bright sunshine again.

'Now you can look,' he instructed.

She opened her eyes—and gasped at the scene before her.

Below, thronged with large and small boats, was Portofino harbour and, beyond it, a wooded promontory topped by an imposing *castello*. Beyond that was the Mediterranean, its calm blue surface streaked by the white wakes of motorboats, the sound of their engines like the distant humming of bees.

'Nice, don't you think?' asked David.

'Nice is an understatement. It's . . . it's *paradise*!'

They were standing on a wide clay-tiled terrace, furnished with white chairs and loungers with white canvas cushions. In front of her was a balustrade beneath which, when she placed her hands on the warm stone and looked over, she could see the inviting sparkle of the swimming pool.

He said, 'Before we do anything else, let's have a swim, shall we? I'll get your case from the car, and show you where you're going to sleep.'

Five minutes later she was alone in a large lofty bedroom with the same lovely view as the terrace. David had told her to pack a bathing-suit, and the only one she possessed was a modest navy blue two-piece which only fairly recently had supplanted the even more decorous one-piece suits which had been regulation wear when she was first sent to boarding school.

David, when she ran downstairs to join him, was already in the water, surging along with a leisurely but powerful crawl.

It wasn't until he climbed out that she saw his bathing suit was as brief as it could possibly be, and that every inch of his tall, lithe, muscular frame was as deeply tanned as his face.

Suddenly the pallor of her own flesh seemed as nasty as the whiteness of the grubs sometimes found under logs and stones. She longed to be as brown as he.

That evening they had their dinner at a table outside one of the bars which ringed the waterfront piazza with its trees pruned like huge parasols.

Although the main tourist season was from June to September, the place also attracted visitors at Christmas and Easter, and the church which stood on the ridge linking promontory and mainland was golden in the blaze of floodlamps which made it stand out against the darkening sky.

They started their meal with a pasta called *tortellini*, each piece stuffed with chopped chicken.

'This shape is supposed to have been inspired by Venus's navel,' said David, as he sprinkled his helping plentifully with Parmesan cheese.

For the main course they had fried chicken with white beans flavoured with herbs, and a salad tossed in olive oil which reminded Bethany of the Suffolks.

'I must send a postcard to Cressida.'

She had finished her letter to her friend and posted it at London Airport. How staggered the Suffolks would be when they heard where she was, and with whom!

'Do you realise that yesterday morning I hadn't met you?—

And here I am, actually in Italy. I can quite see why you weren't interested in taking over from Margaret. Who would be there when they could live here?'

'Many people would. There are much worse places to be than a fine old English country house, even if the weather is unreliable. As a boy, when my parents were alive, I was very fond of Blackmead. But I must admit I prefer more sun than England has to offer.'

'Is it sunny here most of the winter?'

They were eating cheese now—ripe Gorgonzola—and, as she looked up at his face after pressing a piece on her bread, she realised that he was watching someone at another table.

There was a light in his eyes which she could not describe, and which died away when he redirected his gaze to her face, and replied to her question.

Later, while he was paying the bill, she was able to look behind her at whoever had caught his attention and caused that disturbing expression.

Since all but one table on that side of the pavement café was empty, he could only have been staring at a woman who was sitting by herself, reading a novel. Bethany could see the title. It was a French novel.

Just then the waiter brought her what looked like an ice, except that it was dark red in colour. The woman's hair was also red; Titian red, and her eyes were green.

She was not young. About David's age. She was wearing a green silk shirt. When she leaned forward to take up her spoon, it was possible to see the upper curves of her lightly browned breasts where the shirt was open at the front. She had full red lips, and gold hoop ear-rings, and many kinds of rings on her fingers. Bethany could see that she was very attractive, and wondered why she was alone.

The woman did not glance at them as they left their table. She was giving all her attention to what she was eating, filling her spoon and lifting it slowly to her mouth as if the dark red substance was the most delicious dish she had ever tasted.

'Shall we stretch our legs?' David suggested.

They strolled the full length of the waterfront, which branched to right and left of the piazza, on one side being a narrowish walk in front of an assortment of tall, colour-washed houses, and on the other being considerably wider, with berths for large sea-going yachts.

Afterwards they walked up the steep, lamplit way to the church, its forecourt paved with small cobbles, some black and some white, arranged in an attractive design.

From it, there was a fine view out to sea as well as over the little harbour, its still dark waters reflecting the lights of the cafés and houses, and the many craft at their moorings.

When they returned to the piazza, David asked her if she were tired. But Bethany, having slept on the plane, had never felt less tired. So they walked again in the direction of the ship's chandlery and the plaque in the rock-face which said that Guy de Maupassant had written his novel *Bel-Ami* at Portofino.

It was as they were returning from this stroll that they again saw the redhaired woman. She was coming towards them, her book tucked under her arm, her hands in the pockets of her skirt. She walked with a swing from the hips. Her shoes were wedge-heeled espadrilles with tapes criss-crossed round her ankles.

This time she did notice them, looking first at David and then at Bethany.

However, before they came abreast, he paused to admire the sweeping lines of a large American yacht, out of Newport, Rhode Island, on which there were no signs of life although a gangway led from her afterdeck to the quay near where they were standing.

As he was looking at the vessel, the woman also paused there. But she was looking at him, not at the yacht.

'*Buona sera.*' Her voice was unusually deep.

'*Buona sera.*' He gave a slight bow.

They exchanged long appraising glances, both of them smiling slightly, as if sharing a private joke.

Then the woman ascended the gangway, stepped lightly on board and walked forward towards the bows, and out of their sight.

CHAPTER THREE

AFTER eight days of unalloyed happiness, Bethany flew back to London to spend two nights with the Suffolks before returning to school with Cressida.

As soon as the girls were alone, Cressida said, 'You should have heard Mummy raving when I read her the letter you posted before you left England. She was nearly berserk with anxiety. She said it was absolutely scandalous that anyone, even your stepmother, could be so unfeeling and unscrupulous as to let a girl of sixteen go abroad with an unmarried man they didn't know anything about. Daddy was equally furious. Then the next day Sir David rang up from Italy, and asked if we would meet you off the plane and put you up for a couple of nights. That calmed them down and made them realise he wasn't the vile seducer he might have been.'

'He doesn't want to be called Sir David,' said Bethany. 'He prefers being plain Mr Castle or, professionally, David Warren.'

'You're so beautifully brown,' said Cressida. 'You make me feel like a corpse. Tell me everything . . . every detail.'

Bethany described the villa, the breakfasts of fresh bread and honey, and going very early to Rapallo to shop in the market near the church for fruit and vegetables and strange Mediterranean fish, quite different from cold water species.

'When we've finished the marketing, we go to Massone's for ices. There's a dark red one called *mirtilli* which is made from the bilberries which grow on the hillsides round there. Oh, the ices, Cressida! Flavours you never get here. Fig . . . chestnut . . . peach . . . all delicious.'

Cressida's problem was plumpness.

'Which would make *me* burst out of my jeans. But you don't seem to have put on a pound, lucky thing,' she said enviously.

Later, in a tactfully roundabout way, Mrs Suffolk questioned Bethany about David and his way of life.

'Cressida says my letter worried you. I'm sorry about that, Mrs Suffolk.'

'We're very fond of you, Bethany. When you wrote that your uncle was an artist, it conjured alarming visions of your being embroiled with a colony of second-rate expatriate painters, some of whom might take drugs and so forth. I must admit we were horrified. Didn't you feel any misgivings about going abroad with someone you'd never heard of before he pitched up at the Manor?'

'I had heard of him,' Bethany answered. 'From Cressida, actually.'

'From Cressida?' said her mother, looking baffled.

'Yes. Ages ago ... years ago, she overheard you talking to someone about the row between David and my father. Mrs Suffolk, do you know what that row was about?'

Laura Suffolk was a woman of a very different stamp from Lady Castle. She exerted a sensible discipline over her daughter, but her rules were never unreasonable. She would listen to and sometimes be swayed by Cressida's point of view, and her daughter could ask her anything and be sure of an honest answer.

Now, for the first time since she had known Mrs Suffolk, Bethany saw that her friend's mother was disconcerted and even embarrassed by her question.

After a pause, she said slowly, 'No, I don't *know* what caused it. I heard various conjectures about it. I had friends living in that neighbourhood, and they used to gossip to me sometimes. But only your uncle knows the truth of the matter—or at least his side of it—and I think you should ask him, my dear.'

'I did. He admits he did something very bad, but he said it needn't make me distrust him, and that there were extenuating circumstances.'

'Yes, I should think there probably were. Anyway, it's a long time ago, and people change as they grow older. He was very young ... a mere boy.'

For Bethany her last summer term at school seemed to pass with interminable slowness because of her eagerness to return to Italy. David wrote to her once or twice—his letters illustrated with amusing pen and wash sketches—and she wrote to him every week.

In the fortnight before the exams there was one of England's infrequent heatwaves. All the other O-level candidates complained that temperatures in the high seventies didn't help them with their last-minute swotting. Bethany did hers in secluded parts of the school grounds, wearing her navy two-piece, more concerned about reviving her tan than about the dreaded exams.

She had decided that she was definitely going to be a linguist, and was only concerned about getting good grades in the language papers. Her results in the other subjects were a matter of indifference to her.

At last it was over, her school career. The wide world and womanhood beckoned.

On her last night in England, the Suffolks took her and Cressida to the new hit musical at the London Palladium. They had rented a house on Hydra, one of the Greek islands, and were flying to Athens the next day. Cressida's mood was as excited as Bethany's.

This being her third flight across Europe, she arrived at the airport feeling an experienced traveller. The day before, Mrs Suffolk had taken both the girls shopping, and insisted on buying some holiday clothes for Bethany as well as her daughter.

Now, in a new blouse and skirt, and with longer hair, she felt she looked much less waif-like than she had on her first flight to Italy.

David would be waiting for her at Genova. The flight was on time, so he would not be kept hanging about, perhaps regretting the bother of having to come and meet her when he would rather be painting.

She had made a resolution always to be ultra-considerate, never to make him regret taking on responsibility for her. Even if not a burden in other ways, she was bound to be a drain on his income.

The aircraft began its descent, and the cabin crew moved down the aisle, checking that seat-belts were fastened and trays in the upright position. A few other people on board were obviously holidaymakers, but most of her fellow passengers were Italian or British businessmen who were re-packing their briefcases with the papers they had been studying during the flight.

And I'm going home, thought Bethany happily—for already

the Villa Delphini felt far more like home than Blackmead Manor had ever done.

It was easy to single out David in the group of people waiting to greet the air travellers. Although some Italians were tall, he was the tallest man there, his straight sun-bleached hair all the more striking among the dark heads surrounding him.

She wasn't sure how he would greet her; with a handshake or a kiss. She was pleased when he opened his arms, inviting her to hug him, which was just what she wanted to do.

When they drew apart, he said teasingly, 'I expected to find you still haggard and heavy-eyed from the strain of the dreaded O-levels, but you look full of beans.'

'And feel it! Oh, David, it's super to be back —and not just for eight days this time.'

'It's good to have you back, sweetie,' he said affectionately. 'There's a celebration lunch waiting for us at the villa, and as soon as we get there I'll open a bottle of champagne and we'll drink to the end of schooldays and the beginning of Life with a capital L.'

How perfect he was, she thought adoringly, as the car winged along the *autostrada*, into the darkness of the tunnels and out into the sunlight again. So tanned. So immaculately clean in his pink cotton shirt and white pants, his brown ankles bare above navy blue canvas aspadrilles.

She was cooler now, with the hood down and the slipstream blowing in her hair. But outside the air-conditioned airport, while David was loading her luggage into the boot, it had been swelteringly hot, at least ten degrees hotter than at Easter.

She could hardly wait to change into the new blue bikini which Mrs Suffolk had bought for her, then stand under the outdoor shower on the pool terrace before diving into the pool itself.

'So what's new since your last letter?' David asked, with a smiling glance at her.

She told him about the show they had been to the night before. As they drove into Rapallo, she sang one of the best of the songs to him. She had to substitute de-da-de-da for some of the words, but the tone she could remember perfectly. She had always been able to pick up a tune at first hearing.

He seemed impressed by this ability. 'I didn't realise you were musical. Can you play an instrument, or is singing your forte?'

'Having just heard my voice—what a question!' she answered, laughing.

'I think you have a charming voice.'

'Really? I'm afraid Miss Hawker—our choir-mistress—didn't share your opinion. Not that I particularly wanted to be in the choir. *Nymphs and shepherds, come away . . . come away* is not my kind of music. I'm an Aznavour and Bryan Ferry fan.'

'What about instrumental music? Did you have piano lessons or anything?'

'No, I can't say I ever wanted to. Having an ear for a tune doesn't make me a musical genius.'

'Perhaps not, but it's a talent which might have developed into something more, and perhaps still could,' he replied. 'I saw a harp for sale in an antique shop in Genova this morning. How does that appeal to you?'

'I love the sound of a harp. I've never felt the urge to play one. I'm going to adopt your suggestion and become an extremely brilliant linguist,' she said, in a tone of playful boasting.

The beaches at Rapallo and Santa Margherita were almost invisible, hidden beneath rows of coloured umbrellas and supine bodies. Even the sea was crowded with bathers. All the benches in the promenade gardens were packed with elderly people watching the passing throng.

Towards Portofino the traffic became a bumper-to-bumper queue of cars in both directions. Their journey back to the villa took twice as long as at Easter. But at last they were able to break away from the stream of crawling vehicles and shoot up the hill leading to the Villa Delphini.

David parked the car in the shade.

Having unclipped her seat-belt, Bethany sat for a moment feasting her eyes on the apricot walls and the painted architectural details of the house she had thought of so often during the term.

Last time all the shutters at the back of the house had been closed. Today they were open, some of them fully, and some with their lower halves pushed out at an angle to the upper parts, and propped in position by stays.

David came round the bonnet to open her door for her.

'I don't know about you, but I'm parched. Before I unload your baggage, I need some of that champagne!'

They walked towards the front door. Unexpectedly, it opened before they reached it.

'I wasn't sure if I'd heard the car coming back or not. I was half asleep by the pool,' said the woman who emerged. She was wearing a short cover-up of gauzy green Indian cotton over a bikini. Her eyes were masked by large dark glasses.

Even before she took them off, Bethany had recognised her. It was the redhaired woman who had gone aboard the American yacht on her first night at Portofino.

'I hope you've got the champagne on ice, Francine. We're both very thirsty,' said David.

He introduced them. 'Bethany, this is Madame Valery, whose superb cooking you'll soon have the pleasure of sampling.'

'How do you do?' Bethany held out her hand.

Her first reactions to the sight of the Frenchwoman were surprise, puzzlement, and an acute disappointment that she was not going to have David to herself for the rest of the day.

'How do you do, Miss Castle,' the older woman said formally, before they shook hands. Then her face broke into a smile; a warm smile which made her green eyes sparkle. 'But if you don't mind I should prefer to call you Bethany, and you must call me Francine, please. Will you be offended if I make what the English call a personal remark?'

Evidently this was a rhetorical question, as she didn't wait for an answer but went on, 'You are looking much, much prettier than when I first saw you one night down at the harbour. Then you were more a child than a woman, but now it is the other way round. I can see you have begun to arrange yourself. The longer hair is much more becoming to you.'

'Thank you,' said Bethany, warming to her.

They went through to the supper terrace where, in the shade of the awning, a gold-foiled green bottle was up to its waist in crushed ice.

There was a sound like a sigh, and a wisp of vapour escaped as David eased out the cork, then filled the three flutes on the tray. He handed one to Francine, one to Bethany and, taking up the third glass himself, said, 'In the words of Jonathan Swift—May you live all the days of your life. To you, *signorina*.'

They raised their glasses and drank to her, and she murmured another shy 'Thank you' and sipped the pale sparkling wine with lips which quivered a little because she was so very happy.

The lunch Francine had prepared began with a spectacular mousse, part chicken, part ham, the whole thing decorated with hardboiled eggs and asparagus tips under a clear glaze of aspic. With it was a salad which was a revelation to Bethany; it contained not only the usual ingredients but also nuts, raw mushrooms marinated in orange juice, small florets of raw cauliflower, and little curly, crunchy bean sprouts.

Afterwards came a beautiful *tarte Tatin* made with pears instead of the classic apples, the grainy texture of the pears a perfect foil for the sweetness of the caramel. Finally there was *dolcelatte* cheese, with a basket of fresh black figs.

'You remember the American yacht which was berthed in the harbour when you were here before, Bethany?' said David. 'She had come from the Caribbean, with Francine as her cook. Unfortunately for her owner, but fortunately for me, I managed to induce her to give up seafaring and cook for me for a while.'

'For a while,' the Frenchwoman repeated.

It sounded as if she did not mean to stay in Portofino for too long.

After lunch, Bethany unpacked her belongings in the room which had been hers at Easter. A vase of white carnations had been placed on the writing table, and she wondered whose thought it had been—David's or Francine's.

Their manner towards each other during lunch had not been at all lover-like. But she felt it was not very likely that the Frenchwoman's role in the ménage was only to cook and keep house for him. Presumably she was what was known as a living-in girl-friend.

Meditating over their relationship, Bethany found that her growing liking for Francine made a liaison between them less unacceptable than it had seemed at first thought.

It was not to be expected that a man of David's age, with

his virile good looks and his charm, would have led a celibate life. He must have had relationships with many women but, as yet, never found the one whom he wanted to marry; the great love of his life.

Bethany stared at her reflection in the huge, damp-spotted old mirror which reflected the bed and the antique tapestry hanging on the wall behind it.

How long would it be before she was fully grown-up? One year? Two years?

Legally, girls in England were free to marry without parental consent at the age of eighteen. But most people thought that too young to embark on a lifelong relationship. Probably nineteen was the earliest at which the majority of older people would consider a girl ready for marriage.

Her own nineteenth birthday was two and a half years ahead of her. It seemed a long way away. Thirty months. One hundred and twenty weeks. Eight hundred and something days . . .

A tap at the door interrupted her reflections. Francine put her head round the jamb.

'Have you everything you need in here, Bethany? Enough shelves for your books? Enough hangers for your dresses in the *armoire*?'

'Yes, thank you, more than enough. I didn't bring very much with me.'

Spread out on the bed, waiting to be arranged, her personal possessions did look remarkably sparse for a girl in her seventeenth year. Most of them were books, these being what she had usually asked for for her birthdays and at Christmas.

'May I come in and chat to you?' Francine enquired.

'Of course . . . please do.'

'That I like very much,' said the Frenchwoman, noticing a sea-green sundress draped over the end of the bed. 'It's a Laura Ashley, I think—yes? Her clothes are in excellent taste, and pure cotton is the only thing to wear in a hot climate. Synthetics are useless. Even when houses are air-conditioned, as in America, I prefer to wear natural materials.'

'You've lived in America?' Bethany asked.

'Yes, it's where I went first after leaving my husband. I've a sister who is married to an American, and it seemed a good place to start my travels. For the previous ten years I had lived in a small town in France, and I wanted to see all the places I had only read about. San Francisco . . . New Orleans . . . Martinique . . . Lisbon . . . Alicante . . . Monte Carlo. Now I have seen them, but there's still a long list of other places where I want to go before I'm old.'

'Were they as you imagined them, or were some of them disappointing?' Bethany asked.

'No: different sometimes, but never disappointing.'

Francine sat down in a chair by the tall, wide-open french doors which gave on to a small balcony. She had a carrier with her from which she produced a length of satin partially trimmed with lace edging. Slipping a thimble on the second finger of her right hand, she began to continue whipping the lace to the satin and, while she sewed, to talk.

It was the first of many conversations. As yet Francine had not been to England, and was curious to know all that Bethany could tell her about it.

As the days passed, while David was out making sketch notes, or composing a painting in his studio, a friendship established itself between the woman and the girl.

As well as cooking magnificently, Francine was a talented needlewoman who concentrated her skill on designing and making the most exquisite underclothes. She had been to a convent school where the nuns not engaged in teaching children were famous for their beautiful needlework. Some of the pupils stayed on at the end of their ordinary schooling to learn the fine stitchery practised by the Sisters.

'I could not help being amused, and also sad on their behalf, whenever I saw those poor women, who would always be virgins, spending their days sewing lingerie which we, who are not virgins, wear when we hope or expect to be undressed by a lover,' she said to Bethany. 'Imagine going to your grave with lips which have never been kissed, and a body which has never been caressed. I'm sure some of them must regret it— when it is too late to change their minds. It's more difficult for a bride of Christ to renounce her religious vocation than for a woman to escape from a marriage which was a mistake.'

'Was yours a mistake?' asked Bethany.

'Very much so. I married a boy because he was handsome, and I couldn't wait to find out what making love was like. When I was eighteen—twenty years ago—girls like me, in small provincial towns, dared not go too far before they were married. Those who did usually got into trouble.'

Francine paused to re-thread her needle. As usual she was busy with her sewing.

'If we had had children, I should still be with my husband. But no babies came, and after some years I thought: What am I doing, wasting my life in a town I don't like with a man who doesn't amuse me? Even love, with him, was a let-down—he enjoyed it, but I didn't much. So one day I said I was leaving. He was angry, not because he loved me, but because I was a good housewife. It was inconvenient for him to have to find someone else to cook his meals and to sleep with him.'

She raised her green eyes to look at Bethany. 'Don't you make the same mistake, *chérie*. Don't marry your first love— or not unless you are very sure he is also going to be your last love. They are the same person sometimes, but not very often.'

When Bethany received her examination results—A grades in two foreign languages, and B grades in four other subjects— David said, 'Well done, sweetie. You deserve a treat. How about a trip to Florence?'

'Oh, David—could we? Can you afford it?'

Having just finished reading a book about the extraordinary Medici family who had been in the forefront of the Italian Renaissance, she was eager to visit the city which had been the scene of their power and their grandeur.

'I'm doing rather well at the moment. My pictures are going to be shown at the Kennedy Galleries in New York, and the Laing Galleries in Toronto; both of which have a large clientèle of people who think nothing of spending thousands of dollars on a painting which takes their fancy. Certainly we can afford a week in Florence. Not at the Excelsior, but there are other hotels which are equally nice and not as expensive.'

They decided to postpone the visit until late in September, by which time the soaring temperatures of high summer would have dropped to a more comfortable level for city sightseeing.

Although they shared a bedroom, in Bethany's presence David and Francine were not demonstrative. She had never seen them kiss each other, even in a casual fashion; nor had they ever again exchanged the strange secret smile she remembered from their first encounter.

But a few days before they left Portofino, something happened to disturb her placid acceptance of the relationship between them.

Waking up between midnight and one, hot and thirsty, she went down to the kitchen to help herself to some mineral water, several bottles of which were always to be found in the refrigerator.

A couple of weeks earlier they had been adopted by a stray cat which, while they were away, would be fed by Maria, the cleaning woman. The animal had been named Caterina, generally shortened to Cat. She reminded Bethany of Mossy, a little striped female cat she had loved when she was much younger.

Mossy had been given to her by an old lady who lived in the village half a mile down the road from the Manor. Provided the cat was spayed before she produced any kittens, Lady Castle had not objected to her. One summer, when Bethany was thirteen, Mossy had been hit by a car, but the vet had patched up her injuries. The accident left her with a limp, and Margaret Castle said she should have been put down. While Bethany was away at school, she had Mossy destroyed, justifying her act by saying that the cat had become incontinent and to keep her would have been insanitary.

Whether or not this was true, the shock of coming home for Christmas to find Mossy gone, and the sense of betrayal she had felt, had made Bethany seethe with impotent rage for a long time afterwards.

While she was drinking the refreshingly cold water, Cat left the box which was her bed and, purring, wound herself round and between Bethany's ankles. She bent down to pick her up and scratch her gently behind the ears in the way which Mossy had enjoyed.

Presently she put the cat back in her box, and switched out the lights before returning to her room.

David's bedroom door was opposite the head of the staircase. As she stepped on to the landing, her bare feet making no sound on the cool, smooth tiles, a noise from within made her check. It came again, slightly louder; a sort of soft moaning sound interspersed with staccato gasps.

Was one of them having a nightmare? she wondered, listening.

Believing them to be asleep, and with no intention of eavesdropping, she moved closer to the door and stopped breathing, the better to hear the low groans of one of the sleepers.

'... no, no ... oh, no ... stop ... please stop ...' The pleading, frantic voice was Francine's.

There was a low laugh. David's laugh. Then a cry, and a different appeal. This time she was begging him not to stop.

When Bethany realised that what she could hear through the door were the sounds of people making love, and the stifled cries of a woman close to unimaginable ecstasy, at first she was rooted to the spot.

Then, terrified that they might sense her presence, and come to the door and find her there, apparently spying on them, she fled to her own room at the far end of the landing.

Profoundly disturbed by the incident, she lay awake for a long time, trying not to imagine what they were doing in the wide, elaborately draped bed which had been one of the furnishings David had bought with the villa.

So far it had not been difficult to close her mind to the private side of their relationship. After what she had overheard, it would be impossible. Even now, against her will, her mind's eye was showing her pictures of David and Francine engaged in the various acts of love illustrated in a book which had circulated among the members of the Upper Fifth during her last term.

The book had amplified facts which Bethany had known for a long time. But it hadn't interested her as much as it had Cressida and some of the other girls. Now she wished she had never looked at it, for then her imagination could not have presented her with such graphic images of what might be happening in the large moonlit bedroom at the far end of the house.

She remembered the Frenchwoman confiding that her husband had been an unsatisfactory lover. Obviously David made love with much greater skill. Perhaps Francine would fall in love with him, and forget about carrying on with her travels. Perhaps he would ask her to stay with him permanently. That she was a few years older was probably not too important, unless he wanted to have children, which he didn't seem to. Francine was immensely attractive, and good-tempered, and a wonderful cook. What more could he want of a woman?

The next day, and for some days after, Bethany continued to feel disturbed by what she had accidentally overheard.

Even while they were driving to Florence, she could not help wondering if they would rather be by themselves, without her sitting behind them.

But soon the excitement of arriving in one of the world's fabled cities drove everything else from her mind. It was a little before lunchtime, and David parked the car on one of the bridges spanning the slow-flowing Arno and took them to have a club sandwich at Harry's Bar, a riverside restaurant popular with Americans.

As in Rapallo, the shops in Florence were closed between one o'clock and half past four. After their snack they returned to the car to drive to the hotel he had chosen.

The Hotel Villa Belvedere was a few kilometres out of the heart of the city, and the first-floor room he had booked for himself and Francine had a large sun-roof outside it, with a view over the rooftops of Florence, dominated by the dome of the cathedral, and of the surrounding low hills.

Bethany's room was on the second floor, at the back of the building, but it had a private bathroom and a pleasant outlook over the garden of a neighbouring villa.

'As soon as you've hung up your things, come down and share our sun-roof,' said David, who had accompanied her upstairs to see that her room was satisfactory.

'I think I shall swim and sit by the pool,' she answered.

'Just as you wish. We'll take it easy till about four, and then we'll go out and see the town.'

The hotel had a small free-form swimming pool surrounded by reclining chairs, about half of them occupied. Bethany spent the next couple of hours there. Whenever she looked up from her book, she could see David and Francine through the railings round the roof of the hotel's breakfast room and bar. Several of the best bedrooms had a share of this sun-roof, but at present there was no one else up there. Francine appeared to be dozing, and David was drawing. He sketched at every opportunity; always carrying a pad and a black pen or sepia crayon.

Presently, when she glanced upwards, they had gone inside, perhaps to sleep, perhaps to lock the door and make love.

At a quarter to four she had a shower, and put on a jonquil-coloured dress, one of several Francine had run up for her on a borrowed sewing machine. Then she went downstairs to the garden bar and waited for them to join her, which they did about half an hour later.

For Bethany, strolling through the heart of the city for the first time was a magical experience. She had only to raise her eyes above the level of the shop fronts to feel herself back in old Florence. Here, in the Quattrocento—the fifteenth century—tables had been set with knives and forks, while in England, and the rest of Europe, people were still eating with their fingers.

Here, in these narrow streets between the tall, splendid *palazzos* with their jutting eaves, Michelangelo had walked, and Benvenuto Cellini, one of the world's greatest goldsmiths.

Florentine bankers had held the purse-strings of Europe, with agents in every major city. She knew that one group of bankers, headed by the powerful Bardi and Peruzzi families, had financed King Edward III of England in his battles against the French to the tune of 1,365,000 gold florins. When he had declared himself bankrupt, he had toppled the entire structure of Florentine banking. Only temporarily. Soon the zestful, driving ambition of the city's leading men had made Florence richer and stronger than before.

David, who had first come to Florence before she was born, thought it was being ruined by the noise and fumes of heavy traffic, and that a much larger area should be made a pedestrian precinct. But his two companions had no faults to find. Bethany was enchanted by the strong aroma of the past, and Francine declared she had never seen a greater *embarras de choix* of fashionable shoes and clothes in a city which was not a national capital and had a population of less than half a million people.

About half past six they had drinks in a pavement café in the Piazza della Signoria, the great open space in front of the Palazzo Vecchio.

Before they sat down to relax, David had shown them a profile cut in one of the lower stones of the palace wall. It was said to have been chiselled by Michelangelo, working 'blind', with his hands behind his back, for a bet.

In the centre of the piazza, he had drawn their attention to a stone which marked the spot where Savonarola, the fanatical Dominican friar who, four years earlier, had exhorted the Florentines to burn their vanities, including some of Botticelli's paintings, had himself been burned to death for heresy.

'Tomorrow while you two are going round all the museums, I am going to enjoy an orgy of shopping,' said Francine, as she sipped her Negroni cocktail. 'I am interested in the work of some modern artists'—with a smile at David—'but not very much in old masters.'

'Don't you want to see Botticelli's *Birth of Venus*, and Michelangelo's David?' Bethany asked her.

'I have seen it already ... over there.' Francine waved a hand in the direction of the statue of a naked man on a plinth by the door of the palace.

'I mean the original David in the Accademia. That one is only a copy.'

'No, you and David can go together. I am what you call a philistine,' said Francine. 'I would rather go window-shopping in the Via Tornabuoni and find myself some bronze kid sandals.'

Bethany was amazed and rather shocked that anyone should come to Florence and deliberately ignore its treasury of masterpieces.

But David laughed, and said, 'Okay, *carissima*, you do your thing and we'll do ours, and we'll all meet somewhere for lunch. Talking of food, are you girls hungry tonight? Could you manage a pizza?'

It was the first time she had heard him call the Frenchwoman by the lovely Italian word for darling. He was not a man for casual endearments, except for the 'sweetie' he sometimes used to Bethany herself.

Did it mark a significant advance in his relationship with Francine?

The pizzeria where he had eaten as a student was no longer in business. But he soon found another very like it, a place called La Nuova Campana—The New Bell—in a narrow street off the great open space surrounding the green, white and pink marble-faced cathedral known as the Duomo.

As a waiter showed them to a table, Bethany noticed he was wearing a wide tight cummerbund, made of some stretchy black fabric, with his black trousers and white shirt. All the waiters were. Although it suited the slim ones, it looked like a corset on the paunchy ones.

There were many kinds of pizza to choose from. David suggested they should each order a different one and share them.

Bethany was watching one of the cooks, a young man with curly hair dressed in a spotless white sweatshirt, as he kneaded and shaped the pizza dough, when suddenly he caught her eye and winked at her.

She blushed and quickly looked elsewhere. She guessed that he often winked at girls in the restaurant, but she couldn't help feeling a little pleased. She had noticed many Florentines looking admiringly at Francine, but the cook with the mop of black curls was the first to show interest in her.

The following day she and David spent much of the morning in the Uffizi Gallery. At the riverside end of the long courtyard between the two wings of the gallery there were many young art students stationed beside their easels. On these were pinned portraits of each other to give prospective sitters a sample of each student's skill. Some of the portraits were straightforward likenesses, and others were charcoal caricatures.

As David and Bethany watched one student at work on a portrait of a pretty German tourist, others beckoned them to pose for them. None of them seemed to be charging more than a few hundred lire.

'Why don't you have a portrait done?' David suggested. 'Your face isn't fully formed yet. It will be an interesting memento of Florence and your middle teens. That chap over there seems quite talented.'

Rather against her inclinations, he persuaded her to sit to a bearded student in a red shirt and much-patched jeans.

When the portrait was finished, the young artist sprayed it with a fixative and rolled it up. David paid him his fee, and Bethany, relieved to stop being the cynosure of a small crowd of onlookers, murmured, '*Grazie. Arrivederci,*' and retired behind the screen of her sunglasses.

They found Francine already at their rendezvous, the chair beside her laden with parcels.

'What is that?' she asked, indicating the roll of paper in David's hand.

'A portrait of Bethany. What do you think of it?' He

unrolled it for her inspection.

She stared at it critically for some moments.

'It's quite good, but the mouth isn't right. Why get a student to draw you when you have an artist in the family?—A much better artist than this one.'

'It wasn't my idea, it was David's. Have you ever done portraits, David?' Bethany asked him.

'Not since I was a student. Perhaps I might have a crack at a sketch of you this afternoon. I think half the trouble with this was that you were shy of being drawn in public, and it gave you an unnatural expression. With me you can relax. Now let's hear what Francine's been up to. What have you got in all those parcels?'

'I'm afraid I have been very extravagant,' Francine admitted.

She said it in a tone and with a look which made Bethany realise that David must have financed her shopping expedition, and that probably she had no money except what he gave her.

In effect she was what, in some of the old-fashioned novels in the library at the Manor, had been referred to as 'a kept woman'. True, she earned her keep by other means than they had, being his cook and the mistress of his household as well as his mistress in the other sense.

But Bethany couldn't help feeling that, unless she were married to a man, she would not enjoy spending his money. If she herself ever had a lover, she would want to be independent of him financially. Otherwise their relationship would be flawed by a mercenary element which, for her, would spoil it.

'But I have not bought presents only for myself,' Francine went on. 'I have gifts for you two as well. For you, David, a shirt which, if you don't like it, they will change.' She showed him a striped blue shirt, rather lighter than his vivid eyes. 'And for Bethany a belt and some ear-rings.' She put two parcels in the girl's lap.

The belt was a twisted skein of strips of white and gold kid with a tasselled fastening. The ear-rings, which Bethany had expected to be from a cheap but chic range they had looked at the night before, turned out to be hoops of what looked like gold.

'They are actually a present from David which he asked me to choose for you,' Francine explained.

'A reward for being a good girl and doing well in your exams,' he added.

'But I thought this trip was my treat. These aren't *real* gold, are they?' she asked, delight mingled with dismay at his extravagance.

'In Cellini's city, what else? The craftsmanship here is still of a very high order, and very competitively priced,' he added, reaching out a long brown hand to pick up one of the earrings and examine it.

The hoops were not plain but twisted. They were made for pierced ears, she noticed.

At the same moment, Francine said, 'I've arranged for you to have your ears pierced the day before we go back. The actual piercing isn't painful, but sometimes the lobes are a little tender for a day or two afterwards, so it will be better to have them done at the end of the holiday.'

'Thank you, David. They're lovely. I shall treasure them always.' Bethany stood up to brush a soft kiss on one of his cheeks.

'Yes, thank you, David, for my presents.' Francine kissed the tip of two fingers and applied them lightly to his other cheek.

'My pleasure, my dears.' His smile included them both.

In the afternoon, at the hotel, he did a sepia sketch of Bethany which captured with much greater accuracy the tender young lines of her mouth, and the downward sweep of her lashes as she read a book while he drew her.

The pose was characteristic, her chin on the heel of one hand, and her other hand unconsciously playing with a strand of hair behind her ear. He included her long slender legs, crossed and crossed again in the posture of a girl still enough of a child to become completely engrossed and oblivious of the world around her.

But a girl who was also a woman, as he showed by the curves of her breasts under a clinging jersey sun top, and by the smooth grace of her thighs exposed by her short shorts.

At the bottom of the drawing he wrote *Bethany—sixteen going on seventeen*, and his name and the date.

He said, 'I must draw you again this time next year. Twelve months make great changes at your age.'

Next day they persuaded Francine that, even if she saw nothing else, she must see the Museo degli Argenti—the Museum of Jewels—at the Pitti Palace.

But it was not the priceless collection of jewels, cameos, silver, crystal, ivory and porcelain which had belonged to the Medici family which made the most lasting impression on Bethany. Even Lorenzo Il Magnifico's personal collection of exquisite vases made from semi-precious stones did not afterwards linger in her mind as clearly and ineradicably as one portrait in a building filled with paintings.

Although she had read the life of the most famous Medici, she had never seen a picture of him. Suddenly, there he was— Lorenzo di Piero de' Medici, a man with long straight black hair, wearing a plain dark red robe with a touch of white at the collar, and thinking about something which amused him and made his wide sensual mouth curl up at the corners, and his dark eyes glint.

Later that morning, and throughout the rest of their time in Florence, she was to see other pictures of him. But none had the dramatic impact of this first anonymous painting of Lorenzo's strong, forceful features and his compelling black eyes.

She knew, as she looked at his face, that if she had lived in Florence in his time, she would have fallen in love with him. There was something about him which had such a curious effect on her that she could almost believe that she *had* lived here, and had known him.

She was still thinking about him as they walked the short distance from the Pitti Palace to perhaps the most famous of the city's sights, the Ponte Vecchio.

There were many bridges spanning the Arno as it flowed through the city, as well as a diagonal weir on which, at the dry end, people sunbathed. The Ponte Vecchio was the oldest of the bridges, and the only one not damaged in the Second World War. It differed from all the others in that both sides were lined with small shops, almost all of them devoted to gold and silver jewellery.

In the centre of the bridge was an open space, the haunt of

university students, itinerant foreign guitarists, and tourists taking photographs.

Leaving Bethany there, sitting in the sun on the wide parapet, entranced by the passing throng, David took Francine into one of the shops for a souvenir more lasting than clothes.

When they came back, the Frenchwoman was wearing a delicately-fashioned two-colour gold chain round her neck. But although she spent the rest of the day taking admiring peeps at it in the mirror in the lid of her blusher box, Bethany had a sixth-sense feeling that what Francine had hoped he would buy her was a gold ring for her third finger.

All too soon it was time to return to the Villa Delphini.

With the lobes of her ears slightly sore, and wearing the small sleeper pins which she must keep in place, day and night, for the next three months, Bethany returned to Portofino in a happier frame of mind than she had left it.

Somehow the feeling of being an interloper, and the lurking jealousy she had felt on the journey south, no longer troubled her. She knew it was probably foolish, but her mind was full of thoughts of a man who had lived and died five hundred years ago.

Autumn in Portofino was like summer in more northerly places, and early winter as warm and dry as a fine autumn. At Christmas the three of them went to one of the Italian ski resorts.

Soon after Christmas came Bethany's birthday; the happiest birthday of her life. By now she was speaking good Italian, and keeping up her French and German.

After that it was sometimes cold and wet. But interspersed with the bad days were days, sometimes weeks, of good weather when she and Francine would lie in a sheltered part of the garden and top up their tans.

A week or two before Easter, David had to take some paintings to London. He went by himself because it was a business trip. He would only be away for two nights.

Francine drove him to the airport. When she came back, she dropped a bombshell.

Walking into the kitchen where Bethany was giving Cat a saucer of milk, she said, 'I'm going away too, Bethany. I made enquiries at the airport, and booked a flight which takes off an hour before David's flight lands. I've known for some time there was no future in staying here, but I've put off the final decision. Now I've bought my ticket and I'm going . . . and I'm not coming back.'

CHAPTER FOUR

'NOT coming back?' Bethany stared at her, dumbfounded. 'Francine! What do you mean?'

'Make me a cup of coffee, will you, *chérie*.' The Frenchwoman sank on to a chair. She looked desperately tired, all her usual vitality drained out of her.

'I had hoped that David and I might establish a permanent relationship, but I know now that isn't possible—or only as things stand between us which, for me, is not good enough,' she said heavily.

Cat, having lapped up the milk, was licking the fur round her mouth with her pink petal tongue. Francine watched her cleaning herself, but without really seeing her.

'You are older now,' she went on, 'I can talk more frankly to you. I don't know whether you realise it, but between leaving my husband, ten years ago, and coming to stay here with David, I lived with a number of men. In some people's eyes that makes me a bad woman. But I think there are many, many women—respectable housewives trapped in a disappointing marriage—who would be like me, if they had no children and the courage to live as they pleased. Anyway, whatever others think of me, *I* know I am not a bad woman. Always I have looked for love . . . for permanence.'

'I think you're a wonderful person,' said Bethany. 'I—I've been hoping you and David would get married.'

The Frenchwoman's eyes filled with tears. She blinked them away. 'Thank you, *chérie*,' she said huskily. 'I love you, too— I love you both. Unfortunately, David does not feel the same way about me. He is kind . . . sometimes he is tender . . . but he doesn't love me, and never will. I don't think he will ever love anyone. It's my belief that, a long time ago, something happened which has left him incapable of any deep feeling for a woman. Physically, he is still virile, very much so. But, emotionally, he has been castrated. It is impossible for him to give his heart because, in that sense, he has no heart.'

Bethany had made coffee for them both. She placed one

cup beside Francine, and the other on the other side of the kitchen table.

Seating herself, she said anxiously, 'But surely, Francine, if you love him, it's better to stay here and have *some* happiness than to go away and have none?'

The older woman shook her head. 'I am thirty-nine, which is four years older than David. Although I take care of myself, in a few years' time my looks will begin to go . . . a little sag here'—touching her jawline—'and a little droop here'—touching her breasts.

'It is only when a man loves a woman that he doesn't notice these things, or accepts them uncritically. I once met a woman in her seventies whose husband was still her lover. To everyone else they were old. Very healthy, very fit—but still old. Yet one could see that, to each other, they were still attractive and desirable. In fact, after I had known her for some time, she confided to me that if people took the trouble to maintain slim and supple bodies, making love was a pleasure which need never come to an end.'

She poured some milk into her coffee. 'I'm sure she was right. But of course at your age even people of thirty seem old. The idea of very old people making love must strike you as obscene.'

'I don't know. I've never thought about it. But you and David don't seem old to me.'

'David will keep his looks a long time. There is a certain type of Englishman to whom age is very kind. His hair turns white but remains thick. As he grows thinner, the shape of his bones becomes more noticeable. Bones do not age as flesh does. David's eyes may fade a little, perhaps, but as they are so much bluer than most blue eyes, they will always make women look twice at him.'

There was a sadness in her voice which made Bethany ache with compassion for her.

'Dearest Francine . . . don't go,' she begged. 'We need you here. I'm sure David will be terribly upset if he comes back and finds you have left him . . . without even saying goodbye to him.'

'I said goodbye to him last night. We . . . kissed as if for the last time. He knows I am nervous of flying, and he thought it was that which made me not want to sleep but to spend the whole night in his arms. When he comes back he will understand. He will know that I *knew* it was the last time for us.'

Francine drank some coffee and straightened her sagging shoulders. 'I shall be unhappy for a while—yes. That is inevitable. Everything in life has its price, and this past year with David and you has been worth some tears . . . some loneliness. But who knows? I may yet find love. But not if I leave it too late.'

All that day and the next, they talked about life and love, and Bethany did all she could to persuade Francine to change her mind.

However, the Frenchwoman was not to be budged, and she was so much more experienced, so much wiser about the male sex, that eventually Bethany concluded that she must be doing the right thing.

But without her the Villa Delphini was not going to be the happy, comfortable house it had been since the previous Easter.

Before they set out for Genova, Francine gave her the address of a small hotel in Paris where she intended to stay for two or three weeks. Apart from going ashore at St Tropez and Monte Carlo while on the American yacht, she had not spent a night in France for almost a decade, and had never been to Paris before.

'If David finds that he misses me, he must come and tell me. But he won't,' she said, with a sad shrug.

'Have you enough money to keep you until . . . until something turns up?' Bethany asked anxiously.

'Yes, yes—don't worry about me. I shall probably get a job in Paris. Someone who cooks as well as I do can always make a living. In the meantime I have enough to live on for several weeks. You know all the pretty lingerie I have made since you came to Italy? I couldn't wear all those things. I sold most of them to a woman who has an underwear shop in Rapallo. She gave me quite a good price for them. Even in this country, fine hand sewing is not so easy to come by as it once was— television is responsible for that. Also my designs are very feminine, very sexy. By the way, you'll find a parcel on your bed; I made one set specially for you. Keep it for your honeymoon, *chérie*.'

On the drive from Portofino to the airport neither of them

could find anything to talk about. Francine's cloud of red hair was confined in a sleekly coiled chignon. She was made up and dressed for Paris. She looked very sophisticated and elegant.

But when the time came to say goodbye, regardless of her careful eye make-up, she drew back from their final embrace with tears pouring down her cheeks. Bethany was also in tears. After Francine had disappeared through the boarding gate, she made a beeline for the women's cloakroom, there to recover in private.

David's flight was an hour behind schedule, which prolonged the ordeal of waiting to tell him the bad news.

Having only hand luggage with him, he came through Customs in advance of his fellow passengers.

'Hello, sweetie. Sorry you've had to hang about. Where's Francine?'

'She . . . she's not here, I'm afraid.'

'Not here? Where is she?'

Bethany was taking driving lessons, but she hadn't yet passed her test. He knew she could not have come to meet him on her own, except by bus.

'Don't tell me the car has conked out,' he said, frowning at the prospect.

'No, the car's outside in the car park.' She drew in her breath. 'Francine is on her way to Paris. She took off a couple of hours ago. She's gone for good, David. She's left you.'

'What?' He looked as aghast as Bethany must have done when Francine told her she was leaving.

After some moments, he said, 'Why? Did she tell you why?'

She nodded. 'She's in love with you, and she thinks you don't feel the same way. I have her address in Paris if she's wrong about that,' she added hopefully.

For perhaps half a minute or longer, David stood still, staring at nothing, oblivious to the hurrying throng around him.

Eventually, as if speaking to himself, he said, 'No, she was right about it. I liked her. I was very fond of her. She was a damn nice person—terrific in bed, and a bloody marvellous cook. But I wasn't in love with her.'

Then he seemed to return to full consciousness, and looked somewhat embarrassed by his frankness.

'Let's get out of here,' he said abruptly. 'I've had enough of the rat race. I want to get back to peace and quiet.'

Taking her arm, he propelled her briskly towards the exits.

'I think she might have waited to tell me herself, instead of leaving you to do it for her.'

Now that he had had time to take in what had happened in his absence, he sounded very put out, but not at all like a man whose whole life has been knocked sideways.

Again it was a largely silent journey. Bethany ventured to enquire how his trip had gone, and David replied that it had gone well. That was all the conversation they had.

When they reached the villa, he said he was going to have a shower. Having eaten on the plane, he didn't want any lunch.

Bethany, having had no appetite for breakfast that morning, now found herself very hungry. She went to the kitchen and cut herself a hunk of bread. While she ate it, she peeled and chopped a salad of mixed fruit, and topped it with a carton of natural yogurt.

From now on, she realised, their meals were going to be her responsibility. She had never done any cooking, but had often watched Francine at work. Perhaps, if she bought a good cookery book, it wouldn't be too difficult to keep David reasonably well fed. He himself was not helpless in the kitchen. The first time she had come to Italy with him, they had eaten out a good deal, but not all the time. He had cooked several simple but appetising meals for the two of them.

It wasn't until much later that Bethany went upstairs and found Francine's parting gift, swathed in tissue, lying on her bed.

The 'set' she had referred to included a nightgown and dressing jacket, a camisole top and French knickers, and a slip. They were all made of white silk satin embellished with *découpé* work. This, as she had once explained to Bethany, was the reverse of *appliqué* embroidery. In the latter, a contrasting material was applied to the surface of the main fabric. In *découpé*, the decorative material was applied to the underside, after which the uppermost fabric was slowly and carefully snipped away.

For Bethany's present, Francine had chosen white net, joined to the satin with satin stitch in pale blue silk thread. While the colour of the garments, white with the merest tinge of blue, made them look very fresh and virginal as they lay on the bed, the effect, when she tried them on, was rather different.

The placing of the *découpé* motifs was deliberately erotic, yet in a charming and tasteful way. The transparent net flowers on the front of the camisole were centred over the tips of her breasts, and peering over her shoulder at her reflection in the mirror, she saw that the flight of butterflies on the back of the knickers emphasised the curves of her behind.

It was lingerie made for a girl rather than a woman; but it was also designed to make any man who saw it want to take it off.

'Bethany, are you there?' There was a rap on the door and David walked in. 'Have you any idea where——' He stopped short.

Probably it was only a few seconds before he recovered himself, but it seemed much longer to her. She had turned to face him as he entered. As his observant artist's eyes scanned her figure, taking in the clinging white satin and lingering on the diaphanous flowers on the camisole, she felt a strange thrill run through her, a sensation never felt before.

'I'm sorry,' David said curtly. 'I had no idea you were changing, or I shouldn't have barged in.'

He turned and walked out.

That night they went to Rapallo for supper. It was an above average meal, but few restaurants can compete with the cuisine of a woman who loves to cook, and loves the people she cooks for.

In a country of excellent bought bread, Francine had chosen to bake at home. Her bread, even when some hours old, had always tasted freshly baked because she had known the trick of refreshing the crust by passing it briefly under the cold water tap, and then heating the loaf in the oven for a few minutes.

Her vegetables, invariably steamed to minimise the loss of nutrients, had arrived at the table at the point of perfection, an achievement impossible in a restaurant.

Everything she had set on the table—including the butter, the sea salt, the black peppercorns, the virgin oil and wine vinegar—had been the best and the freshest which she could procure.

But it wasn't only her cooking they were going to miss, but her presence. Her green eyes. Her husky French voice. Her laughter.

As soon as they returned to the villa, David said he had been up late the night before and needed to catch up his sleep.

Bethany wondered if he would, or if, unaccustomed to sleeping alone, he would lie awake thinking of the woman who had shared his bed for so long.

In the morning, when she awoke, the first thing she saw was the face of Lorenzo de' Medici. It was a reproduction of the portrait of him in the Pitti Palace. She had tacked it to the centre of the vast looking-glass opposite her bed. There it covered the worst patch of speckling, and was a focus for her sleepy gaze when she opened her eyes.

By now the events of his life— or such as history had recorded—were as familiar to her as her own past.

At nineteen, Lorenzo had married Clarice Orsini, a sixteen-year-old Roman heiress chosen for him by his family. She had not been the ideal wife for him and, in later years, he had been described as 'licentious and very amorous'. One of his amours had been with Bartolommea dei Nasi, a married woman with whom he had spent many nights at her villa in the country, returning to the city at dawn.

Since visiting Florence, and becoming fascinated by Lorenzo, Bethany had often daydreamed herself to sleep at night by imagining herself as a beautiful Florentine who had caught his eye at a banquet or as he was riding through a village.

However, on the morning after David's return and Francine's departure, she did not spend long lying in bed, gazing at the picture of her hero. There was work to be done in the kitchen if David was to come downstairs to find freshly-ground coffee and hot bread waiting for him as usual.

For several weeks, life at the villa felt out of kilter because Francine was not there. Then, gradually, as people must, they began to adjust to her absence.

David had his work to occupy him, and Bethany had the housekeeping to cope with as well as her language studies.

Another and worse shock was in store for her.

One day, while he was in Rapallo having the car serviced and his hair cut, a letter arrived from England. Recognising Cressida's hand on the envelope, she looked forward to reading an amusing account of her friend's lively social life.

But this time Cressida's letter was not the usual badly typed but entertaining record of what had happened since her last one. It was a brief note to tell Bethany that Mr and Mrs Suffolk's car had been in collision with that of a drunken driver. Her mother had been killed outright. Her father had lived for a few days, but with such appalling injuries it was better he had not survived. The letter ended with the news that Cressida's aunt was taking her back to America with her, in the hope that unfamiliar surroundings might help her to get over the shock.

Giving her aunt's address there, Cressida concluded, *You'll understand if you don't hear from me for a while. I feel as if the world has come to an end.*

For Bethany, for whom Cressida and the kind and sympathetic Suffolks had long been her only sheet anchor, their death was infinitely more painful than the loss of the father who had never seemed to feel any love for her.

When David returned, she was lying on the sun-bed on the terrace, where she had sat down to read the letter, exhausted by a storm of weeping.

When she heard him enter the house, she raised herself into a sitting position. As she had failed to hear the car returning, it was too late for her to rush upstairs without him seeing her tearstained face.

'My dear girl, what *is* the matter?' he asked, as soon as he saw her.

For answer, she handed him the letter.

David read it, his brows drawing together. 'God! What a damnable thing. When did this arrive?'

'Oh . . . about an hour ago, I suppose.'

'And you've been here alone, my poor baby.' He sat down beside her, produced a large unused handkerchief, and put his arm round her shoulders.

She leaned against him. 'David, how can she bear it? They were such darling, perfect parents. Poor Cressy . . . poor little Cressy!'

'Poor little Bethany,' he said gently. 'You loved them, too, didn't you?'

'Yes, but now I have you. She has no one. Why them? Why them *of all people*?'

She began to cry again.

David held her, and let her assuage the first piercing pangs of grief in the age-old and natural way, so much better than any modern sedative.

When she was calmer, he talked quietly to her of life and death, and of the Suffolks' happy marriage which must make their deaths more painful to Cressida but, at the same time, less tragic than the death of people who had never lived to the full.

'Yes, I suppose you're right,' she sighed. 'But it seems so cruel, so unfair, that some beastly drunk should have cut off the rest of their lives. They weren't very old, only forty-something.'

'It is unfair. Life is unfair. Why should I have the luck to be born with a talent which allows me to live in a place like Portofino, with plenty to eat and no problems, while some other poor sod—sorry!—chap spends his life sweeping Underground platforms, or stuck in the hell of a car factory? Or, worse than that, waiting for the famine that he and his family won't survive. The world is full of unfairness, sweetie. You should know that better than anyone. You had a raw deal yourself until very recently.'

Bethany gave a long shuddering sigh. 'Living here makes up for all that. You've been so kind to me, David.'

He had been stroking her hair which now fell in thick silky tresses down to her collarbones; bones which no longer had deep salt-cellars above them as they had when she first came to Italy. She had filled out a lot during the winter.

Now David's other hand moved to her chin. He turned her face up to his.

'As things have turned out, it's just as well I did bring you here. Where should I be without you? You really are my general factotum now.'

As he had in her room at the Manor, the night she had wept for joy at the prospect of leaving there with him, he kissed the tip of her nose.

And then, as she mustered a watery smile, his expression changed. His blue gaze shifted to her mouth. She thought he was going to kiss her properly, and her heart seemed to leap in her breast.

But perhaps he had never intended to do any such thing; an instant later he was on his feet, saying bracingly, 'Why not nip up and have a quick shower to freshen you up? I'll deal with the lunch today.'

For several weeks after that, Bethany would often wake up in the morning with a feeling of something amiss. Then, with an aching sense of loss, she would remember that the two people for whom, next to David and Cressida, she had felt the warmest affection were no longer alive, and her closest friend was now an orphan like herself.

Although she tried not to show the persistent depression cast on her by the death of the Suffolks, it was difficult to hide it altogether. David, too, seemed out of sorts; restless, dissatisfied with the work he was producing, easily annoyed by other people, although never irritable with her.

One evening when they were both in the kitchen, she cooking, and he with Cat on his lap and a glass of Chianti in his hand, he said, 'Have you read *The Wind in the Willows*?'

'It's one of my favourite books—or was, when I was younger.'

'Mine too. It may have been my copy of it you read. Do you remember the chapter in which the Water Rat met the Sea Rat and invited him back to his hole for lunch?'

Bethany said, 'And the Sea Rat talked about his voyages and made poor Ratty so restless that he would have gone to sea himself if Mole hadn't stopped him. Is that how you're feeling, David?'

He smiled at her. 'You're very quick on the uptake.'

'Perhaps, later on, Ratty came to resent Mole's interference. It might have been kinder to let him go to sea and have some adventures,' she answered. 'I don't ever want to become an encumbrance to you, David. If you want to go off on your travels, you can leave me here perfectly safely. I shan't mind being alone in the least.'

'That wasn't what I was getting at. Yes, I am having a bout of wanderlust. It's two years since I've been somewhere new, and I've a strong urge to travel—taking you with me. Where shall we go? Any suggestions?'

'I don't know where you haven't been.'

'In Europe, not many places. But I haven't been south of

the Pyrenees. Shall we take a look at Spain?'

Two days later, leaving Cat in the care of Maria, they set out for Spain. On his trip to London, David had met another artist who had spent six months living and painting in a small Spanish seaside town midway between Valencia and Alicante. He had given David the address of an agency which handled the leasing of the many holiday houses in the area, and which would be able to offer them a selection of accommodation.

It was May. On the hills and along the sides of the *autostrada* which, later in the day, merged with the French *autoroute*, the broom was in bright yellow flower.

Their first night stop was to be at the world-famous hotel and restaurant Oustaù de Baumanière at Les Baux. It had been awarded three stars by the Michelin travel guide, signifying that it provided superb food, the epitome of French cooking, fine wines, faultless service and elegant surroundings.

It was not far from Salon-de-Provence, which was where they would have to leave the *autoroute* and cut across country by lesser roads before rejoining it near Montpellier.

However, this plan was frustrated when David took the precaution of ringing up to book two rooms from a telephone at a service area.

'They only have one room vacant tonight, so we'll have to think again,' he told Bethany, having made the call while she was in the women's washroom.

'Oh, dear! What a disappointment. I know how much you wanted to eat there. If I hadn't been with you, you could have done,' she exclaimed regretfully.

'Fine food needs to be eaten in good company to be enjoyed to the full,' was his reply. 'Never mind, we'll stay there on the way back. Let's see what else the Michelin has to offer. Arles is an interesting place, I believe. It may have a starred place to stay.'

It was early afternoon when they drove into Arles. David had decided to try a hotel called Mas de la Chapelle, a few kilometres north of the town. It was listed in the Michelin as having only seven bedrooms, an ancient chapel, a large garden and a swimming pool.

The large inviting-looking pool was the first thing they saw after parking the car alongside a number of others.

'Let's hope they're not full up here,' he remarked, as they

followed a pointer marked *Reception* which indicated that they should go round the corner of the building to the left of the pool.

This brought the chapel into view, its façade much taller than the buildings attached to either side of it. On the ridge of its roof was a bell turret, and there was a stained glass window in an arched frame above the arched door. But what caught Bethany's eyes was the weathered stone statue of the Virgin on the lawn outside the chapel, her plinth encircled by a bushy plant with grey foliage and tiny yellow flowers. Nearby was a large stone-kerbed pool with reeds growing in it.

'Oh, I do hope they have two rooms free,' she said, having fallen in love with the place.

To her relief the proprietress did have two rooms vacant. One was above the other, and both overlooked the quiet lane by which they had arrived at the hotel. Beyond the lane were fields.

Both bedrooms were doubles. David said he would have Number 3 on the ground floor. Bethany's room was Number 6. It was decorated in navy blue and white, the wallpaper and duvet-cover instantly recognisable as Laura Ashley designs.

The reminder of Mrs Suffolk, who had long been a Laura Ashley enthusiast, brought a tinge of sadness to Bethany's pleasure in the charming room with its adjoining navy and white bathroom.

David was already in the water when she joined him at the pool. As she tossed her towel over a deck chair and stepped out of her flip-flops, he climbed out at the deep end, his tanned and muscular back glistening and rippling in the sun. She watched admiringly as he dived off the springboard, and then followed suit.

After the long drive, it was wonderfully refreshing to swim in a pool of sufficient length to allow them to strike out properly rather than reaching the other end after two or three strokes.

When they had been in the water for some time, two French families came to swim. Already the mothers, between them, of half a dozen children, both wives were pregnant again.

Presently, sitting on the pool deck and watching the new-comers disport themselves, both David and Bethany were amused by the antics of two of the youngest children.

As happily at home in the water as a couple of baby frogs, they particularly enjoyed diving. Each time the little girl stepped on the springboard, she would delight in making it bounce. But she always waited for the movement to subside before she plopped into the water. The little boy's idiosyncrasy was to dive off the side of the pool with his arms held tightly to his sides.

Their beaming grins as they surfaced, and their puffs and pants as they swam to the side for another go, made David chuckle aloud. Bethany, who had also been watching the other members of the party, thought how pleasant it must be for children to grow up as members of a large, happy family which included boys as well as girls.

She had missed those close ties herself, but perhaps she might yet enjoy them as the mother of a lively brood.

Presently David said he was going for a walk. He did not suggest she should join him, and she thought he must want to be on his own. In a conversation with Francine, he had once remarked that most creative people needed a certain amount of solitude.

Perhaps being in France reminded him of Francine, and made him regret letting her go. It might even be that his restlessness and his decision to come on this trip had more to do with missing her than wanderlust. Yet now, even if he wanted to contact her, how could he, if she had moved on from the hotel which had been her destination? It was possible that, when Christmas came, she would send them a card giving her current address. Bethany was inclined to think that pride would prevent Francine from making even that gesture. In which case she was lost to him for ever.

How dreadful for him if, too late, he had come to realise that she did mean something to him, she thought worriedly. Surely there must be ways of tracing people if the need were desperate. Presumably Paris newspapers had agony columns. And if an advertisement had no success, he could engage a private detective. Somehow she couldn't see David, if he wanted to find her, accepting Francine's disappearance as insurmountable.

He returned from his walk about an hour after Bethany had gone to her room to have a bath and wash her hair. She was sitting on the bed, painting her nails with clear varnish, when she heard someone whistling in the lane and knew it was him.

But when she peered out of the window—the room's outer wall was immensely thick, and the outside end of the aperture was protected by lyre-shaped metal bars—he had passed beyond her range of vision.

The cheerful jingle he had been whistling had not suggested that he was a man troubled by the belated discovery that he wanted his former mistress back.

A few minutes later he knocked on her door.

'It's not locked,' she called to him.

When he walked in she was surprised to see him carrying a posy of wild flowers.

'A nosegay for you, *mademoiselle*.'

'David, how pretty! Thank you. I'll put them in water.' She went to the bathroom for a glass.

There was a round lamp table in a corner of her room, covered with a circular cloth which matched the duvet cover. Before she put the posy on the table, she examined the flowers which composed it.

'How enchanting wild flowers are if you look at them closely. They've been practically sprayed out of existence in England, poor things. Obviously the French are more civilised in that respect.'

'So it seems. Would you like an early *apéritif*? Later on we'll have a drink in the garden, but I feel like one now before I shower.'

Before bringing her the flowers, he must have returned to his own room for the canvas shoulder bag in which he had packed the lunch they had eaten en route. They had drunk only water with their bread, cheese and fruit. Now he produced two small glasses and a bottle of the dry white Frecciarossa wine which was what he usually uncorked whenever they had fish for supper.

'I'm not sure that someone of your tender years should be encouraged to drink wine as often as I do. I must try to cut down my *vino* consumption while we're in Spain,' he remarked.

'You only drink a glass or two at dinner, and sometimes the odd glass with lunch. And you hardly ever touch spirits. As for me, my years are not as tender as all that. I'm seventeen and a half now. Well . . . almost.'

The double bed was an old one given a new lease of life

with a coat of French navy paint, with some details picked out in white. The mattress felt younger than the frame. Bethany pushed a pillow against the headboard and leaned on it, her bare feet tucked beneath her.

'In eight months' time I shall be of age,' she reminded him.

'So you will. Free to do as you please. I had to wait until I was twenty-one. Not that my father was an intransigent parent. It was John who disapproved of my bent for painting.'

Bethany didn't want to be reminded of the past. She said, 'Where shall we be tomorrow night? Somewhere in Spain, presumably.'

'Yes, but probably not too far over the border if we're going to spend the morning looking round Arles. There's a Roman theatre and an arena to see, and I want to go to the Musée Réattu where they have works by Picasso and Gauguin. Van Gogh lived in Arles for two years, but a man I met on my walk told me the houses he lived in were destroyed in the second world war.'

She sipped her wine. 'It's fun, travelling like this, isn't it?— Not knowing where we shall be tomorrow . . . who we shall meet . . . what we shall see.'

'I've always enjoyed it,' he agreed. 'But it's good to have a base, too.'

She remembered how, a few days ago, she had told him that, if he preferred to travel by himself, she would not mind being left alone. Now she knew that, beautiful as it was, Portofino would have been lonely without him.

In a flash of enlightenment she saw that home was not a place but a person. For Cressida home had not been the flat by the Thames, but the presence of her loved and loving parents. She herself, until David had come, had never had a home. Now home was not the Villa Delphini. Tonight it was Mas de la Chapelle, because he was here.

Wherever he was was where she felt happy and secure.

Presently he returned to his room, leaving her to get ready for dinner.

While she was packing for the journey, she had come across a packet of hairpins and some tortoiseshell combs bought in Rapallo months ago with the idea of copying a hair-style in one of Francine's magazines.

Her experiments at the time had not pleased her, but on

impulse she had brought the pins with her, and tonight her efforts were more successful. She went down to join David for dinner with her hair in a passable facsimile of the sophisticated chignon worn by Francine on the day of her departure, and wearing her Florentine ear-rings, and a dress which the Frenchwoman had made for her which David had not seen before. It was black with white flowers scattered on it, and she wore it with the shoulder ties unfastened and tucked inside the shirred top to make it look strapless.

He was in the garden before her, sitting on a white metal chair, drawing the flowing lines of the stone Virgin's robe. Earlier Bethany had noticed that, incised on the statue's pedestal, were the words JE VEILLE MES ENFANTS. I watch over my children.

David rose as Bethany approached and put aside his sketch pad.

'Don't stop. Finish your drawing. I'm going for a wander round the garden,' she said, strolling past him.

It was cooler now, though still sunny. The trees and bushes, and the grass, still had the lush freshness of early summer. Somewhere nearby, on a court hidden by the tall hedges, people were playing tennis. The clop-clop of ball against racquet reminded her of her last term at school. She felt a different person from the awkward, ungainly schoolgirl of less than a year ago. In Italy she had burgeoned like a shrub transplanted from an exposed position to a sheltered one.

She wondered if David had noticed her hair and her dress. She felt sure he must have done, although he hadn't made any remark.

When she joined him there were tall glasses of lemonade on the white sunbrella-shaded table beside him. He was still working on his sketch, hatching in the shadows cast by the sinking sun.

'I ordered soft drinks as we'll be having some more wine with our meal. You look very grown up tonight. I like the new hairdo.'

'Thank you.'

'I'm glad you have the sense to realise that it isn't necessary to plaster on make-up to look older. With your skin and colouring, you don't need it.'

He turned to a clean page and began to draw her.

Actually Bethany had spent some time on her face, using a light moisturiser, a trace of oil on her eyebrows, a very discreet touch of blusher, and some gloss on her lips. Her eyebrows and lashes were dark enough not to need any artificial emphasis, and she thought it was probably the improvement in her diet under Francine's régime which had cleared up some minor skin problems of the year before, and left her with a clear complexion.

By the time she had drunk her lemonade, David had completed his second sketch.

Had he flattered her? she wondered uncertainly, when he showed it to her. She had thought she looked nicer than usual, but the sketch made her look . . . almost beautiful.

Was her neck really as graceful as he had made it? Her eyes as large? Her hair as lustrous?

'Goodness! You've made me look quite glamorous,' she said lightly.

'I draw what I see. You've developed into a lovely girl,' was his casually-stated response. 'Let's go in and have dinner, shall we?'

The old chapel had been converted into a gracious dining-room with pink-clothed tables, rose-red velvet chairs, and copies of mediaeval tapestries on the lofty stone walls.

It was an unforgettable evening, and not only because the food was superlatively good.

They began with *saudre en papillotte*, an unfamiliar fish which came to the table still wrapped in the paper in which it had been cooked.

They were then brought a small mint sorbet to refresh their palates for a succulent escalope of veal in a wine sauce, served with courgettes as perfectly seasoned and as tender without being over-soft, as if Francine had cooked them.

After this came the cheese trolley, from which they both chose to try the small round soft-textured Chèvres. Finally they had home-made apricot ices.

While they were eating this feast, and Bethany was noticing the white china swans which served as vases on the tables, the large Chinese jar filled with country flowers standing in an alcove, and the antique *armoire* in one corner, there was music playing. Unobtrusive, suitable music, the volume set at just the right pitch to allow the diners to converse in normal voices without their conversation being audible at other tables.

The first time the music caught her attention was when Gershwin's *Rhapsody In Blue* was playing. Later she recognised the melody of Charles Aznavour's *She*.

This was an orchestral recording without a vocalist. But Cressida had played Aznavour's English-language recording so often in her room at the flat that Bethany knew the lyrics by heart.

> *She may be the face I can't forget*
> *A trace of pleasure or regret*
> *May be my treasure or the price I have to pay*
> *She may be the love that cannot hope to last*
> *May come to me from shadows of the past*
> *That I remember till the day I die*

Suddenly she was reminded of Francine saying, 'I don't think David will ever love anyone. It's my belief that, a long time ago, something happened which has left him incapable of any deep feeling for a woman. It is impossible for him to give his heart because he has no heart.'

Was it true? Was the tall, attractive, talented man beside her an emotional cripple? Somehow she couldn't believe it . . . couldn't bear to believe it.

Because she had fallen in love with him.

Fortunately David was giving his whole attention to his food at the moment when the realisation hit her.

In a flash of enlightenment, she understood that she had begun to love him a long time ago; but then he had seemed to belong to Francine, and she had taken refuge in a teenager's romantic fantasy inspired by a man as dark as David was fair, Lorenzo de' Medici.

'I'm not certain we should have dined any better than this at the other place,' he remarked, glancing at her.

'No, it's excellent, isn't it? I wonder what the food in Spain will be like? Apart from seeing pictures of *paella*, I don't know much about it.'

'I shouldn't expect it to compare with the food in Italy or France, but I'm told they have some excellent wines,' he said.

They had coffee outside in the garden. The floodlit façade of the chapel and the green-shuttered house alongside it were

reflected in the surface of the pool. It was country-quiet, but
for the soft music drifting out from the dining-room.

'At one time this place must have been a farm,' said David.
'*Mas* is the southern dialect word for a farmhouse. There must
be several hundred Chapel Farms in Britain, wouldn't you
say?'

'Yes, but usually taking their name from a rather ugly red
brick nonconformist chapel, not one like this. It's more like
the private chapel of a *château*,' said Bethany.

'Yes, possibly one of the *châteaux* which were destroyed
during the Revolution. When I'm paying the bill in the morning, I'll ask.'

But when, next day, they were leaving, after having coffee
and croissants outside in the early sun, neither of them remembered to ask the proprietress to tell them the history of
the chapel.

What Bethany did do, just before leaving, was to pick one
velvety pansy from a large bed of heart's-ease in the garden,
and slip it between the leaves of the notebook which was her
travel diary. Not that she was likely to forget any detail of
their stay at Mas de la Chapelle.

It was Wednesday, and Arles was crowded because it was
market day. All along one side of the tree-shaded Boulevard
Emile Combes there were two rows of stalls, with a jostling
throng passing between them

They bought *pain au son*, bread with bran in it, and
tomatoes, apples and Brie. Bethany also bought a bag of
Provençal herbs, and looked with interest at vegetables shaped
like small melons but labelled courgettes, and at snails vainly
trying to escape through the meshes of round wire baskets.

Having put their provisions in the car, they looked at the
Roman remains and came out on the Boulevard des Lices
where they had another cup of coffee in a pavement café before
going in search of the Musée Réattu.

The waiter told them it was near the river, by which he
meant the Grand Rhône which flowed through the town
before spreading to form the delta called the Camargue, a
region of white horses and black bulls bred for the *course
libre*, the bloodless bullfights of France which, in Arles, took
place in the ancient arena.

On the way to the museum, they passed a shop called

Souleiádo, its windows displaying dresses and accessories made from Provençal prints like those which she remembered seeing in a shop called Brother Sun in London, while shopping with Cressida and her mother.

David saw a skirt which he liked and insisted on buying for her. It was a wrap-around made of cotton the same dark red colour as her favourite *mirtilli* ice cream.

While he was in the shop, he found out that *souleiado* was a word invented by the Provençal poet, Mistral, to mean the moment when the sun came out and illumined a landscape.

Later, when they were once more on the *autoroute*, Bethany thought that the moment when a landscape was transformed by sunlight was like the moment when life was transformed by the state of being in love.

Yesterday she had been happy. Today she was in heaven.

Their first night on the other side of the border was not an auspicious beginning to their sojourn in Spain. They spent it in Barcelona which, accustomed to the peace of Portofino, they found a very noisy city. Their hotel was comfortable enough, but without the charm of Mas de la Chapelle, and the food was of indifferent quality.

'I hope this isn't typical,' said David, at dinner, as he removed two limp strands of white tinned asparagus from his *ensalada especial* which also contained tinned tuna.

The excitement of being in an unknown country made Bethany less critical. They were in the part of Spain known as Catalonia where the people spoke Catalan as well as Castilian Spanish. Already, from signs along the *autopista*, she had picked up a few words of Catalan.

No fumeo si us plau, on a board above petrol pumps, clearly meant *No smoking, please*; and she had been interested to see the difference between *Open day and night* in the two languages. The Spanish was *Abierta dia y noche*, and the Catalan was *Oberta dia i nit*.

So far, what they had seen of the countryside, from the Pyrenees—which, in spite of the heat, had still had snow in the hollows of the highest peaks—to Barcelona, had not differed greatly from the landscape of southern France.

The next morning was marred by two incidents which made her begin to fear that, instead of being a joyous adventure, the trip would turn out to be a disastrous flop.

The first happened in Valencia which, unlike the city of Tarragona further north, had no motorway bypass, so they were forced to drive through the city centre.

Almost immediately it was clear that the modern city of Valencia was not as gay and colourful as the song of that name made it sound. At the first major intersection, whenever the traffic lights were against them, motorists were plagued by gypsy children—unkempt but not undernourished—ostensibly wanting to clean their windscreens but actually begging.

Being in an air-conditioned car, David and Bethany had their windows closed. When a girl of thirteen or fourteen flourished a filthy-looking rag in the direction of his screen, he wound down the window to wave her away.

Immediately, she and another girl poked their unbrushed heads inside the car, whining, 'bonbones . . . bonbones . . .' and looking to see what was on the back seat.

Their dark eyes were so avaricious that, instinctively, Bethany reached an arm over her seat to grab hold of her bag and the camera which she felt they might snatch and run off with.

David said sharply, 'Beat it!' and began to wind up the window. As he did so, the older girl attempted to give him a spiteful nip on the neck with her long dirty nails. However, he was too quick for her, and she had to withdraw her arm or risk being hurt herself.

Bethany had always felt a good deal of sympathy for gypsies, especially the children who, without parental encouragement, had little chance to gain the education they needed to escape from a life of scrap-dealing and petty crime. But the vicious attempt to pinch David had alienated her goodwill towards these Valencian *gitanos* who seemed a more hostile breed than the English gypsies she had encountered.

Another unpleasing impression of the provincial capital was struck by its architecture, or at least what they saw of it on their way through the city. The new high-rise apartment blocks were hideous, and the much more attractive old buildings, smaller in scale and with many fine wrought-iron balconies, were falling into dingy dereliction.

'Not impressive!' was David's curt verdict. 'But perhaps on the way back we should take a closer look. I was told that the

Bellas Artes museum of painting was well worth a visit.'

South of the city, the *autopista* re-opened, giving wide views across rice fields and orange groves to the ranges of barren sierras more in keeping with Bethany's preconception of Spain.

In the centre of the road, between the north and south-bound carriageways, oleander bushes were in flower—mostly white and dark pink, but some a delicate peach colour.

There was almost no other traffic heading south which, in view of what happened next, was providential.

They were travelling fast, but no faster than was reasonable and safe in a car built for speed on a road designed to allow it. Far ahead, she noticed a small saloon parked on the hard shoulder.

As they drew closer to it, she was horrified to see an elderly woman leaving the car and, without so much as a glance in their direction, walk slowly towards the centre line of olean-ders.

'Good God!'

David's harsh exclamation was accompanied by a warning blast on his horn, and as rapid braking as was possible at the speed they were travelling.

The woman gave a startled glance towards them, and mer-cifully, ran for the centre. Had she dithered, dodging this way and that as many jay-walkers were apt to do, he would have been powerless to avoid hitting her. Or perhaps, in attempting to miss her, going off the road and killing himself and his passenger.

What he said when the danger was past was not couched in his usual language. But Bethany, also much shaken by the close brush with a horrible accident, felt the terms in which he expressed himself were excusable in the circumstances.

It had all happened much too quickly for them to take in the other car's registration. The woman had not looked Spanish, but a northern European of almost unbelievable stupidity.

'Not fit to be on the road,' David said furiously.

A few kilometres further on there was a line of toll booths where, speaking Italian which had many similarities to Spanish, he reported the woman's crass folly, and hoped they would take her to task.

The remainder of the journey was uneventful. Having set out early, by lunch-time—which in Spain as in Italy began at one-thirty—they had reached their destination.

A snack at a beach bar, followed by a swim in the sea, relaxed them. But Bethany could sense that David, whose eye for shape and proportion was more highly developed than most people's, was not impressed by the way the original fishing village had been developed into a much larger resort with a marked lack of overall planning or regard for aesthetic consideration.

Her heart sank at the possibility that he was not going to like Spain and find here the mental refreshment he seemed to need. For herself, she didn't find this stretch of coast as lovely as the green coast of their part of Italy; but being with him was more important than the surroundings.

By early evening they were installed in a hill-top house called La Casa de los Angeles. The name derived from the owners' collection of angels; a stone angel in the courtyard, a terracotta angel playing a lyre on the wall of the living-room, and more in other parts of the house.

It was a comfortable house, with a swimming pool, not far from a general shop, and only a few kilometres from the inland town of Benisa where they would do most of their shopping. The surrounding countryside was mostly given over to grapes growing on low-growing vines, more like French vines than the tall ones she was used to in Italy.

That night they ate at a restaurant suggested by the agent for the house. Again the food was mediocre, which displeased David and prevented it from being the lighthearted occasion she had hoped for.

'Tomorrow I'll cook our meals,' said Bethany, when they returned to the House of the Angels. 'Would you like a cup of coffee now, David?'

'Not for me, thanks. I'm bushed. I'm going to turn in. Goodnight.'

He went to his bedroom, leaving her to wonder if it was only the alarming near-miss that morning, and the disappointing evening meal, which were responsible for his terseness. Perhaps he had something else on his mind.

CHAPTER FIVE

DURING the following two weeks, Bethany's mood fluctuated between euphoria and gloom. When David smiled and was friendly, she was on top of the world. When he was withdrawn and taciturn, she was cast into depression.

For a while he became deeply absorbed in the shapes of the terraces of land known locally as *bancales*. Many of the dry-stone retaining walls which supported the terraces were said to have been built by the Moors. Recently, the outbreak of tourism had meant that a nation formerly dependent on cultivating every metre of fertile soil was now, in parts, giving up its agricultureal heritage for easier ways of making a living. Neglected terraces were reverting to scrub, and unrepaired walls were collapsing.

From the hilltops near where they were living, the *bancales* resembled the lines on a contour map, and David spent morning after morning drawing them from different vantage points. It was a departure from his usual work, as indeed were the sketches of Bethany which occupied his evenings.

When they returned to Portofino he was going to paint a large portrait of her, and these were preliminary drawings to help him decide on the final pose.

Every afternoon they would bathe from the wide beach near the town of Calpe and the towering Peñon de Ifach, an enormous outcrop of rock rising out of the sea. The Spanish called it the *sapo* because, from certain angles, it resembled an open-mouthed toad.

After swimming, David would sketch beach scenes of the kind he might later work up into one of his usual genre paintings. With a cruelly observant eye, he drew not only the young girls sunbathing or parading by the water's edge in monokinis, but also the much older women who had joined in the mania for toplessness, even though their bosoms were huge or pendulous.

In Bethany's observation, even people of her age looked more attractive with the tops of their bikinis in place. Bare young breasts were not unattractive, but they looked more alluring when a little was left to the onlooker's imagination.

On the whole, she liked Spain, although not as much as Italy. But David saw much to criticise, and although most of what he said was true—the town of Calpe *was* unspeakably hideous, and most of the *urbanizaciónes* built for foreign occupation *did* disfigure the landscape with their clusters of badly-built houses—she felt that his readiness to find fault was a symptom of some hidden worry, some deep unease.

Every third night they ate at a restaurant where, again, their attitudes differed. She, brought up by an old-fashioned nanny to eat whatever was put in front of her, and later inured to the dull stodge of boarding-school food, found it easier to tolerate the shortcomings of the local cuisine.

David, who detested fried food and loved well-cooked vegetables, became increasingly irascible in restaurants where most things were fried and the only vegetables were uninspired salads and chipped potatoes.

They did find one acceptable place, Los Pepes in the seaside town of Jávea, and another, on the outskirts of Calpe, where the stuffed mussels and lemon sorbet were memorable. But even there he didn't like the décor or the third-rate paintings which hung, for sale, on the walls.

It was almost a relief when, after three weeks in Spain, he suggested going home. Bethany didn't know why the trip had gone sour, but she was terribly afraid the reason might be his lack of any company but hers.

Yet when two or three expatriate couples living near the Casa de los Angeles had invited them to parties, he, although normally quite gregarious, had turned down their friendly overtures.

'They're all retired people, with nothing to do but drink and gossip. We have nothing in common with them'—was his answer when she had ventured the remark that it might have been interesting to mix with some of the other foreigners.

They returned to Italy by a car ferry from Barcelona to Genoa. Once back on Italian soil, David seemed to recover the more relaxed mood of the time when Francine had been with them.

He began his portrait of Bethany, using gouache rather than the traditional oils because it was closer to the medium in which he was most experienced, but had certain advantages over watercolours when the subject was a portrait.

All through the golden month of June, he painted not one but many portraits of her. She spent hours sitting to him. Sometimes they talked. Mostly they were silent, thinking their separate thoughts.

He painted her in the faded sea-green Laura Ashley sun-dress, and wrapped in a Chinese yellow shawl. Lying down, half asleep, in the sun. Sitting up, with Cat on her lap. He painted her under the pool shower, her brown skin shiny, her hair wet; and in the Provençal skirt with red roses twined in her hair.

It was the time of the year when the lime trees were in flower, and every light gust of breeze wafted their sweet, heady fragrance. She had missed this the year before, being still at school.

One morning when, having passed her test, she had driven to Rapallo by herself, coming back with her basket laden with peaches and cherries, David said, 'This afternoon I'd like to do a nude study. Would that bother you?'

'Not at all,' she answered.

Why should it bother her to pose for him without her clothes on when she longed for him to make love to her?

She had taken down the picture of Lorenzo de' Medici. Now David was the central figure in all her daydreams.

He must have given some thought to the nude study before he mentioned it. After lunch, he asked her to pose by the pool, which was not overlooked by other houses, sitting on a blue towel. She had to lean back on her hands and lift her face to the sky, one leg bent at the knee, the other dangling in the water.

It was not an easy pose to hold for more than five minutes at a time. He made her have frequent rests.

It was during one of these rest periods, when she was sitting with both knees raised and her head and shoulders bent forward, that they heard the front door bell ringing.

'I'll answer it,' said David. 'You'd better cover up in case it's someone I have to ask to come in.'

He propped his drawing-board on the easel, and covered it with a piece of cheesecloth. But, when painting outside, this was usual when he left his work unattended for any reason.

By the time he returned, followed by a young Italian, Bethany was wearing her bikini. David introduced the young man as Giancarlo Salviati, the son of the owners of the neighbouring villa.

Later, when they were alone again but Giancarlo had been invited to join them for supper, he said, 'His father is a Milanese manufacturer with several houses. They only use this one occasionally. Usually they send an advance guard of servants to open the place up before they arrive. I should guess that, as Giancarlo's here on his own for a fortnight, he must be in Papa's black books. I expect he'll ask you to go out with him. I'll make sure he doesn't mistake you for an anything-goes girl and try a heavy pass.'

'I don't particularly want to go out with him,' shrugged Bethany.

'Why not? It's time you tried your wings. Seventeen and a half is late for a girl's first date nowadays.'

'I've had my first date already.'

David looked puzzled. 'When?'

She drew in her breath, and dared to say, 'With you . . . at Mas de la Chapelle.'

He gave her a long, intent look. 'You can't count that as a date.'

'I don't see why not. You brought me flowers. I wore a new dress and put my hair up. We had a fabulous meal in a lovely setting. It was by far the nicest evening I've ever had.'

'The first of many, no doubt. Before you're much older you'll be taken to a lot more exciting places than Mas de la Chapelle,' he said repressively.

'That's for me to judge, don't you think?'

She was hurt by his brusque dismissal of the French hotel as a place to be remembered. She went back to her place by the pool and, taking off her bikini, resumed the pose.

For about half an hour they were silent, until David said, 'You can dress now. I've finished for today.'

He had been working in his bathing suit and a wide-brimmed straw hat which shaded his eyes from the strong light. Standing up, he tossed this aside and took a running header into the pool.

There was an explosion of spray, some of the diamond-bright drops raining on Bethany's warm skin. While David began to swim a fast crawl back and forth, she dressed and walked round the pool to look at the painting.

He had captured all the heat and colour and brilliance of an Italian summer afternoon. The jewel-gleam of the water. The flower-heavy bracts of purple bougainvillea cascading over the wall of the upper terrace. The naked girl on her towel, her head flung back so that her long hair almost touched the sun-baked terracotta tiles.

He had painted her breasts the same golden-brown colour as the rest of her. The other small area of paler skin was concealed by the raised leg. As always, when she looked at his paintings of her, it was like looking at a stranger ... someone like her and yet not like her ... a girl of far greater loveliness than her mirror-image.

If he really saw her like that, surely it could only be the eyes of love which transformed her and made her beautiful? Or was it merely artistic licence?

Amateur artists painted what they saw in front of them. Professional artists rearranged things in the interests of good composition. In the same way, perhaps, he had made subtle changes to her form to achieve the effect he was seeking.

David was still swimming vigorously up and down the pool when she went into the house to squeeze lemons and oranges and, with crushed ice and soda, make a refreshing drink.

When she returned to the garden, she found he had cleared away his things and disappeared into his studio. It had been a rule of the house, since long before her arrival, that no one was allowed to disturb him when the door of the studio was closed.

He did not emerge from his sanctum until the bell rang for the second time, and Giancarlo returned to have supper with them.

From then on, with David's encouragement, the young man spent as much time at the Villa Delphini as he did at his parents' house. And before the end of that week, someone else had entered their lives, and showed signs of becoming another habitué.

Natasha—she said her surname was unpronounceable except by other Russians—came to Portofino, as Francine Valery had before her, on a rich man's yacht. But whereas

Francine had cooked for her passage from the Caribbean, Natasha had been a guest on the much shorter voyage from the French resort of St Tropez.

She had been born in London, and the only Russian things about her were her name and her ancestry. She claimed to be a sculptress, and had been on her way to Florence when the charm of Portofino had beguiled her into lingering there for a while. She was staying at the Splendido, and spoke as if expensive hotels and the houses of the rich were her natural milieu.

However, after a few days' acquaintance with her, Giancarlo decided she was an *arriviste* who was staying there in the hope of meeting a new protector to replace the owner of the yacht who had either grown tired of her, or with whom she had quarrelled.

'She must have enough money to last her for some time or she wouldn't be amusing herself with David', was the opinion he confided to Bethany, one day when he was helping her with the preparations for a lunch *à quatre* by the pool.

Bethany had to concede that, with her black hair and slightly slanting ice-blue eyes, Natasha was an attractive woman. But she didn't like her, and she couldn't understand why David seemed to enjoy her malicious humour.

When she said as much to Giancarlo, he said, 'David told me that you were unusually innocent, and I'd better not lay a finger on you if I wanted to keep on the right side of him. You must be incredibly innocent if you don't know why he's laying on the charm with her. He wants to get her into bed. I'm surprised he hasn't by now. *She* is no innocent. I should think she's lost count of the men she's slept with.'

Interpreting her expression as a shocked look, he went on, 'I know you think David is a cross between God and Superman, but you don't imagine that he never needs a woman, do you? He's a man, not a saint or a monk.'

'I know that. When I first came here, he had a living-in girlfriend. But she was completely different from Natasha. Francine was a darling. I think Natasha is . . . a bitch.'

It was not an expression which came easily to her but, after searching her vocabulary, she felt it was the *mot juste* for the woman at present reclining on a lounger by the pool, wearing a black monokini and a skein of gold chains.

The way Natasha had smoothed sun oil on her pointed breasts had made Bethany cringe with embarrassment at the suggestive movements of the other woman's silver-tipped fingers.

'You're right,' Giancarlo agreed. 'A bitch—but what does that matter? He doesn't want to marry her, only to——' He stopped short. 'I don't know a polite word for what he has in mind.'

They were speaking Italian in which Bethany was now as fluent as David, and with less of an English accent, according to Giancarlo.

At that moment David himself entered the kitchen. He must have overheard the last part of their conversation, and there was an expression on his face which reminded her of his anger after narrowly missing the silly woman on the *autopista*.

Was he furious because he had heard her telling Giancarlo about Francine? Or because she had called Natasha a bitch? Or because of the Italian's last remark?

Whatever the reason for his scowl of annoyance, it was quickly replaced by a less fierce expression.

'Anything I can do to help?' he asked.

'It's more or less ready. Would you take this tray, please, Giancarlo?'

With the men each carrying a large tray while she brought the wine and a litre bottle of mineral water, they returned to the garden.

There was nothing in the lighthearted conversation round the lunch table to presage the vindictive outburst, or its catastrophic aftermath, which was to follow the pleasant meal.

Perhaps David was less attentive to Natasha than he had been before lunch, but, while they were eating, his manner did not suggest any radical change in his attitude to her.

Precisely what triggered her outburst—what she said to him, and what snubbing remark he returned—was something Bethany never found out. In the last few moments before Natasha erupted, she had been having a separate conversation with Giancarlo.

'You rotten bastard! Don't you high-hat me!'

Natasha's savage exclamation made the two younger people turn towards her with looks of astonishment.

Her face was contorted with fury, and the voice in which

she had snarled at him had been quite different from her usual purring tones. Suddenly, it was the voice of a coarse, loud-mouthed woman far removed from the kind of person she pretended to be.

'I thought you were normal,' she said viciously. 'I've met some weirdos, God knows, but never one of your sort before.' She turned to the young Italian. 'You're wasting your time there, Giancarlo. You won't ever switch her on. She isn't interested in you any more than he fancies me. It's each other they fancy. I don't know what the Italians call it, but in English it's——'

'Be quiet, Natasha.'

David didn't raise his voice, but he spoke with a steely authority which, for a few moments, silenced her.

Before she could recover herself, he grasped her by the arm and pulled her upright.

'Bring your things. I'm taking you back to the hotel.'

'Don't bother.' She shook off his hand. 'I'd rather walk back.' She snatched up her bag and her towel and stalked angrily towards the steps leading up to the villa.

Glancing uneasily from David's grim face to Bethany's, Giancarlo rose to his feet. Usually a suave young man, he was visibly disconcerted and embarrassed by this unforeseen turn of events.

'I—I should also go home . . . I have letters to write. The lunch was excellent, Bethany. Thank you. I'll see you later, perhaps.'

With a forced smile at her and a nod to his host, he departed.

David watched him go, then sat down.

'I'm sorry about that. I should never have invited her here. An error of judgment on my part—one of several,' he added, in a strained voice.

He did not look at her as he spoke, but at the basket of figs in the centre of the table. The hard, clenched line of his jaw betrayed that he was gritting his teeth to contain his rage at Natasha's accusation.

Bethany said, very softly, 'Is it true, David? It's true for me. I do love you.'

Still he did not look at her. Leaning forward, he picked up the water bottle and splashed some into his glass. As he set the bottle on the table and lifted the tumbler to his lips, she saw that his hand, over which, normally, he had the perfect control of a masterly painter, was shaking.

'What you feel for me isn't love,' he said harshly. 'It's the natural affection and . . . and hero-worship which a girl usually feels for her father—or whoever stands in place of her father.'

'No, that's not how it is, darling David,' she answered, with gentle conviction. 'I love you as a woman loves . . . as Francine loved you. I've known it for weeks, but I wasn't sure how you felt about me.'

His blue eyes turned on her then, full of hunger and pain and despair.

'For God's sake!' he burst out. 'I'm your uncle . . . your father's brother. There can never be anything between us.'

'Why not? If we love each other. I don't think of you as my uncle—I never have. We met as strangers . . . not as relations. We could marry. It isn't forbidden—I looked it up. We couldn't, or shouldn't have children, but we could marry . . . if you wanted to marry me. Or we could just go on living together.'

Had she misread the look in his eyes? Had she seen what she wanted to see? All at once his brown face was a mask of stern disapproval.

'You're talking nonsense,' he said briskly. 'I don't want to hurt your feelings, and I know I'm largely to blame for this situation . . . that perhaps I've allowed my own feelings to get a little out of hand. But that has to stop—here and now. We must both pull ourselves together and look for more feasible relationships. Apart from the blood tie between us, I'm twenty years older than you are. When you're thirty, I'll be middle-aged. When you're fifty, I'll be an old man.'

She seized on the one thing he'd said which gave her hope.

'But you do love me . . . a little?'

'I'm extremely fond of you. As an artist, I'm captivated by your lovely face and the grace of your figure. You're going to be an outstandingly beautiful woman and, just now, you have a freshness and sweetness which would inspire any painter. The fact is that, since Francine left me, there's been a gap in my life which, to some extent, you have filled. But all that doesn't add up to the kind of love you're talking about.'

'I don't believe you, David. I think you're denying that you love me because of what Natasha said. She made it sound wicked . . . perverted . . . for us to be in love with each other. But it isn't—I know it isn't. What would have been hateful and sordid would have been for you to make love to her as . . . as a substitute for me.'

A flush ran up under David's tan, confirming that she had hit on the reason for his interest in Natasha. Her role had been that of a safety-valve, a device to stop him losing control.

'Oh, David, we could be so happy!' She moved to the chair next to his. 'I'd hardly had any happiness until I came to live with you. Now I'm almost perfectly happy. The only thing lacking is that I want you to kiss me . . . to make love to me.'

Impelled by a boldness of which she hadn't thought herself capable, she half-rose and bent to brush a soft kiss on his mouth.

For a moment, with her hands on his shoulders to prevent her losing her balance, he remained unresponsive. Then, with a smothered groan, he pulled her on to his lap.

It was a long, passionate kiss which made no allowance for her youth and inexperience. But, adoring and trusting him, she could never be alarmed by anything he did to her.

For a second or two she was startled by the famished hunger of his lips; then her slender arms wound round his neck, and she yielded her mouth and her body with all the instinctive ardour of a naturally warm and loving temperament.

She thought she had won; that there was no more to be said; that he could not live without her.

She had begun the embrace. It was ended by David when, still holding her tightly in his arms, he sprang to his feet and wrenched his mouth away from hers.

'Dear God! I must be insane!'

He made sure she was on her feet before taking his arms away, and turning to stride along the pool deck, one hand raking back his thick hair, the other clenching and unclenching in the gesture of a man battling against emotions in turmoil.

After half a dozen paces he turned.

'We can't go on living together—that's out of the question now. This madness won't last. I know it even if you don't.'

'I don't believe it is madness. You love me, David. You've proved it . . . kissing me like that.'

'All it proved was that, for a few moments, I wanted you

. . . or any other willing woman,' he said brutally. 'You would have got the same reaction from any man who's been without sex as long as I have.'

Bethany flinched, and saw his mouth twist with pity.

'Don't make me be cruel to you,' he said. 'I don't want to hurt you—in any way. But you have to accept that I know more about life than you do. What you feel now won't last. It's calf love. We all go through it. Five years later, we look back and thank our stars it didn't come to anything.'

He thrust his hands into the pockets of his white shorts. His eyebrows contracted. 'What's to be done with you?—That's the problem. You still need some looking after. I can't just boot you out and let you get on with it.'

'You really mean to send me away?' She couldn't believe that he could mean it.

'I must. I have no alternative. To allow you to stay, after today, would be unforgivable. I appointed myself as your guardian until you were older, and that responsibility includes defending you against myself,' he said steadily. 'For you wouldn't be able to do so if I were enough of a rat to take advantage of you.'

Two days later, Bethany landed at London airport and was met by the friend of his with whom she was going to stay for a week or two.

Geraldine Porter was also an artist; an unmarried woman of thirty-two who had agreed to David's request that Bethany should be given the use of her spare room for as long as it took her to find a job and suitable accommodation.

Whether Geraldine, a friendly brunette with large teeth, had ever been more than a friend to him, Bethany neither knew nor cared. She only knew that she had been cast out of paradise into the outer darkness of a life away from David.

That he, she was sure, felt equally bereft without her was of little comfort. She knew that, however much he missed her, he would not change his mind. She was never going to see him again.

> *He is not here; but far away*
> *The noise of life begins again,*
> *And ghastly thro' the drizzling rain*
> *On the bald street breaks the blank day.*

Tennyson's lines from *In Memoriam* expressed exactly how she felt; each day a blank, dreary span of slow, dragging hours between nights of merciful oblivion.

When, after a year in America, Cressida Suffolk returned to England, she found Bethany living in a Y.W.C.A. hostel, and working in a shop in Chelsea which specialised in dried and silk flowers.

It had been, at first, a temporary job to tide her over until she found a way of making use of her languages. But it had proved unexpectedly interesting, and by now she had taken the place of the owner's right-hand girl after she had left to get married to a Belgian doctor.

Cressida's parents had left her rather well off. She was still in possession of the flat, which had been let during her absence. But she didn't want to live there again. Within a month of her return, she had bought herself a smaller place, and persuaded Bethany to share it with her.

The trauma of losing her mother and father did not appear to have altered Cressida's vivacious personality. She said there were still occasions when she missed them unbearably.

'But one can't go on grieving for ever. I'm over the worst now. I don't suddenly burst into tears as I used to do for the first three or four months.'

Bethany did not tell her anything about her return from Portofino except that David had shut up the house and gone on a year's tour of India and the Far East.

Even to Cressida, she could not confide the truth about her time in Italy. Sometimes she thought it might have been easier to recover from the loss of her love if he had been killed like the Suffolks. While he lived, she could never forget him; never cease to wonder where he was and if he ever thought about her, or had long since found solace with someone else.

That, in spite of his denials, he *had* loved her, she was still convinced.

Before joining forces with Cressida, she had had virtually no social life. However, once the two girls started living together, she could not avoid being involved in Cressida's party-giving.

At first she stayed in the background as much as possible. But unhappiness, rather than diminishing her beauty, had intensified it. No girl with her ravishing looks could remain in the background for long.

Gradually, she began to accept invitations to go to the theatre or a concert; although always keeping the men who took her out very much at arm's length. This discouraged some of them, but others found it a challenge.

Through her job with a firm of auctioneers whose name was internationally known to collectors of works of art, fine furniture and antique silver, Cressida encountered a great many eligible young men. Those who did not appeal to her, she steered in Bethany's direction, watching their progress with her beautiful friend with an interest tinged with concern.

She remembered her mother once remarking that people deprived of love in childhood often had difficulty in forming successful relationships when adult. It was strange, even worrying, that Bethany never showed the slightest sign of falling for any of the attractive men whom Cressida organised for her as determinedly as a matchmaking mother.

The man who, finally, eighteen months after her return to England, caused a ripple of reaction to disturb the unnatural calm of Bethany's emotions, made his entrance into her life not through Cressida's good offices, but by way of the flower shop.

She was in the back room one morning when she heard the jangle of the door bell. In the showroom she found a tall, well-dressed man standing with his back to her, looking at a display of silk flower arrangements. He had black hair and the back of his neck was dark brown. For a moment she took him for an unusually tall Arab in European clothes.

'Good morning,' she said pleasantly, beginning to smile.

He turned, and her smile faded. He had a fine aquiline nose, and very dark, almost black eyes. But he wasn't an Arab. She was ninety-nine per cent sure that he was an Italian, and that she had seen him before. He had a wide, sensual mouth, slightly quirked at the corners to match the gleam of amusement which seemed to lurk in his eyes.

In an involuntary reflex to her strong sense of recognition, she added, '*Buon giorno, signore. Posso aiutarla?*'

His eyes scanned her slender figure which today was dressed in a straight-skirted black wool crêpe suit with a large sailor collar of white organdie and a black satin bow at the front.

It was a very Italian look he gave her; not as lascivious as a leer, but far more overtly sexual in its admiration than an Englishman of his sort—though young, he looked distinguished and successful—would be likely to give a girl while she was looking at him.

'Good morning. I've come to pick up some flowers which my mother ordered earlier this month.'

He spoke faultless English; the English of a public school man.

'What is the name, please?' asked Bethany.

'Dorset . . . Cranmer Castle.'

'Oh, yes, I remember.'

She did not attend to everyone who came to the shop. The owner of it, Mrs Hastings, also had two part-time assistants. But Bethany had been on showroom duty when his mother had brought in a cutting of the material of some curtains she was having made up, and ordered an arrangement of flowers to tone with the colours in the fabric.

She had also brought in the vases in which she wanted them arranged; two rather rare crystal cornucopias on marble bases. She had seemed a nice, friendly woman with whom Bethany had chatted about flowers and furnishings for considerably longer than usual.

It was only when it was time to enter the particulars in the order book, and the customer had handed over her card, that she had become aware that she was serving the Duchess of Dorset, whose home was reputed to be one of the most beautifully preserved historic houses in southern England.

That night she had mentioned the Duchess to Cressida who had said, 'She sounds sweet, but one of her sons is a stinker. He had a terrific affair with a friend of a friend of mine. Suddenly, while she was still besotted about him, he dropped her—bang!—and started chasing someone else. To give the devil his due, Fiona had been around for a while and ought to have known he was the Son of Casanova type. Even so, he behaved very badly. If his mother becomes a regular customer, and he ever comes to the shop with her, watch out!'

That this tall, dark man was the son who had ditched the unknown Fiona could be taken as read, thought Bethany. He had womaniser written all over him. Not liking men of that stamp, however attractive, she became very cool.

Not that, after that first admiring look, he attempted to flirt with her. In fact he said very little while she was packing up the order. But she felt him watching her.

He paid for the flowers with a cheque drawn on an account with Coutts, bankers to the Queen. When he handed it to her and she saw his name and title printed underneath his sprawling signature, she knew he was not the Duke's heir but a younger son, Lord Robert Rathbone.

'Thank you. Please tell her Grace that if the flowers aren't entirely to her satisfaction, we shall be very pleased to re-arrange them for her,' she said stiffly.

'I will, but I'm sure my mother will be delighted with them. Does she know your name?'

'Castle.'

'Miss Castle?'

'Yes.'

'Thank you, Miss Castle. Goodbye.' With a smiling inclination of his head, he left the shop.

Bethany watched him pause at the edge of the pavement and glance both ways before striding across the road. He carried himself well. Possibly he had a commission in one of the fashionable regiments.

No, if that were the case, he would have his rank in front of his title. Captain Lord Robert Rathbone or whatever.

Why, thinking him an Italian, had she felt she had seen him before: Who was it that he reminded her of?

Later that afternoon, after the shop closed, she had an ap-pointment to have her hair trimmed at a Knightsbridge salon which stayed open until seven. Her hair was still long, but she had the ends cut every six weeks. Tonight she was also having it put up professionally because, later, she was being taken to a dance at the Ironmongers' Hall in the Barbican. It was a twenty-first birthday celebration for the younger sister of the man who was coming to collect Bethany at half past seven.

While she was under the dryer—her hair was too long and thick to be blown dry—she skimmed through one or two glossies, including *Harpers & Queen*.

At the back, in the social section called *Jennifer's Diary* which carried photographs of balls, private views, race meet-ings and similar events, her eye was arrested by a picture of the same dark face which had disturbed her equilibrium earlier in the day.

He was dressed for polo in a short-sleeved, open-necked shirt which revealed broad, muscular shoulders, white breeches and long leather boots with padded knee-guards. The other man in the photograph, which had been taken at Imperial International Polo Day at Smith's Lawn, Windsor, was the Prince of Wales. He was presenting Lord Robert with the silver model of a polo pony given to the best player in all the competing teams.

Even if she had heard nothing detrimental about him before, this would have put Bethany off him. Her father and stepmother had been horsey people, and she wanted nothing more to do with them, whether they hunted, played polo or merely hacked in Hyde Park.

As her gaze lingered on the picture of him—a much taller man than the Prince, with a more aggressive chin—something clicked into place in her memory and she knew who it was he resembled.

Lorenzo de' Medici.

For a month, she forgot Lord Robert except when, glancing through the order book, she noticed that, on her day off, Mrs Hastings had taken another order from the Duchess.

The next time she saw her employer, who had an invalid husband and worked on many of her arrangements at home, she said, 'I gather the Duchess of Dorset was pleased with the cornucopias we filled for her. I see she's ordered something else.'

'Yes, this is a present for a friend. I expect we shall get a lot of new customers through her. She's noted for her excellent taste, and if she talks about us it will be a splendid advertisement. By the way, she remarked on my good fortune in having such an efficient and charming assistant.'

'How nice of her.'

'You *are* a great asset to me, Bethany. My kind of customers like to be served by someone civilised; not some ungracious gum-chewing girl with a couldn't-care-less attitude. It's extraordinary how offhand, even downright rude, some of them are nowadays. Even the children and grandchildren of one's friends. Only the other day in Harrods, I was horrified to hear a girl I know being far from civil to a customer. The decline in good manners is really quite dreadful.'

They had gone on to speak of other matters and, with only a passing thought for the Duchess's dark-eyed son, Bethany had again put him out of her mind.

Had she known what had prompted the Duchess to place a second order for flowers, and to make some discreetly casual enquiries about Mrs Hastings' chief assistant, she would have been dismayed and annoyed.

For when Lord Robert had driven home and carried the cornucopias up to his mother's sitting-room, he had said to her, 'There was an incredibly beautiful girl working in the flower shop. Did you notice her, Mother?'

'Yes, I did. She served me as well. She had a lovely face, I thought. Beautiful, rather sad eyes.'

'I wonder who she is. Her surname is Castle. Do you know any Castles?'

'I don't think so.' The Duchess had looked thoughtfully at her son as he cut open the ties on the parcel for her.

And he, knowing her unexpressed longing to see him give up his wayward pursuit of naughty girls and fall in love with a nice one, had not doubted that she would make it her business to find out all about Miss Castle and, if she passed muster, which he felt sure she would, to arrange for them to meet again.

If his mother didn't do the leg-work for him, then he would have to do it himself, because the girl's cool, reserved beauty had caught his errant fancy more than a little.

The more formal she had become—and she had been as prickly as a nervous porcupine all the time he was in the shop—the more he had wanted to let down her neat, upswept hair, and see what it did to her beauty to be thoroughly kissed.

Which was something which, once he had met her socially, it would not take him long to find out.

When the Duchess discovered that Bethany was the daughter of a Hampshire landowner, and had been educated at a girls' public school, the rest was easy.

In earlier years, it had been other mothers, not his own, who had put their wits to work with a view to getting Robert to the altar. Now, knowing he had had his pick of dozens of eligible young women, and had not shown more than a fleeting interest in any of them, the Duchess felt it was time to exert herself on behalf of any acceptable girl who seemed to appeal to him.

There were several reasons why she and her husband were anxious to see him married. The Duke was concerned about the succession. What she minded most, being happily married herself, was to watch her younger son wasting his time with women who really meant nothing to him.

When a girl she had been at school with, but never much liked, came into the shop with her godmother, and the godmother returned a week later and, after some affable conversation, invited Bethany to an informal supper party, she thought it unusually hospitable on the strength of so slight an acquaintance. It never occurred to her that she was being manipulated.

Her hostess, Mrs Fitzhoward, lived within walking distance of Cressida's flat. The night being a dry one, though cold, Bethany did not have to ring for a taxi to take her there.

Walking through the wintry evening streets, she contemplated the months ahead, hoping the coming winter would be milder and shorter than the first one she had spent in London.

She was admitted to Mrs Fitzhoward's house by a maid who took her coat and showed her into a large room where seven or eight people were already assembled.

Immediately her hostess came forward to welcome her. 'Miss Castle . . . how charming you look in that deep violet colour. Isn't the wind bitter this evening? Come and have some mulled wine to warm you.'

She introduced a young man who had been put in charge of the mulled wine, and who handed Bethany a glass of it. Then she introduced the other people.

The tallest man there, when she would have presented him to Bethany, forestalled her by saying, 'Miss Castle and I have met before, Mrs Fitz. But perhaps she may not remember me as it was a rather brief encounter. Robert Rathbone, Miss Castle.'

He offered his hand. When she gave him hers, he did not shake it as she expected, but lifted it to kiss the backs of her fingers. It was done with the unselfconscious ease of someone accustomed to performing the greeting. Even though she had no intention of succumbing to his charm, like the rest of her sex she could not help preferring the homage to her femininity implied by the courtly gesture to the commonplace shaking of hands.

'I remember you, Lord Robert,' she said, with a polite smile.

'I've been hoping we should meet again.' With the adroitness of a practised philanderer, he had contrived, by an unobtrusive movement, to place himself between her and the people to whom she had intended to talk.

'Oh, really? Why?' she enquired.

If he was going to make a set at her—at least until someone more attractive arrived—she was going to make it uphill work for him.

'Because I wanted to talk to you, and I didn't think you would allow that if I came back to the shop, or that I should be able to persuade you to have lunch with me. But now we have met in circumstances where we can talk at length—or at least for as long as our hostess allows me to monopolise you.'

He had a most disarming smile. It made two deep creases appear in his cheeks. She wondered where he had come by his tan.

Deliberately she sipped her wine and let her glance wander past him in a way she thought very uncivil when she saw other people doing it. Even if trapped by a bore, one had an obligation to listen attentively until one could escape with courtesy. Her present companion was not a bore, but he was a special case. She wanted to put him off her.

'What do you suggest we talk about?' she asked.

'About you . . . where you learnt to speak Italian.'

'I lived in Italy for a time after leaving school.'

'What made you think it was my first language?'

'You look rather Italian.'

'I do have Italian blood in me. My great-grandmother— whom I knew because she lived to be nearly ninety—was born in America of Italian parents. Her grandfather was the son of peasants, but he had a good brain and he made a lot of money in the States. His son made more, and had a daughter who was as beautiful as you are. But by the time she was sixty, she had to go about in dark glasses. Her eyes had been permanently reddened by the belladonna which women in her day used to make their eyes sparkle. You don't put anything in your lovely eyes, do you?'

She shook her head. 'I'd heard you were an outrageous flirt, Lord Robert. Rumour spoke the truth,' she said dryly.

'It's not flirting to tell you you're beautiful. Merely a statement of fact. My mother shares my opinion. She thought you had sad eyes. My first impression was of—How shall I describe it? A touch-me-not expression. It's there again now. Do you make a habit of pre-judging people, Miss Castle? Have you already decided not to like me on the basis of some gossip you've been told?'

He was beginning to fluster her.

'Gossip usually has some foundation, and I know at least one *fact* about you which suggests we haven't much in common.'

'Which is?'

'You're a polo player, I believe.'

'Yes, but I've never known anyone to be up in arms about polo. It's hunting which infuriates some people.'

'Everything to do with horses bores me,' Bethany confessed.

'What excites you?'

'Poetry ... art ... cooking.' She thought it unlikely that they were interests he could claim to share.

To her stunned astonishment, he responded to this in Italian, and in verse.

'Quant'e bella giovinezza, che si fugge tuttavia! Chi vuol esser lieto sia: di doman non c'e certezza.' Then he added, 'I don't know who wrote it. Perhaps you do.'

It was an extraordinary, almost eerie experience to hear him speaking the words composed by one of her heroes, the legendary Italian to whom he bore a strong resemblance.

'It was written by Lorenzo de' Medici. Where did you learn it?' she asked, in a rather faint voice.

'From my great-grandmother. Perhaps she was getting a little gaga when I knew her. She repeated it often enough for me to pick it up parrot fashion. Later on, when I found out what it meant, I thought it a very sound maxim.' He repeated it in English. 'How fine a thing is youth, but how short-lived. Let he who wishes to be merry, be so. For there's no saying what tomorrow will bring.'

He looked down at her, dark eyes glinting.

'I believe I've confounded you, Miss Castle. You had me written off as a twenty-four-carat philistine. But I'm not, you see, I had the luck to grow up surrounded by fine paintings, so if it's art you enjoy discussing I can accommodate you as well as anyone here. As for cooking, I'm not much of a chef myself, but if ever you invite me to sample your culinary skills, you'll find me an appreciative guest.'

Bethany was still taken aback by the way he had switched from English to Italian; sounding so much like David when he spoke that loveliest of languages that suddenly she was overcome by a wave of nostalgia for her life at the Villa Delphini with the man she had loved with such fatal, heartbreaking intensity.

To her consternation, her eyes filled with tears, and her lower lip quivered.

'My dear girl, what have I said to distress you?' Robert Rathbone asked, with swift concern.

He moved closer, screening her from the others. Now she was glad of his strategy in interposing himself between them and her.

'Nothing . . . nothing.'

She pulled herself together, forcing a smile which, because of her chagrin at becoming emotional at a party, of all places, was warmer than any she had given him.

He said gently, 'Perhaps my mother was right. You are sad at present. I'm sorry if something I said was unintentionally upsetting.'

'It wasn't . . . you needn't apologise. Let's talk about art,' she said hurriedly, seizing on a topic which, although it had some painful associations for her, was the nearest means to hand to smooth over the embarrassing moment. 'Er . . . do you prefer oils or watercolours?'

'Oh, without question, watercolours. If I had to select which of our paintings to rescue if the place were on fire, I'd grab the Turners and the Girtins. One of the mysteries of the art world which has always fascinated me is what happened to *The Eidometropolis*. Do you know about it?'

Bethany shook her head, grateful for the way he had picked up her cue and was taking the weight of the conversation, giving her more time to recover her poise.

'It was an enormous panorama of London which Girtin exhibited in 1802,' he went on. 'There are five or six sketches of it in the British Museum, but the panorama itself has been lost. A hundred and eighty years is a long time for a thing like that to be adrift. But I suppose it might yet come to light. There's still a great mass of uncatalogued, unrecognised treasures lying around in attics and lumber-rooms up and down the country. But of course a lot of valuable stuff was either pulped in the salvage drive, or bombed or burned in World War Two.'

When he was not flirting with her, but was talking seriously on a subject which interested him, he was, she discovered, an interesting, pleasant companion.

For the rest of the evening, although he continued to monopolise her—and Mrs Fitzhoward made no effort to disengage them—he said nothing to revive her sense of caution.

To the extent that, when he offered to run her home, she accepted without hesitation.

'Good party?' Cressida asked, switching off the television as Bethany entered their sitting-room. She had not had a date that evening.

'Yes, very good.'

'Who did you meet? Who brought you home?' Evidently the other girl had heard the car drawing up and pulling away.

'Robert Rathbone.'

As Cressida's eyebrows shot up, Bethany added, 'I think he's not as black as he's painted. Maybe certain types of girls bring out the worst in him. He was a bit lechy at first, but later on he was quite nice.'

'Are you going to see him again?'

'I shouldn't think so.'

Truth to tell, Bethany had been surprised and even disconcerted when Robert—they had ended the evening on first name terms—had said goodnight without proposing another meeting.

Admittedly, her intention at the start of the party had been to put him off her. Later on she had revised her opinion of him, and although she would probably have refused to dine with him à deux, had he suggested it, it was mildly unsettling not to have been given the opportunity.

'I think he found me all right to talk to at a party, but

realised I wasn't going to join his other trophies of the chase,' she said lightly.

But had they been privy to Lord Robert's thoughts as he drove to his parents' London house, or seen the predatory half-smile which accompanied them, neither Bethany nor his mother would have gone to bed with minds at rest.

CHAPTER SIX

THE next day it crossed Bethany's mind that, between noon and one o'clock, Robert might appear and suggest taking her out to lunch. But he didn't. As usual she ate her packed lunch in the room behind the shop, and afterwards went for a brisk walk.

She was not disappointed by Robert's failure to appear. It had seemed merely a possibility.

During the following three days she found herself thinking about Mrs Fitzhoward's party more often than she would have wished. Every time the telephone rang, she half expected to hear a deep, slightly drawling voice at the other end of the line.

On the fourth day, when she answered the telephone in the middle of the afternoon, a woman's voice said, 'May I speak to Miss Castle, please?'

'Speaking.'

'This is the Duchess of Dorset's secretary. Is it a convenient moment for her to talk to you, Miss Castle? It's not in connection with flowers, but about a personal matter. She can ring you at home if you prefer it, and if you're on the telephone there. I couldn't find your name in the directory.'

'Our telephone number is listed under my flatmate's name,' said Bethany. 'But I can speak to the Duchess now.'

'Hold on a moment, please.'

There was a brief pause before the Duchess's voice said, 'Good afternoon, Miss Castle. My son Robert tells me that you share his interest in watercolours, and might like to see our collection. I wondered, if you are free, if you'd care to come down this weekend?'

An invitation to stay with his parents at Cranmer was the last thing Bethany had anticipated when considering the various follow-ups which Robert might—but hadn't—made.

'I—I should be delighted,' she answered, in some confusion. 'How . . . how kind of you.'

'My husband has to spend Friday night in London. He can drive you down for lunch on Saturday, and I have an early appointment with my dentist there on Monday morning, so

I'll run you back,' said the Duchess. 'It will be a very quiet weekend with only my sons here, and we don't dress for dinner or anything of that sort when we're alone. Nor will you be frozen—Cranmer isn't the ice-house which most people expect a castle to be. But I should advise you to bring some warm outdoor clothes and comfortable walking shoes. Robert will be sure to take you for one or two tramps with the dogs, he's a tremendous walker. I'm not, and possibly you aren't.'

'I am. I walk a lot, even in London,' said Bethany truthfully.

'Good; then you won't mind being dragged up hill and down dale. I already have your address. Could you give me your telephone number in case of any hitches.'

Bethany gave it, and the Duchess closed their brief conversation by saying, 'My husband will pick you up at your flat at half past ten. Try not to keep him waiting as he's rather a fanatic about punctuality. I'll look forward to seeing you on Saturday. Goodbye.'

Cressida, when she heard about the invitation, said 'Good lord! Perhaps he's fallen in love with you and has honourable intentions for a change.'

Bethany laughed. 'I think that's about as unlikely as the world coming to an end tomorrow afternoon.'

All the same, it was very odd.

It was also a teeny bit gratifying to find that Robert hadn't, after all, written her off as an uninteresting girl with an embarrassing tendency to dissolve into tears—or at least to come very close to it—at unsuitable moments.

One thing she could be sure of; he wouldn't attempt to seduce her under his parents' roof. She could relax and enjoy being a guest at the Castle without wondering and worrying about whether his bad reputation was well founded.

By twenty minutes past ten on Saturday morning, she was stationed on the pavement outside the flat, waiting for the Duke to pick her up.

The weather was still very cold. She was dressed in black wool tights under a grey pleated wool skirt from Marks & Spencer which had black and white overchecks. Above the waist, she had three layers; the innermost being a white cotton rollneck jersey under a black wool sweater under a shiny black ciré Cheryl Tiegs windcheater. This she had borrowed from

Cressida who had bought it in America. Red mitts and a long, soft red muffler completed her outfit, and beside her was a soft-topped weekend case.

At twenty-five minutes past ten, her eyes widened at the sight of a brown Rolls-Royce coming towards her. Knowing that Cressida was lurking at their sitting-room window, Bethany stifled a giggle and waited for the stately limousine to slide to a standstill.

The Duke was not driving it himself. There was a chauffeur at the wheel. He got out, said a polite 'Good morning, miss' before opening the door behind his, then picking up her case. While he was taking it round to the boot, the Duke stepped on to the pavement.

'Good morning, Miss Castle. Allow me to compliment you on being ready and waiting. Punctuality is the politeness of kings, as Louis the Eighteenth is said to have said. But it isn't an adage which commands much respect among your sex, if I may say so.'

She smiled. 'Good morning.'

They shook hands. He was as tall as his son, but otherwise they were not alike. The Duke had grey hair, grey eyes, and a small grey moustache.

After ushering her into the car, he climbed in beside her, and a few moments later she was enjoying her first experience of the smoothness, comfort and spaciousness enjoyed by passengers in a Rolls-Royce.

For about ten minutes he chatted to her. Then he said, 'Well now, we can't make small talk for an hour—or I certainly can't—so I suggest you have a look through these books which I collected for my wife yesterday, and I'm going to read *The Times*.'

Between them, on the wide back seat, lay a black plastic carrier bag on which was printed in gold the name and the three Royal warrants of Hatchards, London's oldest bookshop. Inside it were half a dozen books, including a newly published biography which Bethany was eager to read, but for which she had expected to have to wait her turn at the library.

Having opened it, she did not look up again until the Duke surprised her by saying, 'Here we are.'

Although the interior was open only to private parties by appointment, most people would have recognised the battlements and gatehouse of one of the finest inhabited castles in Britain.

Standing on an island in the centre of a large lake surrounded by a deer park, the castle had been photographed for innumerable travel guides as an outstandingly picturesque example of a well-preserved mediaeval stronghold. Subsequently used by Henry VIII as a hunting lodge, and then given to Piers Rathbone by Queen Elizabeth I, it had been in continuous occupation by his descendants since that time.

Bethany had looked up these facts the day before. Now, after carefully replacing the biography in the carrier, she leaned forward to gaze eagerly at the ancient walls which encompassed more than five hundred years of her country's colourful history.

The Rolls swept down the sloping drive to the lake, and soon they were passing under the arch of the gatehouse into a large courtyard.

Someone must have seen them coming and warned the Duchess. She was waiting to welcome them when the car drew to a halt. But her younger son was not with her, as Bethany had expected him to be.

As his chauffeur opened the door, and the Duke stepped down to greet his wife, Bethany noticed how fondly she looked up at him, and the obvious affection with which he bent to kiss her cheek and say, 'Hello, m'dear. How are you?'

Then he turned to help their guest alight, saying, 'Miss Castle has had her nose buried in one of your books all the way here, and no doubt she'd like to finish it before she leaves.'

'By all means. Which one was it?' the Duchess enquired, shaking hands. On being told, she said, 'I'll have it put in your bedroom. Come and meet our elder son, James. Robert isn't here yet. He's been away all week, but we're expecting him back this afternoon.'

'I'm going up to change, Laura,' said the Duke, as they entered the Great Hall.

As he disappeared up a wide stone staircase, his wife said, 'Perhaps I should mention beforehand that James is confined to a wheelchair. He's a victim of a wretched illness for which, at present, there is no cure. He bears it with enormous courage, and fortunately he has intellectual resources which are some compensation for the loss of his physical powers.'

James, Viscount Hartigan, was sitting by a window overlooking the lake when they entered the room where he was listening to some orchestral music which Bethany did not recognise.

However, he heard them come in, turned his chair to face them, and switched off the music before they reached him. His somewhat haggard good looks—quite different from those of his brother—and signs that he had once been a well-built young man, made his present disablement all the more tragic.

But his smile was friendly and cheerful as he said, 'Forgive me for not getting up, Miss Castle—or may I be informal and call you by your very pretty and unusual Christian name?'

'Of course . . . please do.'

He could only know what her name was by having been told it by Robert. Bethany wondered what he had said about her to his brother.

By the time he came home, about three, she had been shown her green and white bedroom in one of the towers, had enjoyed a delicious light lunch, and begun to feel at her ease with the other members of his family, particularly his mother.

The Duchess was showing her the State Rooms when her younger son joined them. Having bent his tall head to be kissed, he gave her a parcel.

'A present from Paris. Hello, Bethany. Nice to see you again. As you'll have been told, I've been on the other side of the Channel all week, so have had to rely on my parents to organise the pleasure of your company for me. I'm glad you could make it at short notice.'

As he spoke, he handed her a smaller parcel in the same striped silver wrapping paper.

The Duchess was already opening her present, which proved to be a pair of pale grey suede gloves with silk linings. She was delighted, and hugged him.

'Thank you, darling. Very thoughtful of you.'

Bethany wasn't sure that she wanted to accept a present from him. It was a relief when she found that hers was an inexpensive cotton square, shocking pink patterned with white birds, for tying at the neck of a sweater.

She looked up at him. 'Thank you very much.'

'I hope pink is a colour you like. The first time we met you were wearing black and white. The other night, purple. And now black and white again.'

The Duchess said, 'I'll leave you to take over the guided tour, Robert. Have you seen James yet?'

'Yes, I looked in on my way up. He looks drawn. Has he been having a bad week?'

'I'm afraid so. He won't admit it, but one has only to look at him. Don't forget tea at four-thirty.'

She walked away, leaving Robert looking after her with a frown and a troubled expression which Bethany had not seen before. It appeared that, whatever his propensities towards women were, he was a considerate son and concerned, caring brother; and for those qualities, if no others, she had to like him.

'What took you to Paris?' she asked.

'I was only there for a couple of hours before my flight. The rest of the time I was in the country outside Paris. If my father hadn't inherited all this, he would have chosen farming as his career. As things are, his other commitments mean that I often have to deputise for him in the management of the home farm and various breeding experiments in which he's interested. We have a large herd of Charolais—the white French cattle you may have seen grazing in the park—and smaller herds of Old English cattle and sheep. But having been warned of your dislike of everything equine, I won't bore you with matters bovine and ovine.'

'I like sheep,' said Bethany. 'Have you seen that delightful book of drawings of sheep by Henry Moore?'

'Yes, I have it. My mother gave it to me. Would you like to know what my father said about you when I spoke to him just now?' Without waiting for her assent, he added, 'You've won his immediate approval, which is not the case with all my girl-friends. If you want his verdict verbatim, it was—"A very pleasant young woman. Good legs . . . punctual . . . and she reads".'

He looked down at her long, slender legs now clad in some finer black tights into which, finding the Castle as warm as the Duchess had promised, she had changed before lunch.

'He's quite right about your legs. I noticed them myself, the first time I saw you. There's something about a pair of pretty ankles in black silk stockings which is extraordinarily erotic.'

Bethany had a strong intuition that, if she didn't forestall him, he was going to kiss her. They were miles away from the rest of the household, in a part of the Castle never lived in except when the Dorsets entertained royalty or ministers of State. Just before Robert's arrival, the Duchess had answered a question from Bethany by saying that the last people to sleep in the enormous bed in the room in which he had found them had been an ambassador and his wife.

Except when they were swept and dusted, these great rooms remained empty and silent, permeated by an almost tangible atmosphere of the past—or so she had felt a short time earlier.

Now that sense of the past had been dispelled by the aura of virile male magnetism emanating from Robert. She was suddenly intensely aware of the powerful muscles, concealed now under a sweater and tweed coat, which she had seen in the picture of him in polo kit.

Tall as she was, even in low-heeled shoes, he towered over her. To resist him physically would be impossible. She had to stop him before he laid hands on her.

Taking a hasty step backwards, she said in her coolest voice. 'I'm glad your father approves of me, but I think I should point out that I'm not one of your girl-friends in the sense that term usually implies. A friend in the general sense, perhaps. Nothing more.'

'Why not? If you'd been involved with someone else, I don't think you would have accepted my mother's invitation.'

'I'm not involved with anyone else—nor do I want to be. Certainly not on our short acquaintance,' she said firmly. 'If you asked your mother to invite me in order to flirt with me, I'm afraid you're going to be disappointed. I came because I wanted to see the Castle, and all the beautiful things your family has collected over the centuries. I was surprised to be asked, but I'm not so overwhelmed by it all that I'm willing to . . . to start an affair with you.'

Perhaps, knowing little about her, he took her for a naïve girl whose background made his seem so dazzling that she would fall like a ninepin.

He said, his dark eyes amused, 'I don't remember suggesting it. I *was* admiring your legs, but do you consider that tantamount to a proposition?'

Bethany felt herself starting to flush at his sardonic tone.

'I—I'm making things clear from the outset . . . to avoid any misunderstanding.'

'Message received and understood.' He glanced at his watch.

'I think we'd better postpone the rest of the tour until later. It's four-thirty, time for tea.'

The last time she had had toast from a covered silver dish had been the day David had come to the Manor and swept her, as on a magic carpet, to his colourful world at Portofino.

It was the memory of that other occasion which made her a little subdued as she ate the delicious things served for afternoon tea at the Castle. Some she had eaten before; parkin, made with oatmeal, black treacle and ginger, and the homemade bloater paste which her father had preferred to jam, and which the Duke also liked to spread on his toast. But the thick oval cakes of light bread, with a hole in the centre, which the Duchess said were called huffkins, she had never had before.

'I'll show you what we do with them,' said Robert. He split a huffkin and spread it with thick clotted cream. Then he added a dollop of last summer's strawberry jam, and put the halves together again, the cream oozing out at the side.

'My favourite thing for tea used to be thunder and lightning,' he said, as he handed it to her.

She thanked him, and asked, 'What was that?'

'Bread spread with cream and then trickled with golden syrup.'

The Duchess said, 'That was something which Nanny introduced as a special treat when either of you deserved it. She came from Tiverton in Devon,' she explained to Bethany. 'And whenever the boys of Blundell's School had a cricket match against some other Eleven, they would have a special tea afterwards including cream on sliced plum cake, or Robert's favourite, thunder and lightning. I'm speaking of sixty or seventy years ago, when her father was groundsman at Blundell's. I should doubt if those famous cricket teas survived the last war.'

James, Bethany noticed, ate almost nothing. While he was talking and joking it was less noticeable, but when his face was in repose it was clear that he was a very sick man. If his illness was a progressive one, it didn't seem likely that he would ever succeed his robust-looking father.

Let him who wishes to be merry, be so. For there's no saying what tomorrow will bring.

Lorenzo de' Medici had seen his brother Giuliano murdered by members of the rival Pazzi family, and had himself narrowly escaped the same fate. Giuliano had been twenty-five.

Perhaps it was his brother's crippling illness which accounted for Robert's philandering. Yet surely he would get more satisfaction from the deep relationship of marriage than from a succession of shallow affairs?

'You've gone away from us, Bethany?'

As the sound of his voice penetrated her reverie, she jumped and said apologetically, 'I'm sorry . . . I was miles away.'

'Clearly, but where?' he asked teasingly.

'At a cricket match in Devon seventy years ago,' she answered evasively.

Before dinner that night, for which she wore a plain sand wool dress with a bronze kid belt and bronze beads, Robert showed her the family portraits in the State Dining-room.

There were portraits by Kneller and Van Dyck, and by Reynolds, Gainsborough and Zoffany. But the one of most interest to her was the painting of his American great-grandmother by John Singer Sargent, the brilliant portraitist of Edwardian society women.

The ninth Duchess of Dorset had been Viscountess Hartigan when he painted her, wearing a scarlet velvet dress which emphasised her vivid Italian colouring. But her fashionably small, pouting mouth and her gentle, rather cow-like eyes made her very little like her great-grandson, except that she had obviously possessed the feminine equivalent of his physical magnetism. Her charm, as she gazed down from her elaborate gilded frame, was almost palpable. That she had bequeathed to him; but his aquiline nose and strong chin must have come from her father or grandfather.

As well as the State Dining-room, the Castle had another dining-room for smaller but still formal dinner parties. However, that night they dined in a round room known as the Parlour, in one of the towers.

It was here that the paintings bought by the present Duke and his family were hung, and the walls were thick with them.

As the Duchess indicated where Bethany was to sit, and Robert drew out the chair for her, she was startled to find herself facing a picture which, although she had never seen it before, was, in style, disturbingly familiar to her.

'Oh . . . is that a Warren?' she exclaimed.

'Yes, it's mine. Bought in New York a few years ago,' Robert answered, from behind her. 'You must know his work well to recognise it at a glance.'

She became aware that, by remaining on her feet, she was preventing the Duke from seating himself.

Quickly sitting down, she had no choice but to say, 'I do. The artist is my uncle.'

'Your mother's brother, presumably?' said James, from his place next to hers.

Robert was walking round to take the chair facing them.

'No, my father's. Warren is David's middle name.'

'I knew he was an Englishman, but was told that he didn't live here but somewhere abroad,' remarked Robert.

'In Italy.'

'Was it with him and his family that you spent your time there?'

'Yes.' It seemed unnecessary to explain that David had no family. Had the picture not taken her by surprise, she would have preferred not to mention her connection with him.

Inevitably it was a matter of interest to the others, and she had to endure being asked several questions about him until, to her relief, Robert cut short the ordeal by switching the conversation to another subject.

The Duke, having been up late the night before, retired to bed at an early hour, and the Duchess with him. James had gone to his quarters even earlier. He had a manservant to put him to bed and to help him to dress in the morning.

Bethany said goodnight to Robert while his parents were still in the room with them.

He said, with a glint in his eyes, 'I was hoping you would stay and play cards with me.'

'I'm afraid I'm a lark, not an owl, and I was up extra early this morning to do my share of the weekend cleaning. It wouldn't have been fair to leave it all to Cressida,' said Bethany.

'In that case I mustn't be selfish and keep you from your beauty sleep. I'm also an early riser, as it happens. I shall be jogging round the lake as soon as it's light. But I usually burn my candle at both ends,' he told her. 'Goodnight, Bethany.'

Actually she was not in the least tired, and was looking forward to continuing the biography she had begun that morning.

She had been in bed for about forty minutes when her concentration was broken by what sounded like a knock on the door. Although not a believer in ghosts and poltergeists, she was conscious of being in a very ancient building, and she couldn't help looking at the door a little apprehensively. Who would be visiting her at this hour?

'Come in,' she called uncertainly, half expecting nothing to happen.

The door was opened by Robert, still in the clothes he had worn earlier, and carrying a beaker in a silver holder.

'Seeing your light still on from the window of my room, I concluded you were having trouble getting to sleep and brought you a nightcap,' he said, closing the door behind him, and approaching the bed.

Having let down her long chestnut hair, she had braided it in a loose plait to keep it from becoming too tangled during the night. Her nightdress was a modern version of an old-fashioned one, with a high ruffled neck, a ruffled yoke and ruffles at her wrists.

Robert put the beaker on the night table. He straightened and looked down at her, taking in the pigtail, the ruffles—and the book she had been reading.

'You look as virtuous as a Victorian virgin, but I suspect you don't have their respect for the truth,' he said, mock-sternly. 'I believe you came to bed early because you wanted to read, not because you were tired.'

'Well . . . partly, perhaps,' she admitted.

'And partly because you were nervous of staying alone with me after my parents had gone up?'

'When you said "message received and understood", I took it as an assurance that I needn't be nervous,' she responded.

'For the time being, yes; we'll play it your way. Having said that, may I sit down while you drink your nightcap?'

Taking her consent for granted, he sat down on the side of the bed, but too far away to cause her any misgivings.

'What is it?' she asked, reaching for the silver holder.

'A herb tea my mother takes when she has trouble sleeping. I've laced it with a little brandy.'

Strange, how history seemed to be repeating itself. Only this afternoon the dishes for the toast and scones had reminded her of having tea with David. Now here she was sitting up in bed, sipping a nightcap, just as she had on that other occasion.

'I should like to ask you a rather personal question,' said Robert.

Bethany remained silent, watching him over the rim of the beaker.

'It was clear—if only to me—that you didn't like being asked about Italy during dinner tonight. When we met at Mrs Fitzhoward's party, and I quoted some Italian poetry, you were visibly upset,' he went on. 'And this afternoon you told me you didn't want to become involved in a relationship with a man. All that seems to add up to a love affair with an Italian; a love affair which ended badly, and from which you haven't yet recovered. Are those deductions correct?'

For a ghastly moment Bethany had thought he had guessed the truth. Then, as soon as he referred to 'an Italian', she had realised that it wouldn't occur to him that it had been her father's brother she had been in love with.

'I was in love with someone in Italy—yes.'

'I thought so.' Evidently he didn't intend to pursue the subject. Picking up the book, he said, 'This is pretty good, I gather?'

'Oh, yes—excellent. Scholarly—one feels all the facts are reliable—but written in a racy style. No dull bits.'

'I must make a point of reading it. Don't let it keep you up too late. I'm hoping that, if it isn't raining, after breakfast we might go for a walk.' He rose and moved towards the door.

'I'd like that,' she said. 'Thank you for this'—meaning the tea.

His hand on the door-knob, Robert grinned at her. 'That, as I'm sure you're aware, was merely a pretext to come here. Goodnight.'

For the rest of that first weekend, he behaved impeccably towards her. A month later, after seeing him several times in London, she was invited to the Castle again, and Cressida with her. The Duchess, having learned from Robert that Bethany's flatmate had no family other than distant relations, had felt that Cressida might be lonely being on her own for two nights.

At this time Cressida was in love in a more intense way than usual. Much as she would have liked to stay at the Castle, she preferred not to pass up a weekend spent with her heart-throb. She had ceased to be a virgin in America, and Bethany suspected that, during her absence, Cressida would not sleep alone. It might even be that she was regretting inviting Bethany to share with her, thereby restricting her freedom of action.

Clearly she felt it was high time her friend graduated from girlhood to womanhood, and that she could do worse than entrust her initiation to Robert.

'I know I once warned you against him, but that was before you'd met him,' she said. 'Now I've met him too, if only briefly, and he seems a much nicer person than I'd imagined, but obviously very clued up about making love. And, believe me, that's quite important if one doesn't want one's first experience to be a crushing disillusionment.'

'I should have thought it was bound to be if no deep feelings were involved,' Bethany answered, somewhat shortly. 'I'll wait till I care for someone for my first experience.'

And that will be for ever, she thought desolately.

Robert, who had been in London most of the week, drove her down to Cranmer on Friday night. James was not at home that weekend. He had gone into hospital for the checks he had every few months.

On Saturday night the Duchess was giving a buffet supper, to be followed by dancing. Most of the guests would be young. She had told Bethany to bring a suitable dress.

'Mother usually arranges these parties at times when James is in hospital. She feels that to see people dancing, and the girls whom he might have married, makes it worse for him,' said Robert sombrely, during the journey from London.

'Poor James,' she said, with a deep sigh.

There came back to her an echo of David saying, *Life is unfair. The world is full of unfairness, sweetie. You should know that better than anyone. You had a raw deal yourself until very recently.*

But compared with James's raw deal, her own had been nothing.

And not only James, poor Robert, she thought to herself. He must often feel guilty for remaining strong and vigorous while his brother grew increasingly frail.

It was the unalterable things which were hardest to bear: James's incurable illness, her own irreversible blood-tie with David.

On Saturday morning they walked, preceded by various dogs and followed, at a dignified plod by Archie, Robert's grey-muzzled Labrador.

In the afternoon, the Duchess insisted that Bethany should rest for an hour. Although she hadn't expected to sleep, the long tramp before lunch in the fresh country air made her nap for more than an hour.

The day before, in obedience to an uncharacteristic impulse, she had bought herself a new short evening dress. It was made of a brilliant blue silk, overlaid with gold-speckled gauze which fell in handkerchief points below the hem of the underskirt. The bodice was tight and virtually strapless but for two very narrow gold shoulder-ties. It had a diaphanous jacket made from unlined gauze.

With it she was not going to wear any jewellery, for she had none except for her gold ear-rings. Whatever jewellery her mother had possessed had, presumably, been taken over by her stepmother, with whom she had had no contact since leaving the Manor.

The Florentine ear-rings she kept in their box in her underwear drawer. They were still too poignant a reminder of David. Sometimes she wore the gold sleeper pins given her by Francine, and sometimes inexpensive modern ear-rings. Tonight she was going to wear the pins; there hadn't been time to find ear-rings to go with the dress. Anyway, she felt that, among women who on special occasions could adorn themselves with beautiful old family jewels, modern trinkets looked out of place.

When the Duchess, who was wearing a long peony-red velvet skirt with a matching silk shirt, saw Bethany's dress, she said, '*How* pretty! You know just what suits you. I like that colour so much. I have a lapis-lazuli set in my Victorian collection which would go with it marvellously. Bethany, would you like to wear it? It's quite a simple little set—a necklet and bracelet, and a pair of small stud-type ear-rings.'

'It's very kind of you, Duchess, but I don't mind not wearing jewellery.'

'No, no—why should you indeed? Your lovely long neck

doesn't really need any ornament, and a young skin and shining eyes are preferable to any jewels,' the Duchess said, a little wistfully. 'It's merely that my lapis-lazuli might have been made for your dress. Let me show you.'

Bethany had already been shown the contents of some of the drawers in the two Wellington chests which housed the Duchess's collection of antique jewellery. This had nothing to do with the magnificent family jewels she had inherited, most of which were kept in a bank vault in London.

She had begun to collect interesting pieces as a young girl, in the 1940s, spending her modest allowance on coral and turquoise adornments which then cost no more than a pound, and when even a necklace of seed pearls might not be more than a few guineas.

The lapis-lazuli set was so perfect for her new dress that Bethany could not resist accepting the older woman's generous offer to lend it to her for the evening. She wondered if the Duchess was equally kind to all Robert's young women—not that she herself was in the same category as most of them, now that he appeared to have accepted her conditions for continuing their friendship.

At times it puzzled her slightly that he showed no sign of overstepping the mark again. Perhaps, having tried it, he found a platonic friendship a refreshing change from his usual hot-blooded amours. It might even be that he was carrying on a discreet liaison at the same time as seeing something of her.

Somehow, although she had no wish for him to make love to her, she didn't much like the idea of him inviting her to lunch, but dining with a more amenable girl who would let him take her to bed.

When Robert saw her in the blue and gold dress, his reaction was a little deflating. He told her she looked delightful, but there was no gleam in his eyes as he said it. It might have been his father complimenting her, as indeed the Duke did shortly afterwards.

During the evening, she was conscious of being the focus of a good deal of curiosity from guests who had been coming to Cranmer for years, and were friends of the family.

The English aristocracy was a closely interrelated strata of society in which everyone knew everyone else. Although no longer totally exclusive in its attitude towards outsiders—even pop singers could become *persona grata*—nevertheless it was still inclined to look askance at girls who had not made the current, much less formal equivalent of a début.

By birth and upbringing, Bethany and Cressida belonged to the lower levels of the aristocracy. But, after leaving school, they had both disappeared, Bethany immediately, and Cressida a few months afterwards. Now, with no parental backing, they had lost their place in the charmed circle where, in other circumstances, she would have been immediately recognisable as 'the Castles' daughter'.

Consequently she was in a similar position to Cinderella at Prince Charming's ball; a mysterious newcomer at whom, in spite of her pretty dress and charming jewellery, people were inclined to look askance.

Also, in view of Robert's reputation, they were probably speculating as to whether she was another of his easy conquests.

The former she did not mind; the latter she found harder to take.

However, as the evening progressed, there was nothing in his manner towards her to support the idea that she was one of his passing fancies. He behaved rather formally towards her, and much of the time it was necessary for him to concentrate on the other guests.

Towards midnight, he did dance with her more frequently than at an earlier stage of the evening.

'Are you enjoying yourself?' he asked, at the beginning of a waltz.

Every third dance was something slow which the older and less active guests could enjoy, and which gave the younger people a chance to merge in each other's arms.

Robert, however, did not take advantage of this opportunity. One hand at the back of her waist, the other supporting her right hand in a cool, loose clasp, he held her slightly away from him.

'Yes, very much, thank you.'

It was always easy to talk to him. Chatting to some of her other partners had been slightly heavy going, but with Robert there seemed to be an inexhaustible fund of conversation.

While they talked, she was conscious of the solid breadth of bone and muscle under the shoulder of his dinner jacket. The warmth of the banqueting hall, and the exertion of the livelier dances, had not made his face flushed and shiny like those of some of the other men.

He was less brown than when they had met—his tan, she had since discovered, had been the legacy of a three-week villa party at St Jean Cap Ferrat—but still noticeably darker than everyone else there.

When, for a moment, he did draw her nearer to him, to avoid coming too close to another couple, she caught the faint scent of his shaving lotion and was startled by a sudden strong impulse to reach up and touch her lips to his lean, smoothly clean-shaven cheek.

It was an impulse which bothered her from the moment it happened until the party was over.

When the last guests had departed, and the Duke and Duchess had gone to bed, but some of the staff were still about, Robert said, 'If you're not too tired, there's something you ought to see—the view from the battlements by moonlight. There's a full moon tonight. Would you like to go up?' Seeing her hesitation, he added dryly, 'I have no ulterior motive, I assure you.'

'All right,' she agreed, rather doubtfully.

There was a room next to the Gun Room where mackintoshes and wellingtons were kept. He fetched her a mac and a cardigan of his mother's. When she was warmly wrapped up, he led the way up to the topmost level of the battlements.

It was indeed a most spectacular view over miles of brightly moonlit countryside with, immediately below them, the glittering breeze-ruffled surface of the lake.

'You can imagine what a marvellous place this was to play,' said Robert. 'I used to spend hours up here, holding out against sieges and so on.'

As he spoke, the night wind ruffled his thick dark hair. It was easy to imagine him wearing a chain-mail cuirass, with a thick cloak flung back from his shoulders. He had an unmodern face; stronger, fiercer, more compelling than the faces of his contemporaries.

Remembering David, also a younger son, and glad of it, Bethany asked, 'What did you want to be when you grew up?'

Robert shrugged. 'An explorer . . . a racing driver . . . all the usual small boy ambitions which seldom come to anything.

Just as well, in my case. I'm needed here.'

He took her on a tour of the roof-tops, all of which were connected by catwalks and metal ladders.

Climbing down one of the shorter ladders in unsuitable high-heeled shoes, she almost missed her footing and gave a soft gasp of alarm.

He plucked her bodily off the ladder and lifted her down, turning her to face him. She wondered if he meant to kiss her, and again she drew in her breath, pierced by a strange, painful excitement.

'We can go down by way of the West Tower, the one you're sleeping in,' he said, turning away.

A few minutes later, having helped her to remove the raincoat outside her door, Robert said goodnight and left her. As she prepared for bed, she found herself pondering whether he *had* wanted to kiss her—or if only she had wanted it.

In the week after the dance at Cranmer, Bethany found herself in a dilemma.

She knew she should stop seeing Robert. The impulse to kiss him while dancing, and the urge to be kissed by him later, were clear evidence of the dangerous power of propinquity.

Even though her heart wasn't involved—and certainly Robert's heart wasn't—the insidious forces of Nature, at work to perpetuate the species, had nearly made her believe that she would enjoy having him kiss her. Afterwards, she had felt disgusted with herself, and disloyal to David who still had her heart in his keeping.

At the same time she was reluctant to give up Robert's friendship, largely—she told herself—because it meant she would also have to sacrifice her growing rapport with his mother.

The Duchess had begun to take the place which first Mrs Suffolk and then Francine had held in Bethany's affections. She knew herself to be a person for whom, in spite or perhaps because of the early loss of her mother and her bad relationship with her stepmother, close friendships with others of her sex were an important part of her life.

There were girls who claimed they couldn't stand their own sex. But Bethany was deeply fond of Cressida, and the hours she had spent with the Duchess—talking about books and shops, and the arrangement of houses and gardens—was something she would be sorry to forgo.

Although she knew it was unwise, when Robert telephoned to say he had tickets for a new play, she didn't demur. As Christmas approached, she continued to see him at intervals of three or four days.

'He *must* be in love with you,' said Cressida. 'A man courts a girl with one of two objectives—a roll in the hay, or marriage. It doesn't seem to be the hay, so it must be the bridal bed.'

Less than a week before Christmas, Robert came to the shop about ten minutes before closing time. He was laden with parcels in Harrods and Harvey Nichols wrapping paper.

Slumping down in a chair—the shop was empty—he said, 'I've been doing my Christmas shopping and I'm exhausted. I don't know why the stores don't turn off their central heating at this time of year—the heat generated by all those milling bodies is like the centre of a compost heap! I'm tired and hungry and thirsty, and it'll be hours before the traffic thins out. How about inviting me to the flat for a share of home cooking?'

'With pleasure. We've a rather special casserole simmering in the oven tonight. We're going to spend the evening wrapping our presents,' said Bethany.

She was spending Christmas at Cranmer and, rather unexpectedly, Cressida was being taken to Scotland to meet the parents of her lover.

When they arrived at the flat, there was a note on the table.

Change of plan—going out with Robin. May not be back until the small hours. Have borrowed your black evening bag and white chiffon scarf. Hope this okay. Love, C.

'Never mind. All the more for us—and I could eat a horse,' said Robert, reading the note over her shoulder.

'Yes, but *when* is she going to tackle her presents?' was Bethany's reaction. 'She and Robin are catching the train to Edinburgh tomorrow night. How like Cressy to go to a party when she has a million things to do.'

'She's not as conscientious as you are. In fact she's probably relying on you to do them up for her,' he suggested.

'I would if I could, but how can I without a list of who's getting what?'

Robert took off his coat. 'Worry about that after supper. Your immediate problem is what to give me to revive me. I think a stiff gin and tonic might do the trick. Let's both have one. I'll make them while you're having a look at whatever it is which smells so good.'

Having dealt with the drinks, he stood in the kitchen doorway, watching Bethany complete the preparations for their supper. Presently, with directions from her, he laid the table in the living-room. With a programme of carols on the radio, and the room bestrewn with his parcels, and some she had bought in her lunch break, it was all very cosy and Christmassy; much better than the year before, at the hostel.

After supper he helped her wash up, then he watched something on televison while she fetched wrapping paper, shiny scarlet tape and gift tags and began to tackle her presents.

She was dealing with a difficult shape to wrap when he switched off the set and asked if she would like some more coffee.

'Mm . . . yes, please.' She didn't look up.

She was aware of him leaving the room at the same time that, with a frown of dissatisfaction, she decided she was making a botch of it and had better start again.

A few minutes later something warm touched the nape of her neck. She stiffened, her concentration on her task abruptly shattered by the realisation that what she had felt was the lightest of kisses.

As she straightened, not knowing what to do, Robert's strong hands drew her to her feet and turned her towards him, as they had once before, on the battlements.

Meeting his eyes, seeing the light in them, she remembered Cressida's phrase—*a roll in the hay, or marriage.*

This time she didn't wonder if he meant to kiss her. She knew he was going to.

What she didn't know was whether the kiss would be the prelude to a proposition or a proposal.

Either way, it would finish their friendship.

CHAPTER SEVEN

HE touched her lips lightly with his; and then, in an explosion of passion, he crushed her against him and kissed her as someone else had once done.

Bethany thought of David for an instant, before her power to think failed, cut off by a wild surge of feeling. There was nothing and no one in the world but the man holding her in his arms, pressing her to his hard body, bruising her mouth with his kisses until he felt her lips part.

He was gentler then, or his mouth was. His grip was still painfully tight round her shoulders and waist. But presently that relaxed too, and his hands began stroking her back, tracing the line of her spine with the tips of his fingers, and fondling the curves of her hips.

Soon she felt him touching her hair, searching her chignon for the pins and combs which held it up. He took them out one by one until the whole soft silky mass fell down her back like an avalanche. And all the time he went on kissing her, inducing long tremors of pleasure, making her shiver and burn.

Until he took her in his arms, she had not known how much intense feeling had been bottled up inside her. She had longed for this, ached for it, yearned for it—and somehow managed to convince herself that, without love, she wanted no part of it.

But she did; she wanted it desperately. His warm breath mingling with hers. His hair crisp beneath her fingers. His hands sliding under her sweater to smooth the soft skin of her waist.

When he picked her up and carried her to the sofa, she felt a primitive thrill at the easy strength with which he lifted her. He made her feel small and helpless; a weak, pliant, yielding captive with no power or will to resist whatever surrender he demanded.

For a long time she lay on the cushions while Robert kissed her closed eyes, and her ears, and the long smooth line of her throat.

When he lifted her up and gently peeled off her sweater, she submitted like a sleepy child. But she wasn't drowsy, merely dazed with kisses, drunk with kisses.

He held her against his shoulder, playing with her hair, nibbling the lobes of her ears.

'Your skin smells of lilac and roses,' he told her huskily. 'How soft it is ... softer than velvet. Oh, God! You're so beautiful, Bethany.'

She could hear the desire in his voice but, because his caresses were gentle, it didn't alarm her. When he piled up the cushions behind her and lowered her on to them, his eyes on her small, round breasts, she blushed, but she didn't attempt to retrieve her sweater from the back of the sofa.

Robert had shed his after supper. Now, in haste, he unbuttoned his shirt and tugged it free from his trousers. A moment later it was flung aside and he was stripped to the waist, his shoulders and chest still brown from his Riviera holiday. His chest was as smooth as polished leather, although there were fine black hairs on his sinewy forearms and wrists.

He raised her again, reaching behind her for the fastening of her bra and deftly unclipping it. Then the wisp of gossamer nylon and ribbon went the way of his shirt, and he pressed her bare breasts to his chest with a throaty murmur of satisfaction.

It *was* wonderful to be like that, heart to heart, warm skin to warm skin. It seemed the most natural thing in the world; as if she had done this before, in other times and other lives, but had not remembered until now the sweet, trembling sense of completion when their naked flesh touched, and she felt the rapid beating of his heart as if it were her own.

Then he laid her back on the cushions and began to do heavenly things with his hands and lips.

At first Bethany lay with closed eyes; quivering with astonished delight at the rapturous sensations invading every part of her body as he stroked and moulded her breasts, and coaxed their soft tips to swell into tight rosy buds.

She found herself purring with pleasure, her arms flung above her head, her spine instinctively arching. When she peeped through her lashes and saw that his eyes were closed, and that he was resting his cheek on one satiny cushion while playing with the other, she felt herself melting inside.

Her arms folded round him, one hand wandering over his head, exploring the finely shaped skull and the thick, springy, raven's wing hair, and the other discovering for the first time the feel of a powerful male back.

He moved higher, seeking her mouth for another frenzy of kissing. It was as if he were as starved of love as she; except that he knew all love's pleasures, while she was only just beginning to learn them.

It was when she realised that he had undone her skirt, which was made like a kilt with buckles at waist and hip and a gilt pin lower down, that she felt the first pang of misgiving.

Under the skirt she was wearing tights and stretchy micro-briefs. As Robert pushed the waistband of the tights down to the top of her briefs, she gave a stifled murmur of protest. He ignored it and went on kissing her, the touch of his fingers feather-light as they circled her navel, tracing slow, sensuous patterns from one hip-bone to the other.

She was torn by conflicting instincts. She wanted him to stop, but also she wanted him to go on. Every nerve in her body clamoured for her to relax and enjoy the exquisite sensations aroused by his delicate, practised touch.

At the same time part of her mind which was not yet completely intoxicated reminded her that neither of them had spoken a word of love. There *was* no love in their feelings for each other. Only friendship and now, tonight, a sudden upsurge of desire.

As Robert's fingers moved lower, she mustered her failing willpower and attempted to break off the kiss.

For a second or two she succeeded in freeing her mouth, and gasping, 'No . . . no, please . . . I——'

But the rest was cut off by a kiss, and at the same time he touched her in a way which sent ripple upon ripple of ecstasy coursing down her slim thighs.

To give him his due—although she didn't at the time—the force which he used to keep her pinned on the sofa was no more than the normal embrace of a strong and ardent young man, too aroused to realise at once that the girl in his arms was making more than a token resistance.

When he did realise how desperately she was trying to break free, he stopped kissing her and sat up.

'What's the matter?'

Bethany struggled into a sitting position, her legs pinned between him and the back of the sofa. Snatching her sweater to cover herself, she stammered, 'I—I don't want to do this, Robert. I—I don't know what came over me.'

'I do. It came over both of us—and it's too late to stop now, my lovely, so stop playing the shrinking virgin.'

Smiling, he took hold of the sweater and would have pulled it away had she not clung to it.

'That's just it—I *am* a virgin! I've never done this before, and I'm not taking the pill, and——' She broke off, avoiding his eyes, feeling sick with shame that it was she who had let this humiliating scene come about. She should have stopped him at the beginning, as soon as he kissed her neck.

'Oh, come off it, Bethany. What about your Italian chap? You're not going to try to convince me that he never went farther than a little heavy petting, are you?'

She looked at him then, meeting his sceptical gaze with an unconscious lift of the chin.

'The man I was in love with—and still love—kissed me once. That was all there was between us. Until tonight, he was the only man who'd ever kissed me.'

'If you responded to him as you have to me, he must have incredible self-control to stop at one kiss,' was Robert's sardonic retort.

'You don't understand. There were reasons why it . . . it was wrong for him to kiss me at all,' she said, in a low voice.

'He was married, I suppose. In which case there's no point in continuing to carry a torch for him, is there? The thing to do is to forget him—and the best way to forget an old flame is to light a new one. Which we seemed to be doing rather successfully, before you panicked.'

He would have taken her in his arms, but she fended him off.

'You don't believe me, do you? Why should you, I suppose, when I've let you go as far as this?' she said, in a tone of bitter self-reproach. Her eyes filled with tears of chagrin. 'Was this what you always intended, Robert? That, sooner or later, you would make me succumb to you like all the others?'

A sudden flush showed on his high cheekbones. He glowered at her for a moment, then sprang abruptly to his feet. Having picked up his shirt and her bra, he handed the latter to her and, turning away, began to put his shirt on.

With fingers made clumsy by haste and emotional stress, she dressed as fast as she could. There was no quick way to restore her dishevelled hair to order. She could only shake it back behind her shoulders.

'I take it I can leave it to you to think of some explanation why I shan't be coming to Cranmer for Christmas,' she said, as she rose from the sofa.

He swung to face her. 'Don't be a fool, Bethany. Of course you must come. With Cressida up in Scotland, you can't spend Christmas here . . . alone.'

'I can't come,' she answered stiffly. 'Our "friendship"—such as it was—is finished now . . . over and done with. I don't want to see you again, and I can't imagine why you should want to see me, now that there's no possibility of . . . of adding my scalp to your belt. I admit you *almost* succeeded, but you wouldn't again. Not a second time.'

With two swift strides Robert had covered the distance between them, and his hands were hard on her shoulders.

'You think not? *I* think you're deluding yourself. You wanted what was going to happen as much as I did. I believe you've always wanted it, just as I've wanted to make love to you since the first time I saw you. I don't know what caused you to panic just now—unless you're telling the truth, and you are a virgin. There's only one way to prove that, but I've always made it a rule never to be first in the field, so I'll have to take your word for it. But don't try to deny that you wanted me, Bethany. Or that, if I were to kiss you again, it would have the same effect as before.'

Bethany said nothing, her throat thick with tears.

He released her. 'I'd better go.'

He began to move about the room, putting on his outdoor clothes and collecting the parcels and packages with which he had arrived at the shop. She watched him in miserable silence. Who would have imagined, an hour ago, that their companionable supper would lead to this wretched débâcle?

When Robert was ready to leave, he said, in a clipped tone quite different from his usual lazy drawl, 'I can't come to London tomorrow, I have things to attend to at Cranmer. But I'll be in touch.'

She knew that he didn't really mean it. It was merely an attempt to gloss over this awkward end to their relationship. There was nothing more to be said. She couldn't blame him for what had happened. It had been naïve of her not to foresee that something like this had been inevitable from the beginning.

After he had left the flat, she went to the window and waited for his tall figure to appear in the street below.

It had begun to drizzle. Having left his car in the underground park beneath Cadogan Square he had some way to walk. She saw him turn up the collar of his mac, and wondered what impatient, angry thoughts were in his mind.

She felt sure she would never see him again. Suddenly the future seemed almost as bleak as when she had first come to London.

Robert strode out of sight, and she turned from the window. She had several parcels still to wrap, one of them a Christmas present for James. She wondered how Robert would explain her absence from the Christmas house party at Cranmer.

Flinging herself on the sofa where, a short time earlier, he had held her in his arms, she burst into tears.

She woke up, confused and disorientated, to find Cressida bending over her.

'It's two o'clock in the morning . . . time you were tucked up in bed. How come you fell asleep here?' the other girl asked as, groggily, Bethany sat up and found herself still fully dressed and in the sitting-room, instead of where she ought to be in the small hours.

'I—I don't know.'

Even as she spoke, it all came back to her.

'Bethany! Have you been crying?' Cressida exclaimed, in quick concern. 'What's the matter? What's happened?'

Bethany dragged herself to her feet. She felt stiff and cramped from lying in an awkward position, and she didn't need a mirror to tell her that her eyelids were puffy from weeping and her cheeks blotched with tear-stains.

She said huskily, 'Robert came to supper. He . . . he made a pass at me. We . . . I shan't be seeing him again.'

There was a silence while Cressida digested this. Then she said gently, 'Go and wash your face and get into bed. I'll make a pot of tea and then you can tell me all about it.'

In the bathroom, looking at the ravages caused by her emotional breakdown after Robert's exit from the flat, and from her life, Bethany wasn't sure that she wanted to talk about what had happened.

If she hadn't fallen asleep on the sofa, she need have said nothing about it. Cressida would have gone to Scotland not suspecting that her flatmate's Christmas arrangements had collapsed. By the time she came south again, Bethany would have had plenty of time to pull herself together.

As things were, Cressida would be sure to fuss about leaving her alone. What could she say to allay her friend's anxiety and secure her own seclusion during the Christmas holiday?

She was in the act of sliding into bed when the other girl entered her bedroom with a tray of tea things.

'Was it a good party?' Bethany asked.

'Yes, very—but never mind that now. Tell me what's been happening here. I thought you were going to have a quiet evening wrapping up parcels—as I should have done.'

While Cressida poured out the tea, Bethany explained what had happened in the early part of the evening, ending, 'I knew the casserole would stretch to three, and I didn't think you'd mind his being here until the traffic had thinned out and he could drive back to Cranmer without being stuck in a miles-long jam of cars.'

'Not at all,' Cressida agreed. 'But then it turned out I wasn't here and—not being the type to waste unexpected opportunities—he made a determined attack, hm? Did he do it with tremendous panache? Is his technique as good as it's cracked up to be?'

A deep flush suffused Bethany's face. She nodded. 'It was very difficult to . . . to resist him.'

Cressida gave her a searching look. '*Did* you resist him?'

'In the end—yes. Before that . . . things got out of hand . . . it was my fault . . . I should have stopped him sooner . . . but at first it was so unexpected, and then he kissed me . . . and I . . . I——'

She broke off this somewhat incoherent explanation to drink from the cup Cressida had handed to her. The tea was too hot to be drunk yet. It burnt her mouth. She gulped it down, swallowing the wrong way and bringing on a choking fit.

Cressida seized the cup and saucer to prevent any being spilt on the bedclothes. When the other girl had stopped coughing, she said, 'In other words, you enjoyed it—up to a point.'

'Yes . . . yes, I did,' Bethany admitted. 'Until I realised where it was leading, and that, as far as he was concerned, I was just another . . . sitting duck.'

'And as far as you were concerned? Was he just an attractive man making expert love to you? Or did it mean more than that to you? Did it make you realise you loved him?'

'No . . . no. How could it?' said Bethany, forgetting for a moment that Cressida didn't know why such a thing was impossible.

'Very easily, I should have thought. He has just about everything a man needs to make him lovable. Looks . . . charm . . . position . . . money. Not to mention the fatal fascination of being a notorious stud, or'—seeing Bethany's faint grimace of distaste—'if you prefer it, woman-chaser. That's a pretty lethal combination which any girl might find herself falling for. If you haven't, why were you so upset about what happened tonight?'

'I suppose it was partly the disillusionment of finding out that he had been lying in wait, as it were, all the time; and partly disgust at myself for not stopping him sooner.'

Always the more outspoken and direct of the two of them—sometimes to the point of being maladroit—Cressida did not hesitate to ask what was in her mind. 'How far did you let him go?'

For the second time a wave of hot colour swept upwards from Bethany's throat.

'Much too far.'

'Knowing what a funny old-fashioned thing you are, in some ways, I don't suppose it was all that far by most people's standards. It's a pity you didn't take my advice about this sort of thing ages ago, then you could have gone all the way. I don't know who you're saving yourself for, lovey, if Robert falls short of your standards. He's most people's dream man incarnate.'

'I'm saving myself for a man who cares for me as a person, not just as a sex object,' said Bethany quietly.

'But Robert must like you as a person or he wouldn't have

lain in wait, as you put it, for so long,' was Cressida's reply. 'He's been patience itself. A man who had nothing but sex on his mind would have stepped up the pace much, much sooner.'

She sipped her tea before she continued, 'I think you're being rather puritanical to say you won't see him again because of one little pass. Any red-blooded chap would have done the same in the circumstances. Surely you must have realised that *something* was bound to happen eventually? There just ain't no such thing as a platonic friendship between a virile guy and a good-lookin' gal, honey. If you thought there was, you weren't thinking straight.'

'I know. You don't have to tell me I've been a fool. I should have stopped seeing him ages ago, but I didn't want to give up country weekends at Cranmer, and being friends with his mother.'

'Talking of Cranmer, what's happening now about Christmas?' asked Cressida. 'I suppose you haven't given that a thought?'

'I—I'm going to Italy instead,' said Bethany, on the spur of the moment. 'David is back from his travels for a while. He rang up today and said he was having a house party and would I like to join it. So that's no problem.'

It made her uncomfortable to lie, but at least it was a white lie to save Cressida from having her happy Christmas marred by anxiety.

'You've never mentioned it, but I've always had a suspicion there might have been someone in Italy you cared about,' said Cressida. 'Was there? Is that why Robert doesn't have the impact on you that he does on most girls?'

Bethany said evasively, 'Look at the time! We must get some sleep. You'll have to be up at crack of dawn to get everything done.'

'Didn't I tell you? I've managed to get tomorrow off, so I shall have all day to pack and do up the presents. However, I get the message. Whatever went on in Italy, you don't want to talk about it. Would you like to have one of my sleeping pills to get you off tonight? They're only very mild ones, you know. It would stop you from lying awake, mulling things over.'

Bethany shook her head. She never took any pills if she could avoid it, and had several times tried to convince Cressida that she ought not to revert to sleeping pills, however mild.

'I shan't lie awake—I'm exhausted. Thank you for the tea and sympathy, Cressy.'

'Any time. Goodnight, lovey.'

Bethany spent the next day concealing her depression from customers in festive spirits.

She was worried about what Robert would say to his parents, and what she would find to say if the Duchess should ring up and insist on hearing the real explanation behind her son's false one. She was a shrewd and intuitive woman. It would not be easy for him to pull the wool over her eyes.

Bethany had said goodbye to Cressida that morning. The flat was in darkness when she returned after work. She would have liked to take the telephone off its rest and go straight to bed. But there was a possibility that Robert would ring up to tell her whatever taradiddle he had invented to explain her withdrawal from the Cranmer festivities.

About eight o'clock, she was trying to take an interest in a television programme, when the door bell rang.

Thinking it must be one of the other flat-owners calling to invite her to join them for a glass of sherry and a mince pie, and deciding to make her excuse that she thought she might have a cold starting, and had just run a bath preparatory to going to bed early, she went to the door.

To her astonishment, it was Robert who was standing outside.

'May I come in?'

She stepped back to admit him. 'I—I thought you couldn't get up to London today.'

'I didn't think I could, but I've managed it. I had to see you as soon as possible.'

'A telephone call would have saved you coming all this way.'

'I have things to say which can't be said on the telephone.'

'Have you told your mother that I shan't be coming for Christmas?' Bethany asked.

'No, because I hope you will be. In fact I'm hoping it will be a particularly happy Christmas for Mother because she will at last have something—or rather someone—she's wanted for a long time. A prospective daughter-in-law.'

Bethany stared at him in bewilderment. What was he talking about?

He took possession of her hands. His own were cold from walking ungloved on a winter night. Usually he wore gloves to drive in, but left them in a pocket of the car.

'I'm asking you to marry me,' he told her. 'It was only last night, driving home, that I realised how well matched we are. I was a fool not to see it before.'

'Well matched—you and I?' she said blankly.

'I can see you're stunned,' he said dryly. 'As well you may be, after the way I've behaved. You were right, last night, when you accused me of having a reprehensible attitude to your sex as a whole, and even towards you—at one time. However, in fairness to myself, I have to add that it's an attitude which was inculcated in me by the women and girls I met in my early twenties.'

He paused for a moment before going on, 'Even before I inherited my great-grandmother's fortune when I was twenty-two, the fact that I was my father's son—even if only his younger son—seemed enough to make them . . . amazingly accommodating. Frankly, you're the first girl in years who hasn't been ready to drop into my arms like a ripe plum. That may sound conceited, but it was cynicism, not conceit, which made me expect even a girl as beautiful as you are to be a——'

He broke off, evidently searching for a word.

'A sitting duck?' she suggested.

'Exactly. So you see not taking women seriously, while at the same time making the most of my chances, has become a habit with me. A bad habit, I admit, but one which, if you try to put yourself in my position, you may find forgivable. And habits, once established, die hard. It took last night's wrangle to make me realise that I liked you for other reasons than your desirability in the sexual sense.'

'But you spoke of marriage, and for that one has to have more than liking, Robert. One has to have love. You're not in love with me.'

'Or you with me. But in the past, and in other cultures, many very successful marriages have been founded on a much stronger basis than what's known as "being in love". Can you seriously mean to spend your whole life as a single woman because the man you're in love with is already married?'

'I—I've never thought about it.'

'Think about it now. Wouldn't you rather live in the country than in London? Wouldn't you rather have a house of your own, with a garden, than a share of a flat? Wouldn't you rather be coming with me to the Caribbean next month than spending January in England?'

Bethany considered the questions. The answer to all three was yes, but——

'You would like to have children, wouldn't you?' Robert persisted.

Children. From a time in her life which she tried to forget, her memory presented her with a vivid recollection of a hot afternoon in May at Mas de la Chapelle, near Arles, and a man with cornflower-blue eyes watching a little French girl bouncing importantly on the springboard above the deeper end of the swimming pool.

'Yes, I should like to have children.'

'I *must* have children,' said Robert.

He was still holding her hands. She drew them free. 'You're not quite thirty. Need you despair of meeting a girl you can love, and who will love you?'

'I think it's highly unlikely, and I can't put off marrying indefinitely. The latest reports on James' condition aren't good. It would ease his mind as well as my father's to know the succession was safe, at least for one more generation. Both my parents like you enormously. They would be delighted if I told them I'd proposed and you'd accepted me.'

Bethany sank on to one of the upright chairs by the dining-table. A restless night—for she *had* lain awake a long time after Cressida had said goodnight—and a trying day did not make for level-headed thought. This latest development was, in a different way, as shattering as what had happened on the sofa the night before.

Almost as if he could sense the direction of her thoughts, Robert said, 'If we weren't attractive to each other, I wouldn't suggest it. But there's nothing wrong with our chemistry—we proved that last night.'

A teasing glint lit his eyes. 'I don't think you'd find making babies with me too unbearable, would you?'

Remembering the ecstatic moments she had experienced in his arms, she blushed.

'Have you never been in love with anyone?' she asked.

Robert shook his head.

'Then you don't know what agony you would suffer if you met the right person for you, but it was too late because you were married to me.'

He sat down at the table with her. 'I don't think people who are contented with their marriage are in too much danger of falling in love outside it,' was his reply. 'When married people fall in love, it's usually because they're on the lookout for another relationship to make up for the deficiencies—usually sexual—of their existing one, don't you think?'

'Perhaps.'

'I think it's far more likely that, if we really exerted ourselves to make each other happy, we might eventually find we had something pretty nearly as good as the traditional love match,' he went on. 'I'm prepared to try it, if you are.'

'You must give me time to think about it.'

'Of course. As long as you like.' He reached for her hand and, lifting it to his lips, brushed a light kiss on her knuckles.

He said, 'I'm sorry I was rather a swine to you last night. We'd generated a pretty powerful current by the time you called a halt, and having to switch it off put me in a bad temper, I'm afraid. Not that I should have taken it out on you. I began what happened. You didn't.'

'It was my fault as well,' said Bethany. 'I should have stopped you.'

'If, until last night, you'd only been kissed once before in your entire life, you have a lot of catching up to do. I don't wonder you were a little carried away.'

'More than a little,' she murmured, her colour deepening again.

He touched her hot cheek with his forefinger. 'I've never encountered a virgin before. I thought they were an extinct species.'

'You do believe me now?'

'Yes, I believe you. I know some women can shed tears to order, and most of them can act a part. But I should think it's impossible to manufacture a blush unless you happen to be a genuine example of a nice girl who doesn't know half the questions, let alone all the answers.'

In all, he was with her for only about half an hour. After he had gone, she could almost believe she had fallen asleep in front of the television and dreamed his visit. It seemed incredible that she was going to spend Christmas at Cranmer after all; and even more so that Robert had asked her to become his wife.

When he and his parents and brother flew to the West Indies for their annual winter holiday—perhaps the last which James would be able to share with them if his condition was deteriorating—Bethany was still undecided whether to accept his extraordinary proposal.

She envied them their three weeks in the sun on Mustique, the island in the chain known as the Grenadines, where Princess Margaret had a house called Les Jolies Eaux.

The Duke and his family stayed at The Cotton House, originally an eighteenth-century farm, developed into an hotel by the Hon. Colin Tennant, and decorated by a famous British theatrical designer, the late Oliver Messel.

However, although she would have revelled in the sunshine and the wonderful swimming and snorkelling which Robert had described to her, at the same time Bethany was glad to have three weeks on her own to think things out.

Cressida told her she was mad even to hesitate. But Cressy didn't realise the peculiar nature of the marriage Robert had proposed.

It was while he was away that she met her stepmother in Harrods. By this time more than one gossip columnist had linked Bethany's name with Robert's, and speculated as to whether he had finally met his match in Lady Castle's tall, beautiful stepdaughter.

As yet they had failed to regale their readers with the titbit that there was a long-term estrangement between Sir John's widow and his eldest daughter. Perhaps it was to avoid this becoming public knowledge that Margaret's manner was unexpectedly ingratiating.

'Bethany, I scarcely recognised you! What a well-dressed, attractive young woman you've become,' was her greeting, when she accosted Bethany at the ribbon counter.

It was late shopping night in the Knightsbridge area of London, but the shop where Bethany worked did not stay open like the department stores and some of the speciality shops. Rather reluctantly but having no ready excuse, she found herself being swept off to have a drink at the Hyde Park Hotel, not far from Harrods. It was where Sir John had always stayed on his infrequent visits to the capital, and Margaret was spending the night there.

'I'm very glad we've run into each other. I've always regretted that we got on so badly when you were younger. I was jealous of you,' she admitted, when they were seated in a secluded corner of the hotel's lounge and she had ordered a gin and tonic for herself and a sherry for her guest.

'Jealous? Why?' Bethany asked, in astonishment. 'Father and I were never close. There was nothing between us to be jealous of.'

'I was really jealous of your mother. I knew he'd loved her to distraction, and that she'd made him very unhappy. I did my best to make him happy, but he never got over her, or the suffering she'd caused him. I knew you were very much like her, and I'm afraid I allowed some of my intense dislike for her to transfer itself to you.'

'When you say she made him unhappy, it sounds as if she did it deliberately. But she couldn't help becoming ill and leaving him a widower with a baby on his hands.'

'It wasn't that which put him through hell,' said Margaret. 'It was long before that.' She paused, as if measuring her words. 'They'd been married for less than a year when he found out that she didn't give a damn for him. She . . . she'd liked the idea of being Lady Castle. Later on she was unfaithful to him. This is not merely rumour, I assure you; John himself told me the truth about his first marriage. But knowing her to be selfish and amoral didn't break the spell she held over him. Looking at you, I can understand it. You're amazingly beautiful. I don't wonder Lord Robert is in love with you. Are you going to marry him?'

'He isn't in love with me,' said Bethany. 'I mean . . . we're friends, but the rest is pure speculation on the part of the gossipmongers.'

'It would be a very good match for you.'

'Unlike my mother—if what you say about her is true—I'm not interested in social climbing,' said Bethany stiffly. 'Why did Father dislike me? Simply because I was her daughter? I was his child as well.'

At this point their drinks arrived, and it wasn't until she had sampled her gin and tonic that Lady Castle said, 'He was not very good with children, even with Susan and Julia. He wanted a boy, not three daughters. Anyway, it's ancient history now, and I hope you are willing to bury the hatchet, Bethany. If you do decide to marry Lord Robert, I'm sure his family would prefer it if past differences in our family remained unpublicised.'

The remark confirmed Bethany's guess at the reason for her stepmother's affability. As soon as she could, she made her escape. It was not Margaret's treatment of her which she could not forgive, but the cruel destruction of Mossy. Nor did she entirely believe what her stepmother had told her about her mother.

Robert had been away for only two of his three weeks' holiday when Bethany was startled to hear his voice on the telephone. He was not in Mustique but in America.

'What are you doing there?' she asked.

'For some reason lotus-eating palled rather faster than usual this year, so I decided to come home early, via New York. Perhaps I had a premonition that there was something here which would interest me—and you,' he told her.

'What do you mean?'

'You'll have to contain your curiosity until I get back the day after tomorrow.'

He told her what time to expect him and rang off, leaving Bethany to ponder the meaning of his cryptic remarks.

She was able to get time off to meet him at the airport. She wondered if he would kiss her. He had kissed her only once— a peck on the cheek under a bunch of misletoe at Cranmer at Christmas—since that night on the sofa at the flat.

After two weeks in the hot sun of the Grenadines, he was as dark as a gypsy; by far the most attractive man to emerge from the Customs hall.

'Bethany—what a very agreeable surprise!'

He put his arm round her shoulders and gave her a hug. But he didn't kiss her.

'I'm madly curious to know what it was you found in New York which interests you, and will interest me,' she admitted.

'As soon as we get back to the flat, I'll show you,' he promised.

His luggage included several flat rectangular parcels which, later, Bethany knew she ought to have recognised as pictures. They were sketches and paintings of her. He had bought them at the Kennedy Galleries in New York—more than a dozen of them.

'One or two had already been sold before I got there,' he told her. 'There's not much I can do about those, although I've told the gallery to let me know if they come on the market again. I don't want paintings of my wife hanging on other men's walls.'

She was too disturbed by the paintings to make any comment on his confident assumption that she would become his wife.

'Nor shall I hang them on our walls if, for you, they're a painful reminder of past unhappiness,' he went on, in a quieter tone. 'They can stay in the family archives, to be admired by our descendants.'

'What do you mean ... a reminder of past unhappiness?' she asked warily.

Could he tell, merely by looking at the paintings, that David had loved her? None of them was signed, but to anyone who knew his work well, there was no mistaking the inimitable Warren style.

Robert said, 'You'll have noticed that they aren't signed. The gallery was under strict orders to sell them as portraits of an unknown girl by an anonymous artist. However, it was obvious to me that if they were not by your uncle—who has never been known to produce anything other than genre paintings and the occasional landscape—they were strongly influenced by his style. I believe they were done by an artist who was a friend of his, or possibly a pupil. I think they were painted by the man you fell in love with. Am I right?'

There could be no harm in admitting to that. She did not have to add that the rest of his theory was incorrect.

'Yes ... yes, they were,' she answered. 'It's strange to see them again ... after so long. I can hardly recognise myself as that brown-skinned girl with all that hair.'

'I like your hair loose. This elaborate bun is too old for you,' Robert remarked, touching her chignon. 'I prefer it when you let your hair down—in every sense.'

Before she glanced up at his face, she knew she would find him watching her with what she thought of as his Medici expression; his dark eyes glinting with amusement, his wide mouth quirked at the corners.

Suddenly, remembering the only time when he had seen her with her hair down, she wished he would take her in his arms and kiss and kiss her, until she forgot all 'past unhappiness'.

'I hope you didn't spend a great deal of money on these, Robert,' she said anxiously. 'It will have been wasted if we don't marry. I still haven't made up my mind.'

'You will. There's no hurry,' he told her.

Although they were alone in the flat, and there was nothing to stop him from making some light, persuasive love to her, he did not touch her.

Later, when she was alone, Bethany wondered what had prompted David to sell the paintings of her. Perhaps there was now someone else in his life, and he did not want his studio cluttered with pictures of his niece. In that case, why not destroy them? She knew the answer to that: he was not the kind of man who could bring himself to tear up portraits of a girl he had once loved.

Although Robert thought the paintings were unsigned, she knew that originally they had carried David's fluid signature. It had been automatic for him to sign and date everything. Even the pages of the sketch pad he carried about with him were initialled, dated and, often, identified in some way. *Market stall, Arles. Fish restaurant, Calpe. Doorway, Firenze. The plaza, Benisa.*

His very first drawing of her, the sepia sketch completed in half an hour on the sun roof at the Villa Belvedere, had been inscribed *Bethany—sixteen going on seventeen.*

Before he had packed them up to be sent to and sold in America, where there would be no chance of the sitter being recognised, he must have cut away all the signatures. The mounts were cleverly designed to disguise the fact that the paintings had been tampered with. Only someone very know-ledgeable would detect a slight disproportion in what artists called the negative spaces, the empty areas surrounding the subject.

Fortunately Robert, although something of a connoisseur, had not noticed anything amiss, and probably never would if the paintings remained in a portfolio in the archives. *If* she married him. If she didn't, presumably he would re-sell them. It was not as if he had bought them because he loved her.

The next time she went to Cranmer for the weekend, the Duke and Duchess were bronzed after their holiday, and even James had a spurious air of health.

On Sunday morning, while Robert went to church with his parents, who always attended morning service in the village which took its name from the Castle, Bethany stayed with his brother.

They had been listening to Franco Corelli singing *None shall sleep* from *Turandot*, when James surprised her by saying, 'I wish you'd put Robert out of his misery, Bethany.'

When she turned a startled face towards him, he went on, 'He told me he'd proposed to you, but had not yet succeeded in persuading you to accept him. Having been rather a breaker of hearts in his day, perhaps there's a certain justice in his having—metaphorically, at least—to bite his nails while the girl of his choice makes up her mind. But I hope that, in the end, you'll take him on. We all feel you're extremely well suited.'

It was on the tip of her tongue to reply that she didn't think Robert's state of suspense was too unbearable. But then it occurred to her that, if he had chosen to give his brother the impression that his feelings for her were the normal ones, there was no point in disillusioning James.

Instead she said, 'I'm not twenty yet, James. I don't feel myself to be immature for my age, but it is rather young to take on a lifelong commitment.'

'It is indeed; particularly a commitment which, eventually, will involve taking over my mother's responsibilities. A good deal of her time is spent doing things which she doesn't enjoy but accepts as her duty.'

'That applies to most women's lives.'

'I suppose you're right. So it isn't that aspect which makes you hesitate?'

She shook her head.

Robert says you're not madly in love with him, and that worries you,' James went on. 'But, speaking as a mere on-looker, I think romantic love is very much overrated. Liking and laughter are the basis of most lasting marriages. If you study my parents, and other happily married people, what strikes you is the friendship between them. They never seem to run out of things to talk about, and they share a huge fund of amusing memories which they're always reminding each other of. I thought last night at dinner, when you and Robert were almost in tears of laughter about that old man you met on one of your walks, that you're the first girl ever really to share his sense of humour.'

It was a remark which, in the weeks that followed, made Bethany aware—as she had not been before—how often Robert made her laugh. It was not that he told many jokes as such. It was merely his way of putting things, and his keen sense of the ridiculous.

During this time he never pressed her to reach a decision, nor was his courtship an ardent one, in the physical sense. He exerted himself to please her in many small ways, but seemed to expect nothing in return, not even a goodnight kiss after taking her out to dinner or to the theatre. This she found very puzzling.

One weekend, when she was again a guest at the Castle, she and Robert were shopping in the nearest market town when Archie was knocked down by a car.

What could have caused the old Labrador to dash into the path of the vehicle instead of padding along behind his master was something they would never find out. All they knew was that, as they were walking along the pavement on one side of the market place, there was a screech of brakes, a woman's scream, and Archie was lying in the road with bright blood on his thick black fur.

It was clear that he was seriously injured. Even so, it was a terrible shock when, after he had examined the dog, the vet—whose surgery was only a hundred yards from where the accident happened—said, 'We can try to patch him up, but it will be a long and painful business for him. He's had a good run, poor old fellow. It would be kinder to put him to sleep, m'Lord.'

The muscles of Robert's jaw clenched into hard knots under the skin. But his voice was even as he said, 'Go and wait in the waiting-room, Bethany.'

She obeyed him, very upset. She had grown fond of Archie. His sire had been Robert's first dog, a puppy given to him on his third birthday. He had had Archie since he was a boy of fourteen.

As if it were not enough for him to have to consent to and witness the injection which dulled for ever the old gun-dog's adoring brown eyes, afterwards he had to cope with the apologetic driver of the car which had knocked Archie down, and also with a policeman called by an irate woman bystander who considered it to have been the driver's fault.

At last, with the dog's body wrapped in a sacking in the back of the Land Rover, to be buried on the estate, they were able to return to Cranmer. Neither of them spoke on the drive back. His face, when she stole a glance at it, was an expressionless mask. Even if she could have trusted her voice not to betray how close she was to tears, she could think of nothing to say.

There was a place not far from the Castle where many family pets had been buried. Some of the graves had small headstones. Robert stopped the Land Rover near this spot, saying, 'D'you mind walking from here? I shall need a spade.'

He swung himself out of the vehicle and began to stride across the grass towards a small outbuilding which housed motor mowers and other equipment.

Bethany felt she could not leave him to bury Archie without showing in some way her sympathy. Hurrying to catch him up, she slipped her hand into his. 'Robert— -'

As he slackened his long pace and looked at her, she saw the raw pain he had masked on the silent drive back. It showed in the twist of his mouth, and the bright glaze of tears in his eyes.

'Oh, Robert!' she choked, her eyes filling.

The next moment they were in each other's arms, and he was holding her painfully tight.

She felt then, sharing his grief for the animal which had been his faithful companion for so long, that even if she and Robert would never feel for each other the love which moved the sun and the stars, perhaps the affinity between them was enough on which to build a comfortable marriage.

CHAPTER EIGHT

WHEN Robert came to the flat on the night of their engagement party, he arrived thirty minutes earlier than the time he had arranged to pick them up. Half expecting this to happen, Bethany was ready, but Cressida was still in her room, getting dressed.

At Christmas it had seemed likely that she might be married before long. But, like all her previous romances, the affair with Robin had fallen through and, as yet, no one had replaced him in her wayward affections.

Bethany was standing at the sitting-room window when a taxi pulled up and Robert sprang out, looking even more debonair than usual in his dinner jacket. The white shirt emphasised his darkness.

She watched him produce his notecase to pay the driver, adding some silver taken from his trouser pocket. Then, with the engaging smile which made people react with friendliness wherever he went, he said goodnight to the cabbie and waited for the taxi to move on before coming across the road towards her.

As he did so, he looked up and saw her. Again that warm, charming smile transformed his lean, forceful face. She forced herself to smile back, but inwardly she felt sick with foreboding.

As she went to open the door for him, her black silk taffeta skirt made an old-fashioned frou-frou rustle as the hem brushed over the carpet. The white blouse she was wearing with it had come from Tatters, a shop in the Fulham Road which specialised in the lace and embroidered lawn garments in fashion at the beginning of the century. It was made of fine Irish lace with huge sleeves and a tight, low-cut bodice which showed off the curves of her bosom. The sweeping black skirt and the very feminine blouse, linked by a wide velvet belt, were a combination which Robert liked.

Until today, it had been her most earnest intention to please him in every way she could, from wearing the kind of clothes he liked to having a baby as soon as possible after their marriage.

But now, since she had read her mother's letter, her mind and heart were in total confusion.

To have discovered, on the very day her engagement to Robert was made public, that the consanguinity which had seemed an insuperable barrier between her and David no longer—never had—existed, was the cruellest trick life could have played on her.

Robert came up the staircase three steps at a time, his long legs and excellent physical condition bringing him to the first floor landing with as little sign of exertion as if he had arrived there by lift.

Without any preliminaries, he said, 'I came early in the hope of being able to talk to you alone for a few minutes. Where's Cressida?'

'Still dressing. She won't be ready until the very last moment, if then. Your mother has told you what's happened?'

'Yes.' He followed her into the sitting-room and closed the door. Then he took both her hands in his. 'How could you think for a moment that it would matter to me whose daughter you are?'

'I—I knew you wouldn't care on your own account. But, being who you are, you can't want your children to have bad blood in them.'

'My dearest girl, there's bad blood in every old family. Haven't you ever heard what David Cecil says on that subject? I'm surprised Mother hasn't told you. He's one of her favourite sages, and she usually quotes him when she's showing people round.'

'I don't think she has.' Bethany was also a fan of the writer and Oxford don, Lord David Cecil, to whose books she had been introduced by her English mistress at school. 'What did he say?'

'I'm not sure if he said it or wrote it, but the gist was that he found it surprising that England's historic houses should have such a tranquil atmosphere when the men who built them were usually such unscrupulous fighters for power and position. If you knew what unpleasant people some of the Rathbones had been, you might think twice about having their blood in your children,' he added dryly.

'But Robert——'

'I don't want to hear any more about it,' he said firmly. 'It's not as if you were a boy, and your father's other children were boys. In that case it would be wrong to inherit what was rightfully theirs. But, as things are, that doesn't arise. His brother is Sir John's successor. There is nothing for you to worry about. And, I might add, even if it *were* necessary for your mother's indiscretion to be brought into the open, I should still want you for my wife.'

He raised her hands to his lips, kissing first one then the other.

In a lower, less matter-of-fact tone, he said, 'Your lovely face . . . the way you smile at me sometimes . . . your understanding and sweetness when I was rather knocked sideways by what happened to Archie . . . those are the things which matter to me.'

She was so much moved by the unexpected tenderness of his tribute that, for a moment, everything else was driven from her mind. She could only wonder how it was that, for such a long time, he had managed to hide what a very nice person he was under the somewhat cynical suavity of his manner when first she knew him.

They were interrupted by Cressida bursting out of her room in a panic because the tag on the zipper of her red chiffon dress was stuck in the small of her back.

After Bethany had fetched a pair of eyebrow tweezers, and Robert had extracted the loose thread which, caught between the teeth of the fastener, had caused it to jam, it was nearly time for them to be off.

Luckily, although the flat was in a quiet side street, it was only two hundred yards from a busy junction where it was usually possible to pick up a cruising taxi without delay.

As the night was quite mild and springlike, instead of Robert going ahead to get a taxi for them, the girls walked with him, Bethany with her skirt furled to keep it off the pavement.

'Black stockings—always my downfall,' he said, glancing down at her ankles.

The remark reminded her of her first visit to Cranmer when, alone with him in one of the great State Bedrooms, she had been afraid he was going to kiss her.

Had she done what common sense advised, and made that

first visit her last, she would not now be in the trap which was what, in less than twelve hours, their engagement had become for her.

Although there was room for three people in the back seat of the taxi, Robert chose to sit with his back to the driver on one of the tip-up seats. Fortunately Cressida was never at a loss for something to talk about, and she chattered to him throughout the short journey to his parents' house. Bethany only had to appear to be listening to their conversation without actually taking part in it.

But something of her inner unrest must have communicated itself to him. When they arrived, he got out first to help the girls to alight; Cressida first, then his fiancée.

As she put her hand into his and stepped down on to the roadway, he said, in a quiet aside which would not be heard by her friend, 'You haven't got a headache, have you?'

'No . . . why do you ask?'

'You seemed . . . rather subdued, coming here.'

'I'm feeling a little nervous, that's all.'

'You have no need to be. They will all be dazzled by you, darling'—this in a normal tone of voice.

Bethany had forgotten that her future mother-in-law had told her that tonight the Duke was going to present her with a set of jewels first worn by Charlotte, the fifth Duchess.

Only he and Robert were with her—the Duchess having taken Cressida to meet some other early arrivals—when he showed her the *parure de diamants* made for his ancestress.

It was Robert who lifted the diamond necklace from its case, put it round her neck and fastened it for her.

'You had better fasten the ear-rings yourself,' said the Duke, as he handed them to her.

Bethany stammered her thanks for the magnificent present, to which he responded by patting her gently on the cheek, and saying, 'It's not only my younger son you have made happy, my dear Bethany. We are all delighted by this engagement. Now I daresay you'd like to have a few minutes alone together.'

When his father had left the room, Robert said, 'Do you realise I haven't kissed you yet?'

She was standing with her back to him. But they could see each other's faces reflected in the large gilded mirror to which he had steered her, after fastening the necklace, so that she could see the blaze of light round the base of her throat.

Her fingers suddenly unsteady, she fumbled to fasten the second of the graceful drop ear-rings. She had not seen that fierce gleam of desire since the night he had almost seduced her.

Even when he had proposed to her for the second time, and she had accepted him, his embrace had been oddly restrained, his kisses more gentle than passionate.

But now, once again, he was looking at her as he had on that unforgettable night at the flat.

Bethany said nervously, 'If you do, it will smudge my lipstick. I—I don't want to look dishevelled the first time I meet your relations.'

To her relief, Robert smiled. 'All right. I'll dishevel you later, when the party is over. For the moment—just one chaste kiss where it won't disturb your lipstick.'

As he spoke, he turned her to face him, then stooped to touch with his lips the soft upper curve of one breast.

'And if you think that wasn't a chaste kiss,' he told her huskily, 'it proves what an innocent you are ... and what a lucky chap I am.'

The hours which followed were, perhaps, the strangest of her life. No girl celebrating her twentieth birthday as well as her engagement could have failed to feel some elation at receiving so much admiration. Bethany thought it must, in large measure, be the magical beauty of the diamonds which lent her some of their radiance. When, from time to time, she caught glimpses of herself in the drawing-room's many large mirrors, she found it hard to believe that the shining-eyed girl with flushed cheeks and a smile on her lips was herself, in the grip of a heartache so poignant she could hardly bear it.

For as she sipped champagne, ate fresh salmon, answered questions, and thanked people for their good wishes, she knew that, after tonight, there was no possibility of breaking her promise to marry Robert.

Even though he wouldn't be shattered, it would make him look undeservedly foolish. And apart from his feelings, there were other people to consider. How could she let down James, and his father and mother, all of whom had been so kind and generous to her?

As Robert was supposed to have returned to Cranmer after breakfast, she was surprised when, the following day, he came to the shop at lunch time and said he had booked a table at a nearby restaurant.

'Why haven't you gone home?' she asked, as they walked there.

'Aren't you pleased to find me still here?' he asked, glancing down at her with a rather strange expression on his face.

'Naturally I'm pleased, but I thought you were going to be busy at Cranmer for the rest of the week.'

'I shall be—after today. I'm not happy that your uncle wasn't present at the party last night. I think he should have been. I understand why you didn't want your stepmother invited, although she will have to be asked to the wedding, but I think your uncle should have received an invitation to last night's junketing.'

'But, Robert, he isn't my uncle, and I explained why it was better not to ask him. He's not at all a social person, and having to come to London because he felt obliged to would have been a bore and a nuisance to him. Anyway, when I rang up there was no reply, so he's probably on the other side of the world at the moment.'

This was a white lie she had been obliged to tell once before when David's presence at the party had first been raised. She had not rung him up. Nor had she written to break the news of her engagement before it was announced in the newspapers.

'Yes, that assumption was correct. He has been away, but he's expected back tonight. I had a word with his housekeeper this morning,' Robert announced.

Bethany stopped walking. '*You* telephoned the Villa? Why?' she demanded.

He had halted when she did. Now, facing her, he said, 'Why not? There's no reason why I shouldn't have spoken to him, had he been there, is there?'

'N-no, of course not, but——' She broke off.

'Perhaps I'm more of a stickler for going about things in the correct way than you realise,' he went on. 'While I was jogging this morning, it struck me that if his coming here would have been an annoying inconvenience, we should have gone to see him. Even if he isn't your uncle and I don't actually need his permission to marry you, he was, in effect, your guardian. It would have been courteous to present myself to him before our engagement was fait accompli.'

He took her by the arm and began to walk the remaining short distance to the restaurant.

'That's impossible now,' he continued. 'I have appointments tomorrow and the day after which can't be rearranged without a great deal of inconvenience to other people. But there's no reason why you shouldn't pop over to Italy and see him. In fact I've fixed it. As soon as we've eaten, I'm taking you back to the flat to pack your toothbrush, and then we're going to the airport and I'm putting you on the late afternoon flight to Genoa.'

'But I—I can't!' she expostulated. 'How can I drop everything here, and ... and turn up at Portofino without any warning?'

'I've explained the situation to Mrs Hastings. You're on a forty-eight-hour furlough,' Robert said calmly.

By this time they were at the restaurant, and she was forced to contain her reactions until they were seated at a table, and aperitifs had been ordered and menus presented to them.

'As you'll be fed again on the flight, if I were you I should skip a first course and choose something light. What about Sole Maintenon?' Robert suggested.

'Yes ... yes ... anything,' she said distractedly. 'Robert, why have you done this?—Arranged everything without consulting me?'

He put aside the folder containing the menu and picked up the wine list. 'If I had consulted you, you'd have resisted the idea. I think you have a block about Italy which will only be cured by going back. While you're over there, you should make a point of seeing the man who once meant so much to you. With any luck, you'll wonder what you saw in him. Two years is a long time, especially between eighteen and twenty.'

The head waiter approached. Robert ordered their lunch and a bottle of wine. This done, he interlaced his long brown fingers and looked thoughtfully across the table at her.

After a moment he said quietly, 'Last night, not for the first time, I felt there was a spectre at the feast. I don't want him present at our wedding breakfast.'

Bethany's lashes flickered. Unable to meet that level stare, she averted her gaze to the apricot rose in the bud vase. Its petals were the same lovely colour as the sun-baked walls of the Villa Delphini.

She said, in a low tone, 'H-have you considered the possibility that I ... that he ... that we may still feel as we did before I left Italy?'

'That's a risk I'm prepared to take,' he answered. 'Presumably there'll be no problem about getting a taxi to take you from Genoa to Portofino?'

'No ... no, there are always plenty of taxis ... or I could drive myself in a hired car.'

'I would rather you didn't. It's a long time since you've done any driving, and you're used to English traffic now. Anyway you haven't an international driving licence, and without one you can't drive abroad. I would have arranged for your uncle to meet you, but when he rang up his housekeeper yesterday he didn't expect to arrive home until after dinner ... possibly very late.'

'Did you tell her when to expect me?' asked Bethany.

'I told her the time your flight was due to arrive, but I also pointed out that it could be delayed.'

'Had she ever heard of me? She isn't the woman who used to clean the house when I lived there.'

His dark eyes became uncomfortably keen. 'How do you know that if there was no reply when you rang up?'

She felt herself starting to flush. 'I ... David mentioned a new housekeeper on one of his postcards.'

'He must also have mentioned you to her. She didn't question your right to arrive without notice.'

Bethany's head was still in a whirl when he took her back to the flat and waited while she changed into something suitable for air travel, and packed the few things she would need. Even on the way to the airport, she continued to feel a dreamlike sense of unreality.

Robert said little on the way there. He was a fast but careful motorist who liked to concentrate on his driving, so there was nothing particularly unusual in his silence. Yet whenever she glanced at his face, it seemed to her that it might not be merely concentration which made his brown skin seem so tautly stretched over his bones.

Perhaps it had been his awareness of what he had called 'a spectre at the feast' which had made his goodnight embrace a great deal more restrained than she had expected it to be.

Cressida had been taken home by a man she had met at the party. There had been nothing to prevent Robert from kissing Bethany in the taxi, and again in the darkness of the hall after unlocking the outer door for her. Instead, he had confined himself to holding her hand in the taxi, and his goodnight kiss on the doorstep, in view of the waiting taxi driver, had been so brief and light that, had it not been on her lips, it might have been a kiss between brother and sister.

At the airport, he bought her some magazines, then said, 'I won't hang about, if you don't mind. In any case your flight will be boarding quite soon.'

In the circumstances it was difficult to know what to say.

'Well . . . goodbye,' she ventured uncertainly.

'Goodbye, Bethany.' He kissed her hand.

Then, instead of letting it go, he continued to hold it as he said, 'I should have arranged this before our engagement was announced, but even so it's not too late for you to change your mind. I hope you know that.'

For a long, tense moment they stood frozen in the attitude of farewell, her troubled grey eyes raised to his. Then, with a startling change of tone, Robert said violently, 'To hell with this!' and pulled her into his arms.

Not since the night at the flat had he kissed her as he did then. Regardless of curious onlookers, he crushed her against his tall frame, his lips as fiercely demanding as they had been on that occasion, but never since.

How she might have responded, he gave her no time to find out. Before she had adjusted to the shock of being passionately embraced in a public place, and in circumastances which made it totally unexpected, he had let her go.

She was still transfixed with amazement when he strode out of sight.

Much later that day, when Bethany found it impossible to contain her nervous impatience for the sound of David's car coming up the hill, she went down to the harbour by way of the steep, narrow path which the owners of the nearby villas used as a short cut to the village.

She had found the villa little changed. Nor had Portofino altered in the two years sine she had left it. The only difference was that no one recognised her.

Sitting in the café where she had first set eyes on Francine Valery, she ordered a lemon *granita*, and sat quietly absorbing the sights, sounds and appetising garlicky smells of a warm spring evening in Italy.

Memories of the life she had lived here came flooding back, washing over the years between like the sea erasing footmarks on the sand. It was almost as if she had never been away.

After re-exploring the waterfront, she returned to the villa to be met by an agitated Anna.

'Oh, *signorina—che peccato!* If only you had been here ten minutes ago. Had the *signore* heard your voice on the telephone, he would not have rung off so quickly. Unfortunately he was in such a hurry to catch the aeroplane that he didn't give me a chance to tell him there was a visitor waiting for him.'

'What aeroplane?' asked Bethany. 'Where was he going?'

'I don't know. He didn't say where—only that he would ring up tomorrow to let me know when to expect him. I am very sorry, *signorina*. You will think me stupid, no doubt, but truly he was in great haste. "I shan't be home tonight after all, Anna. I can't explain now. I have a plane to catch. I'll ring again tomorrow. I didn't want you to worry about me." Those were his exact words.'

Bethany calmed her, and they had a cup of coffee together. From what the housekeeper told her, she was the first woman, other than Anna herself, to stay at the Villa Delphini since David had returned from his travels.

'He is lonely, on his own in this big house. A man of his age should have a wife and children,' the dumpy little Italian confided.

Clearly she was dying to know Bethany's connection with her employer, but she had to retire for the night with her curiosity unsatisfied.

Without being aware that it had once been the English girl's bedroom, she had prepared that room for her. Before she undressed, Bethany spent a long time on the balcony, looking down at the lights of the harbour.

She wondered if the reason David had not come home

tonight was because he had seen the notice in yesterday's *Telegraph*, and had gone to England to find out what sort of man she was marrying.

Cressida had had a date this evening. Finding the flat in darkness, he might reasonably conclude that both girls were out; his niece—as he must still think of her—with her fiancé. In which case he might decide to ring up the flat first thing tomorrow.

Perhaps I should have rung Robert to let him know I've arrived safely, she thought.

Why had he kissed her like that at the airport? Was it possible he cared for her more than he wanted to admit, and that, if her longing for David proved stronger than her obligation to him, he would be seriously hurt?

Thinking about Robert reminded her of the picture which for many months had been fixed to the damp-speckled mirror opposite the bed. She went to the cupboard where she had put it away. It was still there, rolled up and held by a rubber band.

When she had re-rolled it the other way to make it lie flat, she put the picture of Lorenzo de' Medici on the bed, and sat comparing his features with those of the man she had promised to marry.

As she remembered the shock of hearing Robert say the words of Lorenzo's poem in the original Italian, her thoughts turned to another poet, an Englishman, who had lived long in Italy, and among whose most famous verses were the wistful *Home Thoughts From Abroad*.

Far too restless to attempt to sleep yet, she rose and returned to the balcony.

> *O, to be in England*
> *Now that April's there,*
> *And whoever wakes in England*
> *Sees, some morning, unaware,*
> *That the lowest boughs and the brushwood sheaf*
> *Round the elm-tree bole are in tiny leaf,*
> *While the chaffinch sings on the orchard bough*
> *In England—now!*

As she remembered Browning's poem, with its desperately homesick last lines—*The buttercups, the little children's dower—Far brighter than this gaudy melon-flower!*—she found herself seeing, in her mind's eye, a scene very different from the golden lights and warm darkness of Portofino by night.

What her memory recalled, with great clarity, was a cold winter night in England, and the rippled silver of the lake seen from the battlements of Cranmer Castle.

Since then she had been to Cranmer at snowdrop time and, more recently, when the grounds were golden with daffodils and the smaller, sweet-scented jonquils. Robert had picked a bunch for her to take back to London, and for more than a week afterwards their fragrance—the essence of spring—had pervaded the flat.

Never to go there again; the thought pierced her with a pain she had not experienced before.

It was the same pang she had felt when, living in London, exiled from all she loved best, she had thought she would never come back to Italy.

'Signorina! Signorina! Wake up, please. You must come at once. There is a telephone call from London for you.'

Roused from a deep sleep by an urgent voice speaking Italian, Bethany submitted to being hustled out of bed and along the landing to the extension in David's bedroom. But even when Anna thrust the receiver into her hand, she was still only half awake.

'Hello?'

'Bethany? This is David.'

The familiar voice, not heard for such a long time, and now as clear as if he were standing beside her, made her draw in her breath. All at once she was fully alert.

'David! Where are you speaking from?'

'London. I flew in last night, only to find you'd landed at Genoa a few hours before I took off from there. My fault—I shouldn't have acted on impulse. Never mind. I'll be back in time for a late lunch.'

'David, wait . . . wait! Don't ring off yet.'

'I'm still here. Is something the matter?'

'No . . . it's just . . . I have something to tell you. I—I can't explain everything on the telephone—it would take too long—but the fact is we aren't related. Your brother wasn't my father, and I'm not your niece.'

'Yes, so I understand from Robert.'

'From Robert?' Bethany echoed, aghast.

'There being no answer when I rang the number of your flat last night, I tried his—or rather his parents' number. In fact I spent the night with them.'

'At Cranmer?'

'Yes. It's about the same distance from the airport as Cressida's place. Having been told you weren't there, and why, I accepted the Duchess's very kind invitation to put up with them for one night.'

'I see,' she said, rather dumbfounded. 'Did Robert explain that I only found out the truth on the morning of my birthday . . . *after* our engagement had been announced?'

'Yes, Robert and I had a long talk. He's a nice chap. I like him.'

'I like him, too, but——'

David cut her short. 'I must go now. I'll see you in a few hours' time. Goodbye.'

Bethany had barely time to repeat his last word before the connection was cut, leaving her to wonder if he had known what she intended to say and had interrupted her deliberately.

The hours which followed seemed interminable. The pool being drained, she could not vent her impatience with some vigorous swimming. Her only recourse was to walk down to the harbour again.

This morning she went with her hair loose, and wearing the Provençal skirt which David had bought for her in Arles, and which she had never worn since leaving Italy.

She remembered the name of the shop! *Souleiado.* Would it be *souleiado* for David and for her when they saw each other? Would the world be transformed and made a paradise, as it had been before Natasha had entered their lives?

Looking more like the eighteen-year-old Bethany, except for the absence of a sun-tan, she was recognised by several people who the night before had taken her for just another tourist.

When she returned to the villa, she telephoned Genoa airport to check that the flight from London arriving at two had taken off on schedule. Apparently it had.

When David had referred to a late lunch, he must momentarily have forgotten the plastic meal which would be served in flight. Perhaps he would ignore it, preferring to wait for something more palatable when he reached home. But in case he had already eaten by the time he arrived, Anna persuaded Bethany to eat a light snack at half past one.

The last hour seemed the longest of all. She spent much of it pacing the terrace with the restless tread of a caged lioness, straining her ears to catch the first sound of a car coming up the hill.

When at last she did hear the engine, she found herself as sick with nervousness as she had been the day before, coming up in the taxi and wondering if Anna would tell her that now there was also a Signora Castle at the Villa Delphini.

She heard the car sweep through the gateway and crunch to a halt. Then the sound of voices—two voices, both masculine.

She ran through the house to the front door and wrenched it open. There was David, stooping to unlock the boot and unload his luggage. Waiting beside him, arms folded, was another tall man. Robert.

As Bethany paused, transfixed, in the doorway, they glanced round and saw her. David straightened, but then remained motionless, almost shoulder to shoulder with the other man.

For some seconds neither of them spoke, nor did they smile at her. Their expressions were serious and guarded, almost as if they were waiting to see her reaction.

She looked from one face to the other. As she did so she knew, with a certainty which admitted no doubt, which man would always be dear to her, and which man she loved with all her heart.

Only one question remained. Did the one whom she loved love her?

CHAPTER NINE

ROBERT was the first to speak.

He said, 'I expect you're surprised to see me. I thought it might simplify matters if I came with David.'

What he meant by that Bethany didn't know. Before she could ask, David walked towards her.

'Hello, Bethany. How are you?' He put both hands on her shoulders and bent to kiss her, first on one cheek and then on the other.

It was a form of greeting practised by hundreds of thousands of Europeans every day, its significance depending on the relationship between them. Exchanged by fathers and sons, as well as by women, and by members of opposite sexes, it could be an expression of true affection, or a camouflage for other emotions. What David felt as his lips lightly brushed her cheeks, she had no means of telling.

Anna appeared, talking ten to the dozen and throwing up her hands in dismay because she had not been warned that her employer would be bringing another visitor back with him.

She wanted to carry Robert's case into the house for him. He had to wrest it from her, speaking Italian with a fluency which Bethany had not known he possessed.

David said, 'You can make up the bed for Don Roberto later, Anna. For the moment it will be enough to give him soap and towels so that he can have a shower and change into cooler clothes.'

Still speaking Italian, he added, 'For me a glass of wine and a chat with Signorina Bethany has priority.' Then, switching to English and speaking to Bethany, he went on, 'I'll take my bag up, and also show Robert to his quarters, then I'll come down again.'

As the two men ascended the staircase, Anna lingered in the hall.

'Perhaps Signore Castle does not realise that the title Don, or Donna in the case of a lady, is given only to the children of

180

our highest nobility,' she whispered. 'Is this handsome young Englishman the son of a *duca e duchessa*?'

When Bethany nodded, and Anna gave a hiss of excitement. 'Then he will be used to the best, and must have the new towels.'

She bustled upstairs, leaving Bethany to organise the wine David wanted when he came down.

Although accustomed now to Robert's dark colouring, she had not forgotten the blond streaks in David's fair hair, or the vivid blueness of his eyes. After two years without seeing him, they had as strong an impact as the first time she had laid eyes on him, sitting at the top of the ladder in the library at the Manor.

When he joined her outside on the terrace, the first thing he said was, 'So you're not my niece after all. Was it a terrible shock, finding that out?'

She could have answered that it had been a wonderful shock, but she didn't. She said only, 'It explained a lot of things which had puzzled me. I met Margaret in London not long ago. I don't think she knows I'm illegitimate, but perhaps your brother did—or had strong suspicions.'

David took the wine which she offered, and moved to stand by the balustrade. Gazing down at the calm Mediterranean, he said, 'John suspected every man who looked at Clare of coveting her, and in many cases he was right. They did.'

He turned his head and looked at Bethany. 'You're old enough now to be told the rest of the story. I fell in love with your mother. It was obvious that she and John were totally unsuited, although he was mad about her. Why she married him always baffled me—until Robert told me the gist of the letter she left for you to read on your birthday. All I knew at the time was that she was wretchedly unhappy, and I wanted to comfort her. One thing led to another, and eventually John caught me kissing her. He accused us of committing adultery. We hadn't, but it would have come to that. Quite rightly, he threw me out.'

Watching him, waiting for him to continue, Bethany realised that although at first she had thought him completely unchanged, in fact there were subtle changes.

It did not show much—it never did with fair-haired people—but there were threads of grey as well as blond streaks in his hair now. The lines round his eyes were more pronounced than they had been two years ago. And although he was still under forty, and leaner and fitter than many men fifteen years younger, he was not as limber as Robert, who ran three miles every morning, and whose every movement had the muscular grace of a panther's.

'When I took pity on you and brought you back here, you were like Clare, but not so much like her that I foresaw ... problems,' he went on. 'Francine was living with me then, and you were still a gangling schoolgirl.'

He drank some wine, and continued, 'It was later, while we were visiting Spain and after I'd realised that you were having a bad bout of calf love, that I saw the folly of adopting you. I'd never got over loving Clare, and suddenly I was being haunted by her ghost—except that there was nothing wraith-like about you. You were very much alive; a warm, nubile, lovely young creature, patently eager for love. If I was short-tempered most of the time on that trip, it was because it was a hell of a situation. Every time I looked at you, it was as if Clare had come back to me.'

Bethany was remembering the night at Mas de la Chapelle ... the pink damask cloths ... the white swans filled with fresh-picked spring flowers ... the tender melancholy of Aznavour's voice singing *She*.

> *She may be the face I can't forget*
> *A trace of pleasure or regret*
> *May be my treasure or the price I have to pay*

'So Francine was right when she said you had lost your heart to someone a long time ago,' she said aloud.

'Yes, I'm afraid so,' David said sombrely. 'There have been and will be others, including Francine, with whom I shall find a degree of happiness. But Clare was ... the other half of me.'

He was looking at her as he said this and, for a second or two, Bethany felt that he wasn't seeing her face, but another one, very much like hers.

Then he shook off the momentary abstraction and said, in a much brisker tone, 'I should think Robert ought to have had his shower by now. Why don't you run up and say hello to him properly? He seems to be under the impression that there was someone, when you lived here, whom you loved, and might still love a little. But I don't think that's true any more, if indeed it ever was.'

'It was true. It isn't now.' She moved to where he was standing. 'Dearest David,' she said, in a low voice, 'I'm very glad you were my first love. If I hadn't had you as my examplar of what a man should be like, I might not have recognised Robert's qualities.'

As Francine had once done, in Florence, she kissed the tips of her fingers and pressed them lightly to his cheek.

David smiled, and gave her a gentle push in the direction of the hall. A few moments later she was flying up the wide stone staircase, her hand skimming up the brass handrail, her feet scarcely touching the treads.

When she tapped on the door of Robert's room, he must have thought it was Anna, because he called out, *'Avanti!'*

Bethany opened the door and walked in. It was not the exertion of racing upstairs that made her heart thump against her ribs.

Robert was combing his wet hair. He was standing, barefoot, by the huge, heavy, nail-studded coffer which, positioned beneath a tall mirror, served in that room as a dressing-table. He was naked, except for a towel which covered him from waist to mid-thigh, outlining his high, compact buttocks and the leanness of his haunches.

'Oh, it's you, Bethany.' He put down the comb and turned to face her. 'This is a beautiful house, with one of the most spectacular views I've ever seen. I'm not surprised David decided to buy the place after renting it for a season.'

He spoke in a tone he might have used to a fellow guest at a house-party if, soon after being introduced, they happened to find themselves alone together.

'Yes, the Villa Delphini is lovely. I should like to have it, or a place very like it, for a holiday house. But for all year round, everyday living, I think England takes a lot of beating,' she answered. 'Robert, there's something I have to tell you . . . something rather crucial.'

She saw the slight but, to her, noticeable bracing of his body before he replied, his voice even, 'I thought there might be— that's why I came. Whatever the situation was here, I wanted to know it immediately; not to have to wait for you to call me, or to write. Well, go ahead. Say your piece. Or shall I say it

for you? You want to break our engagement. I can't pretend
to be pleased, but I shan't blow my brains out, or take off for
darkest Africa'—with a smile which didn't touch his eyes.

'No, you're wrong. I don't want to break our engagement. I
want to revise the original terms of our marriage. You see,
I'm in love with you, Robert. Only somehow I didn't know it
until you kissed me goodbye, and then I arrived here in Italy—
only to find that I'd left my heart behind.'

His dark gaze narrowed intently. 'Come here and say that
again.'

She walked towards him. At arm's length, she stopped,
saying softly, 'I love you. I love you. I lo——'

But the third declaration ended in a gasp as he snatched her
into his arms and brought his mouth down on hers.

About an hour later, leaving David to go through the mail
which had accumulated in his absence, Bethany took Robert
on a tour of Portofino. It was while they were strolling up to
the church on the ridge between the harbour and the sea that
he said, 'It was David you were in love with, wasn't it? There
was never a married man, as you led me to believe at one
time?'

'Yes, it was David,' she agreed, thankful that at last she
could be honest with him.

'I guessed it as soon as I saw those paintings he did of you.
Unsigned or not, they were unmistakably Warrens ... and
painted with love as well as with brilliant technique.'

'Yes, but not for love for me.' She told him what David had
told her about his unhappy passion for her mother. 'All the
time he was painting me, he was seeing her ... longing for
her. She's ruined his life really, poor man. It would have been
so much better if he could have forgotten her and loved
Francine. I wonder where she is now, and if she's found
someone else?'

Never having met Francine, Robert could not share
Bethany's interest in her.

He said, 'Did you bring the photographs of your mother
with you? Or are they in London?'

'They're here at the villa, in my bag. I thought I would give
them to David, or one of them.'

Later, when she showed him the studio portrait of Clare

Castle, Robert said, 'One can see a superficial likeness, but she isn't as beautiful as you—or as vulnerable-looking. It's hard to judge from a photo, but I think she looks spoilt and conceited.'

He laid the photographs aside, and reached for Bethany's hands.

'Whereas you, my darling, are the least conceited girl I've ever met. As my brother remarked, after your first visit to Cranmer, it's really rather astonishing to find such an un-assuming nature combined with such ravishing looks. He advised me to waste no time in snapping you up—if I could persuade you to have me. How right he was!'

They spent the first night of their honeymoon at an hotel in London. The next day they were flying to India; first to Delhi and then to Srinagar, the capital of Kashmir. From there they would travel by *shikara*, a type of gondola, to spend three weeks in a houseboat on the romantic Dal Lake.

However, at six o'clock in the evening of her first day as Robert's wife, Bethany was not looking forward to the Himalayan part of her honeymoon but only to the night ahead.

As soon as they were alone, with no possibility of being disturbed unless they chose to emerge or to ring for room service, he took her in his arms and kissed her.

Throughout their short engagement, he had been only a little less restrained than during the time before it. But never for an instant had she doubted the ardour underlying his self-control. Now, as he held her close, and his lips roamed her face and neck, she could feel the strong surge of desire aroused by her instant submission.

Although he seemed very tall, very strong, and aggressively male, she surrendered to his embrace with the happy confidence that, with Robert, her first night of love could not fail to be an unforgettable, wildly sensuous experience.

'Shall we go to bed early?' he murmured, his mouth at her temple.

'Why not?' she agreed, pressing against him. 'It's been a long day.'

He began to unbutton the back of her very plain cream silk dress, and then to untie the fringed sash which went twice round her small, supple waist.

Underneath her going-away dress she was wearing the exquisite underclothes designed and made for her by Francine.

Without haste, and with steady, sure hands, Robert undressed her and carried her to the bed. Then, more swiftly, he stripped off his own clothes, his dark eyes delighting in her nakedness and making her suddenly shy as he refreshed his memory of her breasts and looked at the places he had not seen.

Foolishly perhaps, his gaze made her want to cover herself. Perhaps he sensed this last upsurge of virginal modesty. As he lay down beside her, his hand was light on her waist, and his lips were tender on her mouth.

But then, as the kiss went on, suddenly Bethany found herself wanting him not to be gentle and careful with her; but to hold her more tightly, and kiss her with hungry impatience. He seemed to sense this as well. Even as she realised what she wanted, he gave it to her—a fiercely passionate embrace which left her breathless, all shyness forgotten.

As he raised himself to look down at her, she twined her slim arms round his neck. 'Darling Robert . . . I love you so much.' Her fingers delved in his hair. It was as black and glossy as the plumage of the beady-eyed jackdaws which strutted in the grounds at Cranmer. Thick hair, always clean and well brushed. Nice to touch, like his muscular shoulders and the hard, smooth warmth of his chest.

'How strong you are,' she whispered delightedly.

'How soft you are,' was his husky response.

She found herself rolled on her side, her breasts trapped like doves in his palms, his teeth softly biting her neck, sending quivering signals of pleasure to every part of her body.

It was some hours since he had shaved. The slight roughness of his lean cheeks as he kissed a path down her spine made her squirm with voluptuous pleasure.

Last time, she had been half afraid of him. But tonight there was nothing he could do which she would not welcome and enjoy. When he turned her to face him, her eyes were half closed, her lips parted, her ivory skin flushed with excitement and a dewy sheen on her forehead.

'My lovely girl!' His voice was thick with desire.

She could feel how urgently he wanted her. But that was

only the beginning. Again and again his caressing fingers and lips forced gasps of ecstasy from her before, with one swift stab of pain, their bodies fused. She thought she might die in his arms, so intense was that last storm of feeling.

He revived her with many light kisses on her temples and cheeks. When she sighed and opened her eyes, he was propped on his elbow, smiling at her.

As they stayed locked together, at peace, she realised that, for the rest of their lives, whatever happened, they would always have this lovely way of escaping from the world into their own private Eden.

On his terrace above Portofino, David Castle was opening a bottle of the rare and expensive Bianco delle Cinque Terre; a Ligurian wine—when it was the real thing, not an imitation— of exceptional quality, made from grapes grown on the nearly vertical slopes of an inaccessible mountain. It was said that the annual crop was drunk five times over every year, but he knew the wine which he was about to taste to be authentic. It had been given to him by Giancarlo's father, a connoisseur of Italian wines.

All day his thoughts had been in London with Bethany. He had not been present at the wedding, giving as the reason for his absence a trip to Australia which was not actually due to begin for another three weeks.

The truth was that to have taken the place of her father, and given her away, was a role he could not have endured.

He had lied in telling her that Clare had been the love of his life. In fact—as he was to her daughter—she had been merely his calf love. Capricious and shallow, she had dazzled him with the charm which had already blinded his brother to her unsuitability as the wife of a horse-mad landowner.

He had said Clare was his other half, but it was Bethany who, after he had sent her away, had made him realise that, without her, he was incomplete.

The misery which he had suffered after she had gone to England was something which only she, having shared it, could ever understand. Now, for her the heartache was over; healed by her love for Robert.

Had there been no Robert, could he have revived her young love for himself? David wondered. Perhaps. No, not perhaps—

yes. But it was no use brooding on those lines. People who let themselves dwell on what might have been were a menace to themselves and everyone else. After tonight he must strive to put Bethany out of his mind, and get on with the rest of his life.

Tonight, however, it was difficult not to think of her, and to wish himself in the place of the man who was now her husband.

Remembering her radiant face on the day Bethany and her fiancé had flown back to London, he found some slight comfort in the fact that at least she would be spending her life with a thoroughly likeable man who could give her the moon if she wanted it.

Standing by the edge of the terrace, looking down on the dusky harbour with the lights coming on under the awnings of the waterfront cafés, he raised the first glass of wine in a silent toast to his lost love and her future happiness.

Harlequin® Plus

A CLASSIC LOVER

" 'Love that moves the sun and the other stars,' " quotes Anne Weale's heroine, Bethany, to express the rapture of her feelings. And she could not have chosen better than these words written by Dante, famous Italian poet of the thirteenth century. For of all men, Dante knew what it was to love; his writings about his adored Beatrice have made him one of the greatest classic lovers.

So consuming was Dante's passion for Beatrice that he was inspired to write the epic poem, *The Divine Comedy*, a story of his imaginary journey from hell and purgatory to heaven that portrays Beatrice as his guide.

Born in Florence in 1265, Dante Alighieri was nine when he first set eyes on eight-year-old Beatrice Portinari and fell instantly in love. As a young man Dante wrote a collection of thirty-one lyric poems entitled, *La vita nuova (The New Life)*, which chronicled their relationship: the nine years that elapsed before he met Beatrice again; her disapproval of the passionate poems he had written to honor other women; his open declaration of love to her (which he had kept secret by pretending to write to other women); and her tragically early death at the age of twenty-four. He ended *La vita nuova* with the promise that he would not write about Beatrice again until he could do so in a way "that hath not been written of any woman."

The Divine Comedy fulfilled this promise.

The bestselling epic saga of the Irish.
An intriguing and passionate story that spans 400 years.

FIRST...
The Defiant

Lady Elizabeth Hatton, highborn Englishwoman, was not above using her position to get what she wanted ...and more than anything in the world she wanted Rory O'Donnell, the fiery Irish rebel. But it was an alliance that promised only ruin....

THEN...
The Survivors

Against a turbulent background of political intrigue and royal corruption, the determined, passionate Shanna O'Hara searched for peace in her beloved but troubled Ireland. Meanwhile in England, hot-tempered Brenna Coke fought against a loveless marriage....

IN CANADA
649 Ontario Street
Stratford, Ontario N5A 6W2

IN THE U.S.
P.O. Box 22188
Tempe, AZ 85282

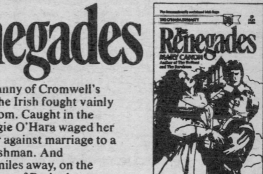

FREE!

A hardcover Romance Treasury volume containing 3 treasured works of romance by 3 outstanding Harlequin authors...

...as your introduction to Harlequin's Romance Treasury subscription plan!

Romance Treasury

...almost 600 pages of exciting romance reading every month at the low cost of $6.97 a volume!

A wonderful way to collect many of Harlequin's most beautiful love stories, all originally published in the late '60s and early '70s. Each value-packed volume, bound in a distinctive gold-embossed leatherette case and wrapped in a colorfully illustrated dust jacket, contains...
* 3 full-length novels by 3 world-famous authors of romance fiction
* a unique illustration for every novel
* the elegant touch of a delicate bound-in ribbon bookmark... and much, much more!

Romance Treasury

...for a library of romance you'll treasure forever!

Complete and mail today the FREE gift certificate and subscription reservation on the following page.

Romance Treasury

An exciting opportunity to collect treasured works of romance! Almost 600 pages of exciting romance reading in each beautifully bound hardcover volume!

You may cancel your subscription whenever you wish! You don't have to buy any minimum number of volumes. Whenever you decide to stop your subscription just drop us a line and we'll cancel all further shipments.